MANDI BECK

Love Hurts
Copyright © 2015 by Mandi Beck
ALL RIGHTS RESERVED

Editing by
Lisa Christman with Adept Edits

Cover design by
Lauren Perry with Perrywinkle Photography

Interior design and formatting by
Christine Borgford with Perfectly Publishable

Dedication

To Ran.
My guy.
My fighter.
My champion.
My husband.

I love you.
Love always, your girl.

Prologue

NOTHING CAN KILL a mood faster than having your cock in some chick's mouth when the woman you love is calling. I sit in the chair, head thrown back, thinking about whether I should answer the call or not. I haven't heard that ringtone in two months. Never did I think that I would miss hearing Iggy Azalea telling me how fucking "Fancy" I am. That's my girl though—she's got jokes.

Two months, two fucking months, and she calls *now*? Snorting, I shake my head, debating how badly I want to hear her voice and know what she has to say. Bad enough to kick this bitch out? I don't know who I'm trying to bullshit. There's nothing—nothing—I want more than to talk to her, to hear that raspy, sexy voice that I've missed so much. Fuck, just thinking about it is making me harder than I've been all night. I need to make a decision before this chick thinks that it's her that has me going solid in her mouth.

My mind made up, I sigh. We've gone long enough without speaking. I just want to talk to my girl, see where her head's at. I don't even care if she's calling to bitch at me, as long as she's calling. Does that make me a pussy? Oh well if it does. I need her and clearly she needs me.

Chapter
ONE

"I CAN'T BELIEVE that you're allowing this to happen, Deacon."

"It's the Princess, Mav. She loves all of this shit. Always has, no matter how hard we tried to beat it out of her growing up," I tell him, shrugging in acceptance, thankful that we didn't succeed.

"Yeah, but she also likes cool stuff. Like sports. Indie couldn't do a hockey-themed party?" he snorts, mildly disgusted.

Shaking my head, I slap him on the back and walk away, heading into the house. Let him tell Indie he doesn't like the party. I'd have one less brother, but it might be worth it to see how *that* whole conversation plays out. I'm not even sure what the theme is supposed to be. There's lace. A lot of lace and feathers…and leather? All over my house. How the fuck does she come up with this shit? Not that I'm complaining. It's actually really sexy. I don't have time to explain that to my dumbass brothers though.

I bound up the stairs two at a time, needing to get ready for this party. I hope like hell that I'm able to stay cool. Today is not the day for me to beat the shit out of Frankie's douchebag boyfriend. It's getting harder and harder for me to see them together. I've always struggled seeing her with other guys, but I couldn't do shit about it. Not without coming clean about how I feel about her, so I've just learned to grin and fucking bear it. Well, that noise is getting old and I'm getting sick as fuck of fighting the urge to claim her ass.

I'm not weak, but this thing with Frankie has me frustrated as hell. I've been a total prick to be around lately and don't have time for any of the bullshit right now. I'm leaving for my next series of fights and the Elite Warriors Federation doesn't give a fuck if I have sand in my vagina over a woman or not. I am a professional MMA fighter and they expect me to act like it. I can't afford any distractions right now—not even the Princess, who is a *huge* distraction.

Striding into my bedroom, I go straight for my music system, firing it up and setting it to shuffle. I enter the bathroom knowing Indie is going to be pissed. I'm sure my playlist isn't what she had in mind for her little sex-themed party.

Jumping out of the shower, towel slung low on my hips, I head back into my room and the walk-in closet, rubbing another towel over my head, drying my hair. After being in the military and told that I had to wear my hair short, I've rebelled since I was discharged and now wear it long. Even though it's kind of a pain in my ass, especially in the cage where fuckers like to pull it like a bunch of girls. I pull a pair of boxer briefs out of my dresser, slip into them, and finish dressing before throwing my boots on. I see that Frankie is at it again when I open the vanity drawer.

Shaking my head, I grab one of the pink hair ties she has replaced my black ones with, yet again, and shove it into my front pocket along with my phone. Checking my watch, I realize that guests are probably arriving and head to the safe in my office to grab Frankie's present. I look in the bag with the two blue boxes that I picked up earlier in the week and smile as I flick the light off and head downstairs. Indie is at the landing, stabbing her fingers at the panel that controls the sound system.

"What are you doing, woman? Why are you being so rough with my shit?" I growl at her, swatting her hands away.

"The DJ is trying to set up and do a sound check but all anyone can hear is your shitty music!" she shouts.

Glancing down at the bag I hold, she jerks her chin in my direction.

"Is that her gift?"

"Yep."

"You gonna show me?"

"Nope," I say as I walk past whistling.

"Are you wearing that? You know he'll be in a suit, right?"

I don't even bother looking down at my worn jeans and plain, black Henley. I don't need to dress up in a fucking suit in order to look good or impress anyone. Who the fuck wears a suit to an outdoor party at the end of May anyway? Douchebags, that's who.

I keep walking but yell over my shoulder, "You say that shit like it matters, Jones!" Running a hand through my still-damp hair, I flex for her, causing my shirt to strain against the muscles rippling beneath. "Doesn't matter what he wears. I'll still look better."

She rolls her eyes, shaking her head in exasperation. Laughing, I wink and make my way outside.

Two hours later, the DJ has all of Frankie's favorites playing. Some of it I love, some I tolerate, and some makes me want to put a bullet in my brain. The Princess has really eclectic taste in music—probably because she's a dancer. Not a stripper, but an actual trained dancer. She did teach a pole dancing class at the gym for a while though, which I found to be fucking hot as hell. She's amazing -- she has a studio in the gym our dads own, teaches classes, and even competes, though not as much as she used to.

Looking around at all of the milling guests and the ones still arriving, I still don't see Frankie. Mav and Sonny are at the bar that's set up on the patio, talking to Indie and one of her friends that I've met but has one of those names that you can never remember. I make my way over to them and ask, "Where's the Princess?"

"Apparently, Annnddrreewww had something important come up at the office. Some hush hush important client or some shit," Indie snarls.

Seething in anger, I begin to shake, "Fuck that! Fuck him! It's her birthday, this is her damn party!"

I grab my phone from my pocket and toss it to Indie. "Call Frankie and tell her I'm on my way!" I turn but before I get very far Indie grabs my arm and holds up her hand to shut me up when I go to speak.

"Slow down, hero." She places the phone in my hand but doesn't let go, forcing me to stay put. "I already called and she's on her way now. That was about five or ten minutes ago, so she should be here any minute."

Slipping my phone back into my pants, I try to reel in my aggravation. I fucking hate this guy!

"God, he's such a fucking tool," Sonny says, before he takes a pull from his beer.

Everyone nods in agreement, but I don't say anything, just grab my drink from the bartender and break away from the group and head back toward the house. I want to be the one to greet her when she arrives.

The kitchen door opens and I see her. She stands there before me and takes my breath away. *Jesus fuck.* I stop my advance and take her in. She's fucking gorgeous. Her long, blonde hair is pulled to the side in some fancy ass braid which falls over her shoulder. Icy eyes done up with dark makeup, making them look smoky, almost as if they're glowing, blue flames. She has this short, gray dress on that hugs every single one of her curves. And my girl has curves on her tight little dancer's body. I don't know what the material is, nor do I give a fuck, but it looks soft and drapes off of her shoulder. The way it hangs leaves the skin there bare, with glimpses of her tattoo playing peekaboo.

Continuing my perusal, I let my gaze linger on the hottest set of legs I've ever seen. For someone that's only five-foot-two, her legs are unreal. On her tiny feet are light pink, fuck-me heels that make my dick instantly hard. I'm so fucked. Bringing my gaze back up, I rest on her face,

"Hey, Princess! I was getting worried about my birthday girl," I tell her, not acknowledging the prick standing beside her.

"I know. I should've called, Deacon, but I didn't think we would be this late," she says apologetically.

Not even glancing at him, I gesture with my head.

"Come, give me some love."

Arms open wide, I smile when she lets go of Andrew's arm and walks right into mine. Wrapping my body around her tiny frame, I look Drew right in the eyes and smirk. I pull back just far enough to grab her wrist, making sure that he's watching as I bring it up to my mouth and place a kiss there.

Take that, fucker.

I watch him watching us for a second longer. To say that he is pissed would be putting it mildly. My smirk morphs into a smile as I look down at my girl. "Happy birthday, Frankie," I say, squeezing her tighter to me.

"Thanks, Deacon. I really am sorry that we're late," she says in that throaty, sexy as fuck rasp of hers.

"No worries, babe. It's your party and doesn't start 'til you get here, yeah?"

I loosen my hold on her, allowing her to step back next to Andrew, who immediately pulls her into his side making the muscle in my jaw tick. I still haven't said shit to him. I guess he's a bigger man than me though because he's the one to finally break the silence.

"Yes, I apologize. I had something that couldn't wait come up at the office and it took longer than I would have liked. I'm in the middle of a very important case." Glancing distastefully around the room, he continues in that pompous ass voice of his, "Thank you for throwing this party for Francesca. I have been so busy at work lately that there was no way I would have been able to throw something together." The condescending tone he uses makes me want to break his fucking face.

Turning away, I lead us through the house and toward the party. Stopping on the patio I turn back to them.

"Yeah, well, we can't all be a prosecutor for the D.A., can we? No worries though, I wouldn't have let you anyway, Drew." He hates when I call him that, which only makes me use it as often as possible. "This is a tradition and you don't fuck with tradition. I've been throwing Frankie her birthday party for as long as I can remember. Wouldn't have it any other way," I say as I glance over at Frankie and wink before I swing my gaze back to his beady, hate-filled eyes.

I love to remind him of my place in her life every chance I get. Meeting his cold stare unblinkingly, I convey my message, *That's right, asshole, you may be here with her, but make no mistake about whose girl she is.* He breaks eye contact and I smile.

Point one for The Hitman.

Sitting at the bar, where it appears my brother has taken up residence, I take stock. The party is going really well -- they always do. Frankie loves everything that Indie has chosen, just like she does every year. If there are two people that know her, it's me and Indie. There is no question that she would like anything that we put together. I did however hear Drew say something about it being crass or risqué or some shit like that. Fucking prude. He probably fucks with his socks on and the lights off. Fuck. I don't even want to think about it.

I look over at Sonny drinking his bottle of *Furious.* "What the fuck does she see in that guy?" I ask, shaking my head in confusion.

"I don't know, brother. She's never really had a type. Even

still, he's definitely not right for her. Indie said that Frankie told her that Drew hates her tattoos. Wants the Princess to get them removed—even offered to pay for it," Sonny conveys, tossing a handful of peanuts into his mouth.

"You're kidding me, right? She's not going to do it, is she?"

Chewing thoughtfully, he swivels his stool in my direction.

"I don't know. I don't think so. Indie said that she flew off the handle at Frankie, was telling her what bullshit it was and all that. Frankie said that she'd think about it. Indie thinks that he's trying to mold her into some country clubber so that she fits in with his associates down at the State Attorney's office or something."

That pisses me off on every level. I've been the one to take Frankie for all of her ink. It's our thing and some of my fondest memories. I have more of my body covered in ink than not, and so many of them have something to do with her or a memory that includes her. When she told me that she wanted some work done, I jumped at the chance to share that bond with her. Now this asshole wants to erase it like it's dirty or something? *No fucking way! Not on my watch!*

I'm lost in thought when I see Andrew make his way to the DJ and say something to him. The DJ nods his head and pulls out a mic, handing it to him.

What the fuck is he doing?

When the song ends, the DJ waves his hand as if to say "All yours." Drew clears his throat, thanks the DJ, and starts talking.

"Francesca, can you please come up here, darling?"

"Darling?" Really? I hate this motherfucker. I. Hate. Him.

All I can hear is the blood pounding in my ears, drowning out everything around me. My eyes following her every move, I watch Frankie glide up to the stage. As soon as she reaches him, he takes her hand and smiles at her. Then he drops to one knee.

What the holy fuck is going on right now?

I don't even realize that I've taken a step toward them until

8

I feel both Mav and Sonny press their hands to either side of my chest and push back a little. I don't acknowledge them, or anyone else for that matter. I just stare at the train wreck in front of me, feeling my heart race, threatening to beat right the fuck out of my chest. I can see his lips move, imagine what he's saying, the promises, but I can't actually make out the words. Still, I hear nothing but the sound of my own blood, a deafening roar through my head, and to myself I just keep repeating, "Please don't say yes. Please don't say yes." I see her nod her head yes and watch him slip the ring on her finger, stand up, and wrap his arms around her, kissing her. I'm not sure whether I want someone to kill me or I want to be the one doing the killing. No, I know what I want. And it's not his pretty boy ass standing next to her, where I should be.

Chapter
TWO

I'M NOT SURE what the fuck just went down, but I do know with every fiber of my being that there is no way in hell I will let him have her without a fight.

Not able to watch the scene in front of me any longer, I drop my chin to my chest and try to take in a deep breath. Willing it all to be some fucked up dream, a nightmare where I lose my girl to someone who can never love her like I do. All because I'm a pussy and thought she'd always be there when I was finally ready. *What the fuck just happened?*

Sonny squeezes my shoulder, breaking me from my trance. I look over and he shakes his head in understanding.

"Do something, Deacon!" Indie is not as subtle in her reaction, her rockabilly self up in my face while she jabs me in the chest. "You cannot let this shit happen! Grow a set of balls and do something!" She pushes her cat-like glasses up her nose and yanks at her brown curls. "If she marries him—actually fucking marries him—we will lose her forever. He'll make her a fucking Stepford wife. Deac, go! Tighten the hell up and tell her that you love her already!" Indie's rambling so fast I almost can't catch all the insults she's hurling at me. The tears pooling in her eyes are the kicker though. "You're a fighter for fuck's sake, so fight for her!"

Finally I blink, her words sinking in. How long has Indie known that I'm in love with Frankie?

Never mind that shit. She's right. I can't let this happen. That's *my* girl and there is no way I'm going to stand by while she marries anyfuckingbody let alone that asshole.

My eyes land on Frankie holding a champagne flute, and I can't help but shake my head in disgust. I turn toward the bar and away from that tattoo-removing, proposing-to-my-girl, fucking asshole standing with a proprietary hand on her back, talking to a group of friends as they gush over her ring. Giving the bartender my drink order, thinking hateful shit until he hands me the drinks, I make my way over to where they're standing. Without saying a word, I pluck the flute from Frankie's hand placing it on the tray of a waiter walking by and put a glass in her hand.

"Vodka cran, tall, extra lime for the birthday girl."

"Thanks, Deacon," she says, smiling up at me.

"I'm sure she would much rather have champagne to celebrate her birthday and engagement, friend," Andrew says in that pompous ass tone of his.

Who the fuck does this asshole think he is?

Sneering at him, "I'm sure she wouldn't -- champagne gives her a migraine, *friend.*"

"No, it does not," Andrew huffs

Frankie looks away sheepishly.

"Does it, Francesca?" he asks, completely shocked.

"Seems like something a fiancé should know about his woman, yeah?" I say, unable to hide the smirk at his ignorance.

He just glares at me with unabashed hate, but I couldn't give a fuck less. I smile wider, even though my jaw is ticking. The only thing stopping me from knocking him on his ass is one of the twins jumping up and down, holding Frankie's hand, the one with that asshole's ring on it, reminding me where I am.

Otherwise the motherfucker would be laid out.

I look at the Princess and noticed that she is smiling, but it never really reaches her eyes. I know my girl, and seeing the look on her face confirms she isn't as happy as she's letting on—she's pretending. Before I can even process what it might mean, I feel someone slip their arm through mine. I look down and see Indie there smiling up at me with a mischievous glint in her eyes before turning her attention to Frankie.

"Congratulations, doll. Now that Drew has had the chance to give you his present, why don't the rest of us do the same? Sound good to you, Deacon?" she asks innocently. Focusing on me again, that evil twinkle behind her glasses reminding me that whether she likes me most days or not, she's on my side.

Indie and I wear matching grins, and she just moved up about ten spots in my book. "Sounds good to me. Let everyone know that the birthday girl will be opening presents and we'll set up at the head table in a few."

I go back into the house, grab my little bag and another drink—I'm going to need it. As I head back outside toward the table, I see Frankie sitting there, smiling and laughing at something Indie is saying. I love seeing her like this. Her laugh is intoxicating, the way she throws her head back exposing her throat makes me want to bury my face in her neck and just inhale her. Turning my attention away from them the smile falls from my lips as I see Andrew off to the side watching them as well. By the look on his face though, he isn't nearly as taken by the scene as I am. Taking long strides to where Indie is now placing packages and cards in front of Frankie, I hand her the bag.

"Save this one for last, Indie."

"Oh, absolutely, sir. I always save the best for last." With a wink and a little fist bump, she turns back to the gifts and Frankie.

I walk over and stand next to Andrew; my brothers,

materializing from seemingly nowhere, following close by. I think that they're worried I might smash my fist into his pretty-boy face. Which they're right to worry. I'm having a hard time remembering why I shouldn't.

When it comes time for my gift, I smile over at Frankie and watch her as Indie walks over to join our odd little group.

"Who is this one from? I didn't hear you say, Indiana."

Only this asshat calls Indie by her given name. She hates when he does it, but he is one of those people that believes in using peoples "*proper*" names, not what he calls "*silly nicknames*."

"Oh, that one is from Deacon, *Drew*. She's going to love it…he always gets her the best gifts. I bet it'll be her favorite present this year!" Indie tells him sweetly, making sure to get that final dig in.

I love how she emphasizes the name "Drew." Like me, she knows how he hates it. All during their little exchange, my eyes never leave the Princess as she looks into the bag and pulls out the first little, blue box. She smiles—a real smile—and looks up, searching the small crowd around her. Finally her eyes find me and she smiles even wider. I wink at her, giving her a nod to go ahead and see what's in the box. My hands are stuffed in my pockets as I watch her, loose limbed and relaxed, my mouth kicked up in an excited smile. Out of the corner of my eye, I can see Drew shifting from foot to foot, looking on edge.

The first box she opens is a charm for her charm bracelet that I bought her years ago. It's a little book…Frankie reads like it's her damn job! If she isn't dancing, she's reading. I hear Andrew exhale, almost as if he's relieved that it's just a charm. *Don't get too ahead of yourself, dick…I'm just getting started*, I think as I laugh softly.

Frankie looks up and mouths "Thank you," blowing me a little kiss before handing the box off to someone. I look briefly in Andrew's direction, just in time to see the cocky, little smile he'd been wearing slip as Frankie pulls another much bigger box from the bag. I glance down at Indie and give her an 'Oh yeah, this is gonna be good!' smirk of my own. We're both brought back to Frankie when we hear her gasp softly. I'm almost certain that I hear our boy Drew groan, but I can't be positive because at that moment, one of Frankie's friends lets out a squeal that only dogs should be able to hear.

The Princess raises her hand to her throat as she looks up at me. I can see the tears welling in her beautiful blues, her lips trembling slightly, and I just smile, motioning with my hand for her to put it on. I can't wait to see his face when he sees what it is. I had it custom made for her. She has one of the girls help clasp the necklace around her neck, gently fingering one of the stones, the one that settles right in the hollow of her throat as it's clasped. A soft smile replaces the trembling lip from moments before. Her fingers touch the other two stones before she lifts her head and our gazes lock. There is no thanks needed—the look on her face tells me all I need to know. I did good, again. Standing, she thanks everyone for the lovely gifts and for coming before she turns to talk to the friend writing all the shit she got down. As she is talking to her, I can feel Andrew-the-douche shooting daggers at me.

"Do you think it is appropriate to be buying another man's fiancée expensive jewelry?" he hisses.

I tense at the word "fiancée." My eyes narrow as I look down on his much shorter than my own six-foot-three frame.

"Hey, Sonny, what did I get Frankie last year for her birthday?" I ask my brother pointedly.

"Jewelry," Sonny replies.

"Mav, what did I get her the year before?" I still have not looked away from a seething Drew, but I can just imagine the shit-eating grins my brothers and Indie are sporting at the little scene playing out between Drew and me.

"Definitely jewelry, bro. The good shit," Maverick says smugly.

"Indie, the year before that?"

Still keeping eye contact with him, I watch as his face reddens more and more with every word spoken.

"Oooooh, one of her favorites. That's the year you had that bracelet made for her. A black and gray diamond anchor. She wears it all the time."

I nod my head in agreement.

"You see, Drew, this is my thing. I get the Princess jewelry every year and that's not gonna change because you came to town, my man," I say, crossing my arms across my chest and widening my stance.

He sneers at me and all but spits out, "The 'Princess.' That sounds so juvenile. You do realize that she is a grown woman and not a five-year-old, right?"

I don't even get a chance to open my mouth before Mav steps up. Towering over him in his anger, his inked up arm and fierce glare make him look as if he's the fighter in the family right now instead of the PR guy and sometimes trainer. My older brother points a finger at Drew-the-dick and says in a low voice, "She's always been the Princess to us, always will be. When you're the only girl raised with three rowdy as fuck boys and two fathers, you're damn right she's the Princess, jackass! You can call her whatever the hell you want, but know this: we for damn sure will call her the Princess whether your pansy ass approves or not."

At that moment, Frankie makes her way up to us with her friend, Jill, in tow, not realizing that she just walked into a bit of a shit storm. Never breaking stride, she doesn't stop until she's right in front of me. I uncross my arms from my chest to pull her in to me as she throws her arms around my waist and squeezes tight.

"Thank you so much, Deac. I absolutely love them both, especially my necklace," Frankie says, giving me another tight squeeze.

I lean back to get a look at the necklace, and at the same time, her stellar rack and smile.

"It looks good on you, Princess," I tell her honestly.

"Deacon, you always find her the greatest little gems. I'm going in tomorrow to buy myself one just like it. Well, maybe not just like it...I'll have to get it with smaller diamonds, big spender," Jill says on a laugh.

I look down at Frankie again as she touches the necklace and smiles back at me. It's three strands of the thinnest, almost invisible platinum, and each strand has a heart-shaped diamond on it making them look like they are literally floating on air.

"Sorry, Jill, it's one of a kind. I had it made for her a couple of months ago."

I hear Andrew's teeth clack together when I drop that little bomb.

"Oh, wow! We were just talking about how he gets you jewelry every year and that awesome anchor bracelet that he had made for you. This boy is so good!" Indie says, goading Drew even more.

Frankie and her friend nod enthusiastically.

"It's true, he is. I'm very lucky," Frankie says before tugging me down and brushing a kiss across my cheek.

"Thank you, for everything," she whispers and places another kiss to my stubbled cheek.

Willing my hard on to calm the fuck down over a simple peck, I answer with a tight smile.

"You're welcome. I'm glad you like them, though I was pretty sure that you would," I tell her, winking.

Laughing at me, she pushes against my chest, but I don't budge.

"I do. I love them so much," she rasps.

Between the stirring in my dick that I'm trying to hide from her and me being completely mesmerized by her beauty, I can only nod and smile at her. Just as I am about to pull her in for another hug, Andrew clears his throat loudly.

"Yes, well, I'm sure you all won't mind if I steal my fiancée away for a dance," he says arrogantly, taking her elbow and pulling her from my arms.

As he leads her away, she glances back at me over her shoulder and mouths "Thank you" and "I'm sorry," then blows me a kiss before she turns to follow him again.

After watching them for two of the longest fucking songs of my life, I am about to lose my shit. I turn to Indie.

"Go have the DJ play something for me and the Princess," I demand.

She looks at me with wide eyes "Me?" she squeaks in a very un-Indie like way.

"Yes, Indie, you. Make sure it's something slow." I throw the words over my shoulder as I stalk to where Drew has Frankie loosely in his arms on the makeshift dance floor.

"My turn," I say, not asking permission for shit.

"Of course. Andrew doesn't mind," Frankie says, beaming up at me.

Oh, but he does. He so fucking does mind. Ask me if I give a fuck though. Ever the gentleman, he hands my girl over to me with a closed smile and a slight bow. Seriously? I don't bother to say shit to him.

I wrap one arm around her waist, taking her small hand in mine, flipping her wrist and planting a kiss there before I pull her in tight and place our joined hands on my chest right over my heart. Frankie's body instantly molds itself to mine seamlessly, as if it too knows it's made for me. As soon as the song starts, I whip my head up and look at Indie, who just shrugs at me from the DJ booth, a snarky, little grin on her face. She probably couldn't have picked a better song, really, but the first lines of "Burn" are a little harsh. My eyes close as the words wash over me *"Oh mama, don't walk away, I'm a goddamn sore loser, I ain't too proud to stay…"* Probably seems that way because it hits so close to home. I shake my head, wrap myself around my girl, and sway gently, her head now resting on my chest, as I listen to my boy Ray Lamontagne lay it all out there for me while I try to figure out how in the hell to tell her that I love her. Not just "We've been friends forever" I love you, but "I want to slam you up against a wall and get balls deep in you until you're screaming so loud that the neighbors know my name" kind of I love you. Fuck me, I hope that this is the long version of this song.

Chapter
THREE

AFTER THE NEXT song is getting ready to come to an end, I still haven't said shit to her. I'm starting to feel a little panicked. I glance around the party and see Andrew heading our way, so without even thinking about it, I take her hand and start pulling her off the dance floor toward the house.

"Deacon, what's the matter? Where are we going?"

"I just want to talk to you; I'm leaving tomorrow." I don't know why I throw that out there. She knows my schedule as well as I do, probably better. I just know I need her away from him and that I need a minute to think. Once we get into the house, I steer us toward the stairs up to my office.

"Slow down...I have short legs, you giant ass!" she jokes.

"Sorry, I forgot you were a little person for a second," I huff out on a laugh, winking over my shoulder at her.

She just rolls her eyes at me, letting me pull her along at a slower pace. Once we get to my office, I have no clue what the hell I'm going to say to her. I walk over to the music system that I left on up here and start scrolling through the music, not really looking for anything, just trying to gather my thoughts. I stop on Kings of Leon and am about to say something. What, I'm not sure, but something...I think...when she starts talking.

"Are you okay? Did something happen?" she asks, her brow furrowed in worry.

I just look at her, take it all in, how she makes me feel just by standing there, just by being. "Are you happy with him, Frankie?" I blurt, startling both of us.

"W-what? With Andrew? Why would you even ask me that?"

"That's not an answer, Princess. Are you happy with him?"

"Yes, of course I am! I can't believe you!" Frankie says in an exasperated tone.

"So you love him?" My eyes locked on her face, I search for the answer that I want—fuck, that I need.

"Deacon, what is this about? Is it the proposal? Do you think it's too soon?" she asks before going on, "I'll admit I was surprised, but I guess I should've seen it coming. I mean, we've moved in together. It's the natural progression, right?" she rambles a little nervously, then starts biting at the pad of her thumb.

"Are you asking me if you should marry him, Frankie? Because if you are, then the answer is no. Fuck no, you shouldn't be marrying him." Crossing my arms over my chest, waiting for that to sink in takes less time than I thought it would.

She sucks in an audible breath, narrowing her eyes at me. "What the fuck do you mean 'no'? What are you saying, Deacon? I thought you liked him, that you were happy for me?"

"Fuck no, I don't like him, Princess! I tolerate him for you, and I'm barely managing that lately," I nearly shout.

"I have no idea what the hell has gotten into you tonight." She points a finger at me, clearly pissed. "I don't need to ask your permission to accept a marriage proposal from my boyfriend. My boyfriend whom I live with. My fiancé who loves me!" Frankie snaps.

Oh yeah, she's pissed, and it's fucking hot. She has her hands planted firmly on her sexy little hips with that stupid ring taunting me. Before I even think about it, I stalk from behind my desk, closing in on her, our bodies almost touching. Her chest rising and falling visibly with how aggravated she is with me. I snatch her hand and hold it in mine.

"It's ugly," I tell her matter-of-factly, like we weren't just in a yelling match.

"What? What's ugly?" Thrown off by my abrupt shift, she stands looking at me like I've lost my fucking mind. Maybe I have.

"This ring—it's ugly," I lean down and whisper in her ear, throwing her off even further. "It's not you. But that doesn't surprise me, because he doesn't know you, not the real you," I tell her with a shrug of my shoulders.

A slight shudder brought on by my nearness rocks her before she shakes it off. "It's not ugly!" she huffs, looking down at it.

I know what I'm doing to her, keeping her off balance by crowding her, touching her. I need this in more ways than one. Standing straight again, watching her for a reaction. "It is, Frankie. You hate it and you know it. Admit it and then admit that you shouldn't be dating him let alone marrying him. I heard you say you live with him and that *he* loves you, but I noticed that you didn't say that *you* love him." The last words leave my mouth and I give her a cocky grin. She can't deny that's how she put it and I feel as if her admission is in my favor.

"Oh my God, I have no idea what your fucking deal is, but you're really starting to piss me off, Deacon!""

The madder she gets, the harder I get.

"Princess, don't get pissy with me. I like it too much."

Smirking at her, I take another step closer, bringing our bodies flush, her having to lean back to look up at me. I reach out and finger the diamonds at her throat, diamonds that I put there, diamonds that she loves because I know her.

"Don't marry him, Frankie," my fingers still playing over her necklace. I haven't taken my eyes off of my hand, watching it stroke back and forth.

"W-why shouldn't I marry him, Deacon? Why wouldn't

I marry him?" I watch as she swallows nervously. "You're not making any sense, are you drunk?" she asks me in confusion.

I finally raise my eyes and meet her confused ones. She's searching my face, my eyes, trying to read me, trying to figure out what the fuck I am getting at. She huffs out a breath that tickles my lips and that's all it takes to push me over the edge. Before either one of us knows what's happening, I have her backed up against the wall, my hands gripping her hips, pressing my rock hard cock up against her.

"Call it off. Call it off and give him back that ugly, goddamn ring." My words are nothing short of a demand.

Her hands fly to my chest to steady herself from my abrupt assault. I don't give Frankie time to do anything else, swooping down and taking her mouth. There's no other way to describe it. I take, and after a second's hesitation, she gives. I trace her bottom lip with my tongue, nipping it, making her gasp, and giving me the opening I need to deepen the kiss, sliding my tongue into her mouth. The sound that comes from her then is part moan, part sob, and it undoes me. At that moment, that one little sound, all of the years of me wanting this woman and not being able to have her, all of that want, that need, bubble to the surface and take over. She slides her hands into my hair and drags me closer at the same time I grip the back of her thighs and lift her up against the wall, her legs instantly wrapping around me, her pink, fuck-me heels digging into the small of my back, making me even harder, if that were possible.

Groaning as I press into her, pinning her even tighter against the wall, I drag her bottom lip between my teeth, kiss across her jaw and down her neck. I lick and taste, inhaling her scent—coconut and lime mixed with a smell that is just Frankie. I kiss my way back up to her mouth.

"Tell him you can't marry him. Tell him you can't be with him. Tell him, Frankie. I'm done waiting," I pant against her mouth, punctuating my words with kisses, not giving her a chance to argue.

I pull back enough to look at her and take in those beautiful, blue eyes, glazed over with want that I'm sure mirrors my own.

"Waiting for what, Deacon?" she asks in a shaky whisper.

"For you, for us. I've kept my mouth shut trying to do what I thought was the right thing, but I can't anymore. I won't. I want you, you belong to me, and you always have, Frankie," I say vehemently.

She looks completely dazed and rightly so. I am coming out of left field with all of this shit. I've been sitting on it for so long, I've lost the ability to ease her into the idea of us. I'm just putting it all on her and hoping she doesn't freak out on me.

I press my lips to her temple, working my way down to her lips already swollen from my kisses. Now that I've tasted her, I don't want to stop. I am already addicted. I lick into her mouth, softly burying one hand into her hair and tilting her head, allowing me better access, letting me deepen the kiss. I can feel the heat of her pussy pressed against my stomach through my shirt and it is killing me. I rock into her, letting her feel how hard I am, swallowing her moan. I'm ready to push her dress up and rip her panties right off when I hear someone calling her name. No, not just someone. Andrew.

"Francesca, are you up there?"

It takes me a second to realize that she is pushing against my chest, scrambling to get down. Fuck me, I need more time. I need for him to not be here. Frankie is too good a person to hurt anyone intentionally. Me? I could give zero fucks if he walked in on us right now. In fact, it would make shit a whole lot easier for me if he did.

"Deacon, put me down, please. He can't find us like this," she says a bit frantically.

I look at her and the panic in her face convinces me to lower her. She tugs her dress down over her perfect ass and legs, but not before I catch a glimpse of the tattoo high up on her left thigh. The lacy garter that does nothing to help with my raging hard on. That tattoo on her thigh is my favorite. Feminine and sexy as hell, even though I hated watching Cage, my tattoo guy, with his hands in between her legs laying ink.

The second she is straightened, she dashes into my bedroom which is connected to the office. One deep breath is all I manage to get myself under control, because about three seconds after I hear the door to the bathroom snick closed, Andrew is standing in the doorway.

"Have you seen Francesca? I've not seen her in a bit and Indiana is ready for the cake."

"I ha—"

"What the hell is that?" he fumes, cutting me off and pointing at the fireplace wall.

"A fireplace?" I mock, knowing that can't be what has him all huffy like a little girl.

"Don't be daft, Deacon. Why do you have a naked picture of my fiancée on your mantel?" he spits.

Naked picture? What the hell is he tal--...Ohhh, *that* naked picture. I glance over my shoulder as he starts stomping toward the frame that does indeed hold a naked-ish picture of Frankie. Before he can reach it though, I'm able to snatch it off the mantel. I don't want him touching it, as crazy as that seems. It's an incredibly intimate picture. An intimate moment between Frankie and I, and I don't want to share it with him, with anyone really. The only reason it is on display here is because no one ever comes in here except for me, the Princess, and my assistant, Carter...and he'd much rather see a half-naked picture of me. I don't think that Frankie has ever even seen it and if she has, she's never mentioned it.

I look down at the picture, remembering that day. It was when I took her for her first tattoo. I had been home on leave for Christmas and was just about to leave the gym to get into some kind of trouble, preferably the kind with tits, but a bar would've done too, when Frankie called me into her dance studio.

"Hey, Princess, I didn't know you were here," grabbing her hand and flipping it, planting a kiss on her wrist while she talked.

"I just stopped in to grab some paperwork when I saw you come out of the locker room. I want to show you something and get your opinion. Do you have a minute?" There is never anything more important to me than Frankie, especially not a random piece of welcome home ass.

"Absolutely, what's up?"

She looked a little nervous which was unusual for her, always so cool and sure, nothing ever seeming to get to her. She walked into her little office at the back of her studio and pulled something up on her computer.

"What do you think of that?"

I leaned over her shoulder to look at the artwork she has on the screen. It's a delicate ribbon of lace with flowers and simple vines stemming from it in places. *"What is it?"*

"It's a tattoo that I want to get on my back. Well, it will start on my shoulder and go across my back to end on my hip.

She ran her hand from my shoulder diagonally down my back to my opposite hip to show me. It took all my strength not to shiver at her light touch. I steeled my jaw and looked back at the computer. It's really girly, elegant, and totally her. Just the thought of her getting ink made me hard.

"I think it's perfect for you."

She gave me an excited peck on the cheek and clapped her hands together. *"Yay! I'm so glad you like it! Will you take me while you're home? I don't want to go by myself and this is totally your thing,"* she said laughing.

Nodding in agreement, *"Ab-so-fucking-lutely! Let me call Cage and see if he can squeeze you in."*

"Today?" she squeaked, sounding a little panicked.

"Whenever would be great, but yeah, hopefully today."

Cage was able to squeeze us in that day. I remember thinking it was hilarious that it was five below zero out and I'd told her to put on one of her bikinis instead of a bra and panties if she didn't want to be laying there completely naked. In the picture, she's lying flat on her stomach on the table, the top to her string bikini completely untied and only one side of the bottoms tied together. Cage is working at her hip and I'm sitting at her head. She has her forehead against my knee and both of her hands grip my jean clad thighs in pain. One of my hands covers hers and the other's stroking her hair, a small smile on my face. I had given my phone to the shop girl to take pictures with so that we'd have documentation of her first tat. I had no clue that the girl was actually a photographer in her spare time and that she would capture such honest and raw pictures of Frankie and I. They were my absolute favorite pictures of her, of us, for so many reasons.

"Keep your hands to yourself, Drew. Jealousy doesn't look very good on you."

He's glaring at me and sputtering when Frankie comes back into the room, which is probably a good thing, since he doesn't notice that she came from my bedroom.

"Andrew, what's the matter? You look angry." She places a hand on his forearm to try to calm him.

"Why does he have naked pictures of you in his office, Francesca?" he asks in a biting tone.

The hand not holding the frame curls into a fist. Gritting my teeth, I try to shake it off. Motherfucker better lock that shit up. I'm fighting the urge to hit him as it is.

"Naked pictures? What are you talking about?" Her head snaps to look at me questioningly.

"You're not naked, calm down," I tell her soothingly, before turning back to the troublemaker. "She's not naked, Drew, and it was a long time ago, long before you, that's for sure."

Frankie looks down at my hands where I am still holding on

to the frame, shielding it from his view. She closes the distance between us and holds out her hand.

"May I see it, please?" she asks in a low, breathy voice.

I look her in the eyes and hand the picture over, never looking away. Her blues widen a bit when she gazes down at the framed photo and then soften as she runs a slightly shaky finger along the image.

"How? Who took these? I had no idea anyone was taking them."

Shrugging, I reply. "It was Stephy. I handed her my phone when Cage started and asked her to take pictures to remember it by."

"The receptionist? She took these with a phone?" she asks a little in awe.

"Oh, for the love of…so, not only do you have naked pictures of her, but they were taken without her knowledge?" Andrew fumes.

Right as I am about to tell him to shut the fuck up, Frankie speaks.

"Andrew, I'm not naked and it's not like he's a peeping Tom. I'm glad she took them. I'm glad he thought to ask her."

He just stares at her with a stunned look on his face, almost like he can't believe that she is challenging him even slightly. She looks down at the picture again and then walks over to the mantel to put it in the only empty space there, where it was obviously taken from. She lets her gaze touch on the rest of the photos that cover every inch of the mantel. I know what she sees. She sees the story of us, from family holidays, graduations, proms, deployments, fights…it's all there and as permanent, ingrained, and meaningful as the ink etched into our skin.

"If you're finished with this little trip down memory lane, Indiana is ready to do the cake," Andrew grits.

That seems to break the spell and brings her back to the here and now.

"Let's not keep her waiting then," she tells him with forced enthusiasm.

They make it to the door before I call out to her. "Frankie?"

She stops but doesn't turn around to face me, and unfortunately he stops as well. "Go ahead, Andrew, I'll be right there," Frankie reassures him.

"If you're sure."

"I'm sure. Tell Indie to light the candles. I'll be right down."

He looks at her for a beat before deciding to leave her with me, the big bad wolf. She still hasn't turned around. I run my fingers through my hair, yanking on it, trying to gather my thoughts.

"I know that I've thrown a lot at you tonight, and I really am sorry, but I'm not sorry about finally coming clean. I've been sitting on it for so long I'm used to the thought of being in love with you, but I know it's got to be overwhelming for you. I never intended to tell you like this. All of these years, I thought about the day I'd actually tell you how I felt, and none of the scenarios ever played out like this."

She turns around at that and stands there, head down, still not meeting my eyes. "What do you mean 'all of these years?' How long have you been in lo—…felt like this, Deacon?" Her voice is so soft I almost can't hear her. I notice that she can't say the word "love" though.

I laugh without humor at her question and shrug my shoulders. "Forever. At least that's how long it seems. I honestly can't remember a time that I wasn't in love with you, Frankie. Like I said though, I know it's a lot to take in."

She still hasn't looked at me and just stands there wringing her hands, staring at the wood flooring, biting the inside corner of her bottom lip like she does when she's thinking.

"Princess, look at me."

Finally, she looks up, but never stops torturing her poor lip.

I speak, hoping she'll stop chewing on her damn lip. "It's a lot and I'm not asking you to decide on anything tonight." I see some of the tension leave her on a sigh at my words. "I'm not asking you to choose him or me this very moment. I'm not asking you to choose me at all. Until you don't," I say in a low, gravelly voice.

"Deacon, I don't know what to say, I don't know what to think. You're my best friend. I can't lose you and I feel like I am," she tells me with tears in her eyes.

I take a step toward her. I want to reach out and touch her, but know if I do, I won't stop and I'd have her up against the wall again in an instant. It's as if as soon as the words left my mouth, I had absolutely no control over myself. My need to touch her, protect her, own her only intensified. I pride myself on my control— it's one of the things that makes me a good fighter—but I am losing the battle right now. One more step in her direction and I have to force myself to stop, shoving my hands deep into my pockets.

"That will never happen. Never. No matter what. You can't lose someone that makes up a part of who you are. We are a part of each other, Princess. That's never going to change."

She looks down at the floor again briefly as my words sink in, before our gazes collide and lock. I see the flash of anger in hers and I'm not surprised really. This is who she is. Fiery, passionate, fierce…and I have a feeling that she is about to unleash all of that on me.

"Why? Why now? All this time you've felt this way and you've said nothing. Nothing, Deacon!" Hands on her hips again, her voice raised, she rages, "You decide that today of all days is a good time to bare your fucking soul?" Glaring at me accusingly, she goes on, "This is unfair, Deacon. So very unfair and selfish. You can't just do this and expect me to drop it all and come running. Where the hell have you been all…you know what? Never mind. I better get back down there before he comes looking for me again," resigned and still obviously pissed.

I shake my head in frustration. The muscle in my jaw pulsating in time with my heart at the thought of her running to Drew's side.

"Fuck him. Don't leave. Don't go down there. Don't go to him," I say forcefully. "Stay here. Be mad at me, whatever. You want to fight? Let's fight it out then." Heart racing, my eyes don't leave her face as I wait for her to give in. I can see the mad in her eyes, the frustration in the way her mouth is in a straight, unforgiving line. My hands are balled so tightly, it's painful. Without another word she breaks eye contact, slowly turns and walks away, leaving me alone as she goes to *him*.

Chapter FOUR

TWO MONTHS SINCE I called Carter and had him get me the hell out of Chicago and away from Frankie. Two months without a word, without hearing her voice. Fine. I can work her out of my goddamn system or die trying. I'm winning my fights, I'm on top of my game, and running on pure adrenaline for these past two months. I'm training like a machine, but not taking care of myself, and I know that my brothers are worried. I have a couple fights coming up back to back, and I'm partying all the time, and for the last month, fucking anything in a skirt just as long as she isn't blonde. I'm a hot, fucking mess over a woman for the first time in my life and I hate it.

We're in St. Louis, and tonight's fight will be the last for the next few days. It's the shortest break I've had in a while, but these last couple haven't been qualifying fights, so I didn't have months off in between like I normally would. Four fights in two month's time isn't what I'm used to, but I welcome the distraction. Mav left yesterday for home to work on promo shit for the next string of fights, so it's just Sonny and I, thank fuck, because one of them is more than I can handle right now.

I'm sore as hell. My face is already bruised and puffy. I took more than a few good hits tonight, just good enough to let the physical pain overtake the emotional pain that has been a constant. I welcome it. Anything is better than the mindfuck I'm putting myself through.

I'm slipping my key card out of my back pocket when Sonny swings the door to our suite open to let me in. His eyes narrow as he takes in the bottle of vodka in one hand and the redheaded Amazon in the other. She is everything Frankie isn't— tall with fake tits, skanky clothes, too much perfume, and no class. All these differences make her perfect. By the barely veiled look of disgust on Sonny's face, I don't think he agrees. "You gonna let me in, brother?" I ask him with a little laugh. He steps to the side, barely.

"Don't you think you should relax a little and put a cold pack on that?" Sonny asks me, pointing at my eye that is swollen completely shut now.

"That's the plan. I'm gonna sit in that chair right there, ice down, have a drink while I let her blow me, and then I'm going to go to bed."

She giggles at that and flops down on the love seat, sitting there eye fucking the shit out of me while I talk to Sonny.

"Jesus fuck, Deacon, really? Why don't you man the fuck up and call her before it's too late? You keep this shit up and she'll be married while you're balls deep in some skank you couldn't give two shits about," Sonny snarls at me.

I glare at him with my one good eye and snatch the collar of his shirt up in my fist, yanking him in close and tight.

"I call her every. Fucking. Day, Jameson. I call her and she ices me every time. I stopped leaving messages after the first month, and now I just hang up when I get her voicemail. So if you want to come at me with some more of your bullshit, save it, because right now, I don't fucking need it." Releasing him, I take a step back.

"Deac, I'm sorry. She never mentions you calling, she just asks how you are. I just assumed...I just assumed..." he drifts off, straightening his shirt.

I clear my throat. "You've talked to her? She asks about

me?" I ask in a voice so low and gravelly, sounding completely defeated, that I don't even recognize it as my own.

"Yeah, one of us speaks to her almost daily, just like always," Sonny reassures me.

I'm relieved that my brothers are in touch with her, and at the same time I'm mad as hell that she'll talk to them, ask about me, but not pick up the phone when I call.

"That's great. Fucking great. I'm glad she's still speaking to you guys. Now, if you don't mind, I've got company, but you're welcome to stay and watch…I'm sure she won't mind."

Ambling over to the freezer to take out two ice packs, I slump into the chair I had indicated earlier. I slap one of the packs on my shoulder, lean my head back and place the other over my eye. Twisting open the cap on my vodka, I pour it right from the bottle down my throat, welcoming the burn. It takes me a second to register the quiet, and I remove the ice pack to see Sonny and Reggie, the head of our security team, standing at the door.

"You staying for the show? If not I'll call you when it's okay to come back. Won't be long, so don't go too far," I call after them as I settle back in the chair with my ice.

Reggie gives me a little salute over his shoulder, "See you later, you dumb fucker."

Sonny gives me a final glance with those disappointed fucking eyes of his and slams the door hard enough to rattle the bottles in the mini bar.

"Wow, he's a dick, huh?" the chick asks in a high-pitched, whiny voice that grates on my nerves instantly. She moves to the floor in between my legs and is working on my zipper.

"Nope, I'm the dick. He's my older brother. No more talking, yeah?" I pull my cock free and stroke it firmly. "You know what I brought you here for, right?"

Nodding yes, she licks her lips, watching my hand as I make a pass over the head of my cock.

"Then why the fuck isn't my dick in your mouth yet?"

Her eyes widen at my gruff tone. I look down at her one more time as she lowers her mouth and swipes her tongue down my shaft. Satisfied that she finally gets the message, I lean my head back and put the ice back over my eye again. This chick is a little slow. It might take her a minute to figure out that this is gonna be all about me, and when I'm finished, she can get the fuck out.

Teeth clenched, I thrust my hips forward as she tries to swallow my length, gagging in the process. She works her way back up, tongue and lips gliding from base to crown. After ten minutes of this, I'm about to just bend her over the fucking couch and pound it out. Grabbing a fistful of hair, I push down hard on the back of her head, forcing her to take me deeper, trying to get this over with. I'm not as close to coming as I want to be when I hear "Fancy" blaring from the phone in my pocket. It takes me a second to realize that it's the ringtone that Frankie programmed for when she calls. I haven't heard that ringtone in two months. I reach into my pants for my phone, pushing her off my cock in the process. Two months, two fucking months, and she calls *now*?

Glaring up at me through narrowed eyes, chick on her knees whines, "Are you seriously going to answer that?"

"I seriously am. You can go," I say, waving her away.

"Oh my God, you really are a dick!" she screeches as she totters to the door, slamming it behind her as hard as Sonny had.

I slide my thumb over the picture of the Princess on my phone just as the chorus of the song is finishing.

"Frankie, I haven't heard that ringtone in so long I didn't recognize it at first," I blurt with a bitter laugh.

She doesn't say anything.

"Frankie?"

Still nothing, but I can hear breathing on the line. My pulse spikes. Something is wrong. Forgetting every ounce of pain, I stand and tuck myself back into my pants. "Princess?"

Nothing.

"Francesca?" I shout into the line. "Baby, talk to me!" Every part of my body is in motion before I know where I'm going. I have to get to her.

All I can hear on the line is a wheezing gasp that fades in and out. In a full panic, I rush to the door to look for my brother and Reggie.

"Frankie, answer me!" I scream, stepping out into the hall.

I see Reggie and Sonny ahead and they both stop at the sound of my voice.

"Deacon?" Sonny asks, worry in his voice as he starts walking to me.

I can feel my heart pulsing in every vein of my body. Never in my life have I been so terrified. Never. I look at my brother, waiting, straining to hear something that would tell me what the fuck is going on. I don't have to wait long before I hear a gurgled, "Help," a gasp for air, "Deac," another shallow breath, "Hurt," in a thready whisper, and then, "Andrew."

The last was barely audible. I go taut with fear and Sonny must see it because he springs into action. He runs into our room and grabs our bags that we thankfully had already packed in order to catch our early flight time. I start barking orders at Reggie.

"Call the cops. Tell them that she's hurt, to get an ambulance over to Frankie's house."

I don't know what the fuck happened or even if she's at home. I hope like hell that's where she is.

"Then call my dad and have him find Guy. He's out of town still; it's going to take him awhile."

I break out into a jog toward the parking garage, fear spurring me forward. Thank God we are only half a mile from the airport. The phone is pressed tightly to my ear, a cold sweat trickling down my spine with every second that passes and she doesn't speak.

Sonny and Reggie are right behind me, moving at the same pace, and somewhere along the way we picked up Trent, our other security guy. I'm on autopilot as we move through the hotel. Terrified out of my mind, I never stop talking to Frankie. Swallowing against the bile rising in my throat, I try to sound calm.

"I'm coming, baby. The police are on their way." Pushing my way through people gathered in the lobby, I move as fast as I possibly can.

"You're going to be okay. I swear, you're going to be okay," I tell her as firmly as I can manage.

Jesus fuck, I hoped that isn't a lie. Please don't let it be a lie.

"Where's Mav, Sonny? Get him on the phone; I need him there! If she's at home, he can be there quicker than the cops can."

I'm striding toward the exit, my mind racing, wondering how long it will take us to get to her, and praying that we will make it in time. The fear causes pressure in my chest, suffocating me.

"I'll call him now. Is she ok?" Sonny asks as he jogs to keep up with me.

I shake my head no, fighting the tears and the panic that are threatening to take over.

"She's okay, she's a fighter. Right?" I ask trying to reassure us all. "Stay with me, baby. We're coming, we're all coming. We'd never let anything happen to the Princess." The words tumble from my mouth on a barely contained sob.

I'm trying to sound calm for her, but the reality is I'm about to break. I've never felt so fucking useless, so absolutely helpless in my life.

I can hear Trent on the phone with the pilot telling him we are wheels up in twenty, to figure it out or he's fired.

Sonny taps me on the shoulder. "I've got him— he's in his truck and on his way to her already. He was out, so he'll be there in five minutes."

"You hear that? Mav is on his way. He'll take care of you until the ambulance gets there," I tell her as relief washes over me.

At least with my brother there, I'll know what the fuck is going on. Because the only sounds coming from the other end of the phone are shallow, wet gasps that can't even be called breaths. Each one of them scaring me more than the last, yet making me pray for the next.

By the time we pile into the SUV and head to the airport, I'm ready to claw out of my fucking skin! I just need to get there. The anxiety of not knowing, the rage at the thought of her being hurt by someone and me not being there to protect her is wreaking havoc on my mind. I can't wrap my head around any of it. Mav keeps Sonny on the phone with him and I make him swear he won't hang up. He is going to have to be my eyes and ears, my connection to her until I get there, and there's no way I can let him disconnect.

"Mav just pulled up, Deac. He said all the lights are off and the door is locked. Are you sure she's there?"

"No. Tell him to kick the fucking door down if he has to. I don't care. We need to find out if she's in there," I tell Sonny before turning my attention back to my girl. My palms sweating, gripping the door handle, I'm ready to bail as soon as the truck comes to a stop.

"Did you hear him, Mav?" Sonny waits and then nods at me, "He's in."

I can actually hear Mav now over my connection with Frankie, as he's calling her name throughout the house.

"You hear Mav, baby? He's there now, there's nothing to worry about, Frankie."

My heart drops when I hear Mav yelling. "Oh God,

Princess! Oh God! Please, please, please. Oh God!"

My eyes fly to Sonny the same time his meet mine. The fear I felt before is nothing compared to what's coursing through me now. Paralyzing me.

Holding my breath, I hear Sonny, "Mav, you're scaring us. What's going on? What's wrong with her?"

Listening to Sonny yell right next to me and Mav crying—fucking crying—over the phone line. It's so surreal, like I'm watching it play out from above, like I'm in both places at once. I can also hear Reggie on the phone with the dispatcher letting them know that my brother is in the house with her, giving them Mav's description so that they won't shoot first, ask questions later.

I hear the utter despair in Mav's voice when he says, "Sonny, I don't know what to do, there's so much blood, so much fucking blood. I don't know where to touch her, she's covered in glass, I don't want to hurt her any worse. Her eyes are closed, she hasn't opened them since I've been here, but I can see her trying to breathe. Fuck, Sonny, where are they?" he bites out the last in full out panic mode now.

I'm listening to him and still talking to Frankie.

"You're scaring, Mav. Go ahead and open your eyes, baby. Tell him to shut up." I'm rambling complete nonsense, but I can't stop.

"Be okay for us. Your Loves need you. I need you, Princess." My head lowered, I shove my hand through my tangled hair.

"I love you, Frankie." My voice breaks, showing the pain I've been trying to hide.

The truck comes to a stop at the airfield at the same time as I hear the police come in and then the medics talking to Mav. One of them is talking to Frankie, telling her his name. That's when he says, "There's a phone lying over here next to her; let the detectives know."

He then asks Mav, "Are you who she was talking to?"

Mav must've come closer to them because I can hear him more clearly. "Not me -- my brother. She called him for help. He got you guys and me over here. He's still on the line."

"I need you to stand back so that I can try to get her stabilized for transport, sir."

My eyes squeeze shut at the thought of losing this little bit of connection to her. "Princess, you have to go. They're gonna take good care of you though and I'll be at the hospital soon. I love you, baby. We all do, so much."

I don't even know if she hears me because the medic is working on her, talking to her. I can hear them in the background, her phone completely forgotten in their haste.

Sonny hands me his phone as we walk up the stairs to the plane, knowing that I need to be able to speak with Mav. As soon as Mav gets on the line, I lose it. The tears come so quick and hot that I have no control over them.

"Deacon, don't do that, bro, you gotta stay strong because she needs us right now. I promise. I. Promise. I won't leave her side." I just nod my head even though he can't see me, taking a deep breath to pull myself together and follow the guys onto the plane.

"What the fuck went on there?" I question.

"I'm not sure. The house is trashed," he relates shakily. "The dining room table is flipped, there's broken glass everywhere. I found her in the bathroom. She went through the shower door. The cops are taking pictures and dusting for prints now." The phone is muffled briefly. "They're taking her to Rush. I'll have to follow them."

We settle onto the couch that runs underneath the windows on one side of the plane, the phone in my hand on speaker. Sonny and I are leaning against each other, and I'm pretty sure if either of us were to move, the other would fall over. I stare ahead as I listen to the inarticulate noises coming from

MANDI BECK

Mav over the phone as he watches them work on her. With every minute that ticks by and every sound he makes, my heart shatters a little bit more. How would I survive if she didn't? The answer is simple: there's no fucking way. *My* Princess? No. Fucking. Way.

I look up at Reggie and notice the tears streaming down his face and I can't deal. Our Princess. Fighting without us, not only for herself, but for us, even if she doesn't know it. I snap back to the sounds coming from my phone and my world stops cold when I hear the frantic *"She's crashing!"*

Chapter
FIVE

IT'S BEEN THE longest two hours of my life. Confined to a plane where all I had were my own thoughts and fears to fuel the devastation taking over, and then the car ride over that seemed like a goddamn eternity, there was just way too much time for me to run through every fucked up scenario and put myself even deeper into a panic.

Finally we're here though. Sonny's running interference with hospital personnel who are trying to stop us in our rush to get to the room the lady at the front desk directed us to.

He can deal with them—no one is going to stop me or slow me down.

I need to find Frankie. See with my own eyes that she is all right.

Sprinting through the hall, I come to a jarring halt outside of the glass-fronted hospital room. I can feel myself falling to my knees as I look at her lying in that bed. Everything light and good and beautiful in my life lies there hooked up to machines, so still and quiet.

My breath hitches as I stagger to my feet, trying to push my way into her room, only to be stopped by Reggie pushing me back, and a nurse barring my entrance. I stop fighting them and sink to the floor again, watching in a daze as they tend to her. My heart physically aches as I take in her tiny, unmoving form.

I won't even fucking think the word "lifeless" because there's no way I'll lose her. No fucking way in hell. I'm not me without her. I'll fight for her to come back to me. I'll fight hard enough for both of us if I have to, and I'll love her even harder. When she does open those beautiful eyes of hers, I will love her fucking harder still.

I don't know how long I stay on the floor like that watching the doctors and nurses flit around her while she just lies there. Still dazed, I'm a little surprised to look down and see that I have my arms wrapped around Indie, who must've crawled onto my lap like a lost, little girl. Which I'm sure is exactly what she feels like at this moment. I feel the weight of a hand on the nape of my neck and another on my shoulder. I look over my shoulder to see if it's Mav; I want to ask him some questions. My breath catches in my throat at the sight of him. His face and hands have blood smeared on them, and his shirt is completely ruined.

"Is that hers?" I force out with a tremble in my voice that I have never heard before.

Mav looks down at himself with confusion in his eyes. When he sees his hands and then his shirt, he flinches like he had no clue that he was covered in blood or where it came from. He looks back up at me completely bewildered, shaking his head. "I didn't know, I didn't even think about it."

Reggie comes over at that moment and takes Mav by the arm. "Come on, I brought in Sonny's suitcase. I'm sure he has something in there. Let's get you cleaned up, my man."

Reggie looks back at us with complete sadness. "Why don't you three wait in the waiting room? They already told you twice that they won't let you in yet and that they'll come get you when it's time."

I just nod and rest my cheek against the top of Indie's head.

"What do you think, Jones, should we stay here where we can kind of see her or should we go into the waiting room?"

I usually only called Indie "Jones" when I was trying to get a rise out of her; I don't know what made me do it now. Maybe I needed to feel closer to her as if that would make me feel closer to Frankie. She sniffles and wipes her nose with the wadded up tissues in her hand

"They'll come get us, right, Deac? Reggie said that they will."

"Yeah, they'll come get us."

Giving in she climbs off my lap. Sonny, who has been quiet the whole time, grasps my arm and helps me up onto my shaky legs. The three of us head back to the waiting area, which is actually close enough for us to still see her room, which makes me feel better about leaving my spot on the floor. Mav and Reggie come back just as we sit down in our seats. Thankfully, we are the only people in there.

"Has anyone been able to reach Guy or Dad?" I ask no one in particular.

"I couldn't reach Guy, but I spoke to Dad and he was going to find him and then drive him here. He was in a meeting at the new gym in Milwaukee," Mav says.

I nod and stare at my hands clasped between my knees. "What the fuck happened? I mean, what in the fuck happened? Did Drew do that to her and why?" I ask, again to no one in particular.

Indie, with her arms wrapped around herself rocking slightly and staring at nothing, looking completely and utterly overcome, finally says in a low monotone voice, "She was leaving him. She called me earlier and asked if she could come stay with me until she figured everything out." Tears clog her throat, sticking to her words. "She said she was already packed and that she'd be at my place within an hour. I was in my office writing and didn't realize how much time had passed when Mav called me from here."

I'm trying to wrap my mind around the words "She was leaving him" when the doctor steps into the waiting room. He's young, probably only a little older than I am.

"Are you Ms. De Rosa's family?" he asks, eyeing me and my banged up appearance warily. Disdain at what he clearly thinks my injuries are from is evident in the tight set of his mouth and the way he puffs his chest out a bit more as if he's trying to tell me to pick on someone my own size instead of slapping around a woman.

We all stand at once and I hold out my hand for him to shake.

"I'm Deacon Love. We're her family, and her father is on his way as well." I see the recognition on his face when he connects who I am and realizes that I am not the woman beater that he first assumed.

"Well, that explains a lot then," Dr. Ashley says almost to himself, losing his aggressive posture.

"I'm sorry?"

"Well, your face for one, but also, it explains some of her defensive wounds. I take it she's trained with you at some time in her life?"

Defensive wounds? My girl was fighting that fucker?

"She has. Plus her father owns gyms."

He just nods and looks at us all solemnly.

"Miss De Rosa has extensive wounds over the majority of her body but the issue that I am most concerned with is the swelling and damage to her brain. The CT scan shows that the trauma she has endured caused hemorrhaging and swelling of her brain tissue. I've had to insert a probe in her skull to monitor cranial pressure. I have placed her in a medically induced coma to allow for her body to be able to rest and avoid any further swelling." Pausing, he takes a breath and goes on, "Until she wakes up, we won't know exactly what we're dealing with. The brain is a very tricky, complex organ. The swelling could have affected many things, but right now we are maintaining focus on the swelling. Beyond that I just don't know yet. In addition to the brain trauma, she has two broken ribs and I thought that she may have fractured one of her arms, if not both, due to the extensive bruising and swelling, but upon seeing her x-rays we've determined that neither is fractured." He indicates his own forearms while speaking, helping me to follow along.

"She was keeping her cover," I realize, both proud and devastated by that. Shaken by the things he's telling us, it's hard for me to focus on his words and their meaning. I just want him to tell me one thing — that she's fine.

Nodding his head in agreement, "It would appear that way, that's why I assumed she trained with you. She has nicks covering most of her body, front and back, but they're all superficial. However there was a large shard of glass imbedded in her neck that caused us some concern, but luckily it missed her carotid artery and we were able to remove it safely and suture it. She'll have a scar, but that's the least of our worries," he says grimly.

"We'll monitor for the next twenty-four hours and go from there. Right now it's a waiting game. I know that's not what you want to hear, but it's all we have at the moment."

"Wh—" I clear my throat and try again. "What happens in twenty-four hours?" I manage to get out.

"Due to the extent of the trauma her brain has suffered, I want to wait twenty-four hours and reassess to see if the swelling has gone down. If so, we will slowly wean the coma-inducing medications and remove the ventilation to see if she is able to breathe on her own." Placing his hands in the pockets of his lab coat, he gives us all a moment to absorb all he has said.

"And if the swelling doesn't go down or she can't breathe without the ventilator?" I can hear the despair in my voice, and it scares me. All of this does.

"First we wait the twenty-four hours," he says stoically.

"Dr. Ashley, what if she can't?" I press. I need more than he's giving me.

"Well, then we'll have to discuss what her wishes are and if she has appointed someone to make decisions for her if she's not able. But I don't want to get ahead of ourselves," he tells us, his words laced with sympathy.

"So you don't think that that's what we're looking at then?"

"I didn't say that, Mr. Love. I said that we need to allow Miss DeRosa's body a chance to rest." His pager goes off, interrupting him. As he glances at it, he says, "I'm the Neurosurgeon on call, I will be here to monitor her. My advice to you is to take the chance to spend some time with her, each of you."

"Are you—are you saying that we should say our good-byes?" I ask in a broken whisper, rubbing the spot that hides my shattering heart.

Indie lets out a sob that startles me into looking back at her. Mav has her wrapped in his arms as she sobs into his chest, her whole body shaking with emotion. I refuse to believe that he's telling me that I should say goodbye to my girl. There's no way in hell that that's what he means. It can't be.

"Whenever anyone suffers such a traumatic brain injury, they have a 50/50 chance of responding to treatment without life-altering complications. I'd say you should treat it as a last chance unless you can live with that regret," he tells us all. "I'm needed in the ER, but I'll be back in a couple of hours to check on her." Nodding at us, he strides away.

He's wrong. He has to be. It's the Princess that he's talking about. She's a fighter— he said so. There's no fucking way she'd be taken away from me. I don't fucking accept that as the truth of the situation. I look up when I feel a hand on my arm. The nurse that had been in the room with Frankie when I showed up is standing in front of me looking at me with the saddest yet kindest eyes I have ever seen.

"Mr. Love?"

I just stare unblinking.

"I have Miss De Rosa's belongings over at the desk. There

are some items of value in there. I think it's best for you to take them."

I just nod—it seems to be all I am capable of at the moment. I follow as she walks to the desk in the center of the hospital floor. She reaches under the desk and punches a code into the safe and pulls out a clear plastic bag.

"The police have some of her things for evidence. You'll have to talk to them about when they will be returned," she says as she hands me the bag.

I stare down at it and my breath catches at the sight of the rust-colored spots and smears that must be Frankie's blood.

Numb with pain, I look through her asking, "Can I see her now?"

"Not just yet. As soon as her nurse has finished in there, I'll let you know and you'll be allowed in. Visiting hours are technically over, but I'll bend the rules a bit so that you're all able to see Miss De Rosa," she says, patting my arm.

My head snaps up. "I won't be leaving her," I say in a voice as cold as steel. She must realize that this is a fight she won't win, because she just stares at me for a second and sighs.

"Mr. Love, I will allow you to stay past visiting hours, but no one else, and if it becomes an issue, you too will be forced to follow hospital rules." Her tone doesn't encourage any argument.

"Yes, ma'am, thank you." I go back to the waiting room and sit in the chair between Sonny and Reggie. Mav sits with Indie across from us, his arm around her shoulders as she stares at nothing, rocking slightly.

"Hey, Jones?" I wait til she looks up at me.

"We'll be able to talk to her soon. So, no worries, all right?" I try smiling at her, though I'm not sure if I'm able to pull it off.

We all just sit there lost in our own thoughts when Reggie's phone goes off. He answers it and hands it to me.

"It's Carter," he says softly.

I take the phone from him and barely have it up to my ear when my assistant starts talking.

"Deacon, are you there? I'm on my way. I'm stopping for food and coffee for everyone, but I'm on my way. I also booked a suite at the hotel across the street so that nobody has to go home to rest and get cleaned up, okay?" He stops to take a breath, so I take that as my cue to speak.

"Thanks, Carter. Can you do me a favor and pick me up a charger for my phone? I left mine in the hotel and I want to make sure Guy and my dad can get a hold of me."

"I have my docking station in the trunk, is that okay?"

"That's perfect. I'm sure she'll want her music."

"Deacon, is sh—...is she going to be okay?"

My world spins on its axis at his question. I refuse to say out loud that she has a 50/50 chance of pulling through, so I pretend like he didn't ask.

"I'll see you when you get here, Carter. Thanks again."

I can hear the break in his voice when he says, "Okay, Deacon."

No sooner do I hit end than I see our dads racing down the hall, looking around frantically. I step out of the waiting room to intercept them.

"Guy, Pop! We're in here."

They spin at the sound of my voice and I jerk my thumb over my shoulder to indicate the room I'd just come from. I look at Guy and it's like a punch to the gut. He looks crazed and like he's aged ten years. Fucking hell, is that what I look like? My dad places his hand on Guy's back and guides him over to where I stand.

"Where is she? Is she okay? I need to see her!" he rattles off in his thick accent.

I gesture with my head to have them follow me into the waiting room. Once inside, they collapse into a couple of chairs, and in a voice as controlled as I can manage, I explain to her father and mine what the doctor told us. I feel my heart break even more as I watch the bear of a man that helped train me into the fighter and man that I am crumble.

He completely falls apart, crying and yelling out, "God, not her too, please not her too." He sobs into his hands.

My dad has his arm around Guy's shoulders with his forehead pressed into his other hand. I see his lips moving, but can't make out what he's saying, if he's talking to Guy or himself. My dad and Guy are two of the toughest sons of bitches I know, and to see them now hurts me on a level I don't even want to touch.

"Per favore no, non la mia bambina. Non la mia bellissima figlia. Io ho bisogno di lei. Non puoi avere anche lei. Ti prego, non prenderti anche Francesca!"

I'm relieved that the rest of his meltdown is in Italian and that I can't understand all of it. Just witnessing his pain is more than enough for me to bear. I can only imagine the bargains he's making, the prayers he's offering up.

Guy lost his wife in a car accident when Frankie was just four. Besides us, they were all that he'd had. Guy's family still lives in Italy and his wife had been an only child whose parents had died long before Frankie was born. By the time she was six, my mom had left us, and Guy asked my dad, his friend since middle school, to move closer to him to help him run the gym so that he could spend more time with Frankie. Within a couple of years, our dads went into business together, opening gyms and training facilities in a dozen different cities and states. Together we make up an odd little family, with the Princess being the center of all of our worlds, and there's nothing that we wouldn't do for each other.

Just then, two officers, probably detectives since they're in suits, their badges hanging around their necks, come into the waiting room and give a wary nod to all of us as a whole, though their eyes linger on me, which is no surprise given the condition of my battered face. We all stand up and move toward them, one of them speaking to Mav. She must've been at the house with Frankie.

"Sir, you said that Miss De Rosa called your brother when we spoke earlier?"

Mav nods his head in my direction, just as I clear my throat to speak. It feels like I've swallowed a handful of sand.

"She called me. I had my brother, Sonny, and my security guy, Reggie, call you and my other brother, Maverick, whom you've already met."

"Yes, sir, we did. Would you mind if we ask you a couple of questions?" the detective asks, her voice not nearly as accusing as her eyes.

"Whatever I can do to help, but you'll have to ask here. I'm not leaving her and I want to be sure I know when I can go into her room."

"Of course, that's fine, Mr...?"

"Love, Deacon Love."

They both take a second to let that sink in, and then just as I had with the good doctor, I saw the recognition on the face of the other detective. I imagine it's because of my swollen shut black eye and the other cuts and bruises decorating my face that make it difficult for him to recognize me on sight. Clearly the EWF billboards with my face all over them don't mean shit when you're just coming off a fight. Detective Adams introduces herself and holds a hand out for me to shake, as does Detective Flores, who goes on to tell me what a huge fan he is. Now is not the time for that shit, and by the look that I give him, he knows I'm not up for autographs and a fucking meet and greet. He has the decency to look embarrassed at least and gets back to work.

"Mr. Love, do you remember what time Miss De Rosa called and what she said?" he asks me.

I explain to them how it all went down, and after about ten minutes of questioning, Detective Adams asks if I'm sure that she said "Andrew" and if I thought that's who attacked her to which I reply, "Absofuckinglutely."

Flores shakes his head and says, "I'm not buying it. Why did she call you and not the police?" suspicion underlying his every word.

I grind my teeth together so hard I swear they are about to disintegrate. The muscle in my jaw is ticking like a time bomb. It takes everything I have not to throw that fucker against a wall.

"Are you insinuating something, detective?" I demand through my clenched teeth.

He seems startled at the gruffness in my words.

"No, no, I'm just curious as to why she thought to call you first."

I had forgotten that Guy and my dad are there until Guy says, "Deacon is always who she turns to first. He's been protecting her, saving her, since she was a little girl."

He has his hand on my shoulder the whole time he is speaking, and when the last accented word leaves his mouth on a breathless sob, he squeezes, in reassurance, solidarity, gratitude. That tiny gesture says so much, and I'm choked up all over again about why we're all there, rallying together.

"If that's all, detectives, I would like to go check if we can see her yet. I'm not going anywhere, so if you need me for anything else, you know where to find me," I tell them. I don't shake either of their hands this time or wait for an answer, just stride away toward the nurse's station.

After what seems like an eternity, the nurse comes into the waiting room and informs us we can go in now, but only two at a time and not for very long. Shortly after he arrived, Carter had taken Guy to the chapel; he had wanted to light a candle for his daughter. I send Reggie to find them while I hold my hand out to Indie. She jumps up out of Mav's hold and clasps my hand in both of hers. I give it a squeeze and hope that it conveys as much of a message as Guy's reassuring touch had.

We walk over to the room and open the heavy glass door, stopping at the threshold, neither of us moving or even breathing. This time it's her who squeezes my hand. I let my chin fall to my chest and take in a fortifying breath. I need strength that I'm not sure I have to walk in there and see my girl so broken. I shake my head—broken, yes, but still here and she needs me. That thought is what propels me forward. Indie and I split at the end of the bed, each taking a side. As soon as we reach her, Indie crumples into the chair sobbing, her forehead resting on the bed next to Frankie's hand, which she holds gently so as not to disturb any of the wires and cords snaking up, down, and around her.

I feel the tears rolling down my face as I look at Frankie. She's beaten, battered, and bruised over every inch of her that I can see, and still she is beautiful. I sit in the chair and pull it right up to the bed, taking her hand in mine. I press a kiss to the inside of her wrist, and let my eyes roam over her face. She is almost unrecognizable. It's absolute agony to see her like this and to know that I wasn't there to stop it from happening. The guilt is as consuming as the pain gripping me.

I've seen so many men look much the same way leaving the cage after a brutal match, but never a woman, never my girl. There is no name for the kind of rage that I feel over seeing her like this. It scares the shit out of me, and at this moment, I'm glad that they haven't found Drew yet, because I know without a doubt in my mind that I would kill him, and nobody would be able to stop me. Not the cops, not my brothers, not even the Princess. I have to shake that shit off right now though, because there isn't fuck all I can do about it until they find him. Right now, Frankie needs me and that's what I have to focus on.

I look across at Indie who is still crying, albeit silently now, murmuring softly to Frankie. To see Indie shaken is a little unnerving, as she's as tough as Frankie, but more in your face about it. I'm a little worried about how she's going to hold up.

They're so tight—they feed off of each other, balance each other out. It's one of the reasons I never worried about Frankie when I enlisted—I knew that between Indie and my brothers that she would be fine.

I let my eyes travel across Frankie in the bed. She's tiny as it is, but lying here like this, she almost looks like a little girl.

Swallowing past the lump in my throat, I lean in and whisper in her ear. "I'm here now, Princess. I told you I was coming. Everyone is just outside the door waiting to love all over you. You know I always get the sugar first though, right? Indie's lucky I even let her come in with me."

I'm trying to keep it light. I don't want her to hear the pain or the straight up fear in my voice.

Indie must've been listening because she gives a little snort, "Yeah, right, I let him come in with me, Frankie, and he knows it."

Before I can say anything else, there's a tap at the door. Mav's standing there beckoning me to the waiting room. I look back at the girls, saying, "Let me just see what he wants real quick."

"Do you need me to come with you, Deac?" Indie says. I think she's nervous about being left alone with Frankie and her own inner turmoil.

"No. Spend some time with her. Guy should be in here any minute," I tell her as I give Frankie's wrist another kiss and walk toward Mav.

"What's up, brother?" I ask expectantly. I know it must be a big fucking deal if he's pulling me away from Frankie.

"You're never gonna believe this, but Andrew's parents just showed up. The cops called looking for him, I guess," Mav says, shaking his head in bewilderment.

"You're fucking kidding me, right?" I seethe, pissed at their audacity. They have some serious balls to show up here.

"Yeah, the detectives are with them now asking them where

he might be and shit. They're adamant that there is no way that he could have done this to her and that it must have been someone that she knew or maybe even a robbery."

"Someone she knew, like who? A robbery? I wasn't aware that anything was stolen."

I'm losing my temper by the second, and I'm ready to charge in there and start ripping people to shit.

"There was nothing stolen, Deacon. It was what it was. Someone beat the hell out of her and left her for dead."

His words slap me right in the face, burning through me. Hearing him say it out loud like that makes me cringe, causing a physical ache in my chest.

I point at him, demanding, "Get them out of here before I take care of it. I don't want Guy to see them and have to listen to them cover for their piece of shit son. We don't want them here. They can go down to the station and pitch their bullshit theories." I turn on my heel, furious, and stride down the hall back into Frankie's room.

As soon as I enter, I stop, taking deep breaths to try and collect myself. But it's no use as I'm met with the sight of Frankie clinging to life in front of me. Never even saying a word to Indie, I just yank the door open and storm out. I stalk toward the waiting room to where I can see everyone standing. The detectives are huddled with the McAvoys talking quietly when I walk right into their little circle, startling everyone. Out of the corner of my eye, I see both of my brothers and Reggie coming toward me, trying to intercept the train wreck they know they are about to witness.

I point my finger in Pete McAvoy's face and all but spit at him "You and your wife need to leave. You can discuss whatever the hell you need to discuss with them somewhere else. I don't care where, but you will not fucking spew your bullshit about your woman-beating son here."

I'm shaking I'm so heated just being near them, saying the

words "woman" and "beating" in reference to Frankie. It makes me sick to my stomach. By this point, I'm flanked by Sonny, Mav, and Reggie and I know they are waiting for the moment that I will completely lose my shit.

Drew's dad chooses that moment to prove that he is as dumb of a prick as his son.

"You cannot possibly think that our son had anything to do with Fran's attack. That is absolutely preposterous."

I feel my brothers both grab on to an arm and tug a bit, making both detectives stand up just a little bit straighter. I'm not going to give in to the temptation to do some serious bodily harm. I need to reel it in and I need to do it quickly. No way did I want to find myself in jail and I know that's where this would end. I take in a deep breath, almost to the point of pain, and slowly exhale.

"I do not want you here when her father gets back to see the damage done to his daughter at the hands of your son." Acid lacing every word, I stand glaring at him.

Pete opens his mouth, but isn't able to get anything past his pompous lips by the time my control slips. I have his shirt snatched up tight and pull him in so close that I can't even see his face. Spittle flies at him as I roar, "Did. You. See. Her? Did you see what he did to her?" I let his shirt go and shove him toward the glass door of her room. He stumbles before he braces himself against the wall. I see him flinch when he catches sight of my girl.

Before I can do any more damage and put my hands on him again, I hear my dad's voice.

"That's enough, Deacon," he says sternly.

I look over my shoulder to see Guy and my pop standing there, looking grieved and shaken. I can't keep this up, especially in front of Guy. No matter how badly I want to.

"Yes, sir, you're right."

Agreeing with him resolutely, I turn back to the McAvoys

who are both standing at the door of her room, a look of total shock on both of their faces.

"You two aren't welcome here. If you don't leave on your own, I will have you escorted out," I warn in a deathly low voice. They don't say anything else as they hurry past us. Just as they are getting into the elevator, I call out, "And her name isn't Fran; she hates that."

I don't wait for an answer or even look in their direction to see if they heard me. It had been more for me anyways.

I tell my dad and Guy that they can go in to see her now, just to send Indie out since only two at a time are allowed. I go back to the waiting room with everyone else, and sit in a chair in the corner away from them all. My head back against the wall, I can feel my body literally shutting down on me little by little before I'm just completely numb from the loss of adrenaline that I've been riding for the past few hours. All I can remember thinking before I get pulled into sleep is if I would ever not feel numb again?

EARLY THE NEXT afternoon, after sitting with Frankie for what feels like days, I'm asked to leave the room so that the doctor can look her over. As I'm searching for a decent cup of coffee, I feel my pocket vibrate. I pull out the phone and see that it's Reggie. He and Trent are at Andrews' house collecting Frankie's things. The minute we got the okay from the police I sent them. There is no way in hell she is ever going back there.

"Yo, man. I'm here getting her stuff and there's FBI all over the place," Reggie whispers, I'm guessing so no one around him hears.

"What the fuck are they doing there? Are they looking for something?"

"Nah, they just seem to be asking questions and they have some geek squad looking fucker here going through the computer. It doesn't make any sense."

"Do they have Frankie's laptop?" I've started pacing, thinking about the possibilities and what the hell the Feds want with a domestic violence scene.

"I already packed it before they asked and told them I didn't know anything about other computers in the house. Do you want me to give it to them?" he asks me, though he already knows the answer.

"No. I don't know what Drew was into, but there's no way I'm letting any of it fall back on Frankie." I don't care that I'm having him do illegal shit for me. I'll risk both of our freedoms if it means keeping her safe. I'm sure I'm overreacting, but I'm not willing to take any chances. "Just bring all of her stuff to my place for now; we can decide later what to do with it."

"You got it, brother. I'm clearing out of here now before they can ask me any more questions."

"Thanks, man. When she wakes up I don't want the Princess to know about any of this though, you feel me, Reg?" I know I don't have to tell him—he's always had my back.

"I feel you," he grunts before disconnecting the call.

What the fuck did Drew's dumbass get mixed up in?

Chapter SIX

INDIE IS SITTING in my usual spot next to Frankie's bed when I come back from grabbing a quick shower over at the hotel that we are all still staying at. None of us wants to be that far from her for any real amount of time.

"Any change?" I ask, even though I already know the answer.

It's been a week, and while the swelling on her brain has gone down almost completely and she's breathing on her own, she still hasn't woken up.

"No, still nothing. I just brushed her hair and braided it for her, painted her finger and toenails. She'll want to look pretty when she wakes up," she says with as much enthusiasm as she can manage, which isn't much at all.

"She'll appreciate how well you've taken care of her, Indie. You're right, she wouldn't want to look like shit, and she'd be pissed at us if we allowed that."

Not that she could ever look like shit, but I was trying to lighten the mood a bit for Indie—hell, for myself too.

"Why don't you go and grab some food? They just ordered Chinese in the room; Sonny said to tell you it's from that place you love so much. Go, go eat while it's still hot. I've got her." I smile encouragingly at her.

I know she's feeling as helpless and off kilter as I am with our girl still out, but I need her to hold it together a little longer. I have to focus all of my energy on Frankie right now, and I don't need Indie breaking down. Truth be told, I think we are drawing strength off of each other and I'm a little afraid of what might happen to my resolve if she shatters. She looks over at the bed and nods.

"You'll call me if she wakes up, right?"

"You know I will, Jones."

"Okay, I'll go eat and maybe lay down for a bit. I can be here in two minutes if you need me though."

I jerk my head toward the door. "I know it. Now get out of here; you're in my chair."

"Prick," she mumbles good-naturedly as she walks by me and out the door.

I sink into the seat she's vacated and take Frankie's hand in mine, careful of her wet nails. I place a kiss on the inside of her wrist and reach into my pocket with my other hand for my phone, plugging it into the dock that I keep next to her bed. "Hey, Princess. I just talked to Jack. Him and Cara were calling to check on you. I told him that I've been playing music while we hang out. He said he's going to put a playlist together for us, but that I had to play you this new song that he heard. Jack says he has no fucking clue what they're talking about, but he digs it and if I blow him any shit for it, he's gonna junk punch me the next time he sees me, so I'm guessing it's a giant vagina song," I tell her chuckling.

I tend to ramble when I'm here with her, but the doctors all think it's good that I talk to her, so I just go with it. Even if they didn't, I'd still do it.

"Let's see what this pussy has us listening to."

I click on the link he sent me and lean forward, placing my arms on the bed beside her and listen to the song with her. I will never admit it to him or anyone else, but I kinda dig it too.

"You loved the shit out of that, didn't you?" I ask once the song ends, shaking my head.

I'm scrolling through the playlists when Mav walks in.

"Hey, brother, how's the Princess today?" he greets.

"Same. How'd it go down at the station?" I ask since he had a meeting with the detectives on her case earlier today.

They still haven't found Andrew, not a hit on his phone or credit cards; it's like he vanished. If he's smart, he'll stay that way, but he proved how stupid he is the day he fucking laid hands on Frankie.

"They've still got nothing. Where the hell could he be? How does a person just disappear like that? It's like he's a fucking ghost," Mav says, exasperated.

He doesn't expect an answer which is good, because I don't have one for him, so we just sit in comfortable silence with our girl, listening to some of the Italian music that she loves so much. It makes me feel closer to her; I can almost hear her singing the words. I have no clue what the fuck they are singing about. I'm about to turn it up when Mav says, "Oh fuck! Who called him?"

My head shoots up and I whip it around to see who he's talking about.

"You know who that is, don't you, Deac?"

I narrow my eyes trying to place the guy leaning against the glass door staring at Frankie with a look of total devastation on his face. I recognize it because it's the same look I see when I look at myself in the mirror. I can't place him right away though and then it hits me.

"Who the fuck told Flashdance? Isn't he supposed to be competing on another fucking continent?"

Maverick just nods. Flashdance, or Cristiano Palomo, as he prefers to be called, had been Frankie's dance partner while I was in the service. He had also been her first serious boyfriend and her "first" everything else. To say I hate him with every fiber of my being would be putting it mildly. My brothers had dubbed him "Flashdance" when they first met him while I was in boot camp. He hated it, so naturally it stuck. This is obviously our thing. He and Frankie were together for two years when he asked her to leave with him to go live in Spain and compete there and in Europe. Clearly he didn't know her if he thought that she'd ever agree to leave her dad. She said no and he left, leaving our girl brokenhearted and without a dance partner. That's when she switched gears and started teaching more than competing and really started focusing on her contemporary dancing.

I see him reaching for the handle when the nurse stops him. He hasn't taken his eyes off of Frankie, so he still hasn't entirely registered Mav and me sitting there until the nurse points us out, most likely explaining to him that only two people can be in here at a time. Cristiano doesn't look happy and I can honestly say I couldn't give a fuck less. In fact, I'm willing to bet that zero fucks are given by my brother and me.

"Can I trust you alone with him, dude? You know he's not going to leave without seeing her."

I glare at my dumbass brother.

"I'm not going to start laying people out in her hospital room, Mav. I'll have the decency to at least take him outside," I say with a smirk.

"You're a bad motha—"

"Shut your mouth," I finish for him.

We look at each other and laugh. I'm pretty sure it's the first real laugh we've shared since we got here.

"This should be interesting," he says as he strides toward the door. "I'm just going to grab some coffee for us. I won't be far and Reggie is in the waiting room if you need him," he calls over his shoulder.

I grunt in answer, my eyes never leaving Cristiano, who is back to watching Frankie. I hate it. I hate this whole situation obviously, but I hate that she is so vulnerable lying here and that people are seeing her like this. My girl isn't weak or timid, she's a scrapper, but also so elegant in everything she does. I like to tell her that she's "Classy as Fuck." A lady in every sense of the word, but still wouldn't hesitate to cut a bitch if need be or tell you to go fuck yourself. Ergo, "Classy as Fuck." Just the thought makes me smile. That ends real quick though when I hear him enter the room.

By the time he makes it over to the other side of the bed, I'm so tense my leg is bouncing and I can feel the muscle in my jaw jumping like mad. I glance up to find him scowling at me.

"What happened to your face, Deacon?" he asks in an accusing tone that I do not fucking appreciate. Not one fucking bit. It's like all of these assholes forget what I do for a living, and why are they all so quick to assume I put hands on her? Just because my job is to hurt people doesn't mean I'm a monster.

My eyes narrow and that twitch in my jaw takes off as I clench my teeth and count to ten, reminding myself that I told Mav that I wouldn't lay anyone out at her bedside—though when I said it I didn't realize how hard that would be.

"What the fuck do you think happened to my face, Flash-dance?" I snarl and he flinches a bit, though I'm not sure if it's from the venom behind my words or the use of his little nick-name.

"I had a fight the night that she called me for help, you fuck," I growl, trying with everything I have to reel in my temper. "Don't think that you can waltz your pretty boy ass in here and start making assumptions and accusations. If you think for one minute that I'll put up with that shit from you, or anyone else for that matter, for even one second, you are sadly mistaken. Sadly fucking mistaken. So I suggest you take that bulllshit somewhere else."

I hadn't realized that I am now standing and leaning toward him over Frankie's bed until Reggie pokes his head in.

"Hey, Deac, bro, you okay in here?" he asks in that scary,

low voice of his.

I don't even bother looking at him, keeping my gaze focused on this motherfucker, when I ask, "We good here, Flashdance, or are you ready to go?"

He looks down at Frankie and shakes his head.

"No, we're good. I'm sorry. I—I wasn't prepared to see her look like this and then I saw you and all of your bruises and I just—just lost my head for a second. I apologize," he says in a quiet voice.

I don't acknowledge his apology, leaning in and kissing the Princess on the head, and then on her wrist, whispering low in her ear, so that only she would hear, that I'm sorry for losing my shit and that she can give me hell for it later. I kiss her again and sit back in my seat, taking her hand and placing one more kiss to the inside of her wrist, taking a second to just breathe her in and let her heart pulse against my lips. It soothes me a bit, that soft throbbing telling me that my girl is still here, still fighting.

Cristiano shifts from foot to foot and clears his throat.

"Can I have a minute alone with her?" he asks timidly.

I look over at him, my eyebrows pulled low and give him a dubious look. "Not gonna happen, I don't leave her unless it's absolutely necessary, and I just got back from grabbing a shower, so I'm good."

He huffs out an exasperated breath, which I ignore.

"Fine, can you tell me what happened to her then? I got a phone call from a friend of ours who happened to see the story on the news and I came immediately. She said that the news wasn't saying much. Is it because they don't know anything?"

Answering him is like torture. I don't want to talk to him at all, let alone hash out what happened that night.

"They don't know much because she hasn't woken up to tell them what went down yet. All they have to go on is that she said Andrew's name when she called me and that they haven't been able to find him since that night."

I can see the shock and confusion on his face.

"Why? Why would he do this to her? I don't understand."

That makes two of us, but I'm not about to bond with his ass over it.

"I called her just a couple of weeks ago when I heard the news that she was engaged," he says more to himself than me.

"You spoke to her?" This was news to me. "Did you talk often?"

He gave a tiny shake of his head.

"No, maybe a few times a year. My girlfriend didn't like it. I called her to congratulate her, but I couldn't do it." He shakes his head again as if remembering. "I told her not to marry him, that I'd move back, teach with her, and compete here."

If I thought I was tense before, not even close. Now I'm about two point five seconds from completely going ballistic at his words. It's as if he doesn't even realize that he's saying them out loud. He almost seems dazed and a little out of it, but still he goes on.

"She was so angry. She said 'Why does everyone keep doing this to me?' I didn't understand what she meant, and before I could ask her, she hung up on me, and I haven't talked to her since."

He's still looking down at her, holding her hand, lost in his own thoughts, and I in mine. I knew what she was talking about. First me and then him…seems like Cristiano didn't realize a good thing when he had it right in front of him either. I'll be damned if I'd give him a chance to change that though. This Rico Suave motherfucker is not going to get in between me and Frankie. I've already let Andrew do that and it nearly killed her. I am done with that shit. I'm ready to fight dirty if I have to, and the way he's looking at her with love and longing in his eyes and the gentle way he holds her hand tells me that I'm going to have to do just that. I'm ready. She's worth it and we both know it.

Before I can voice my plan and start an all-out war, Mav

sticks his head in. "Times up. I gotta get my Princess fix before Guy gets here."

He looks like he's about to argue. I can see how pissed he is that he really has no say, no place in her life anymore that would earn him the right. He just nods and then leans down whispering in Spanish. I'm not fluent, but I understand enough because of Frankie and her love of languages, always spouting off with her multilingual talents. I catch every couple words and they piss me off. I hear "Blah, blah…I'm here now, my love… blah, blah…safe….blah, blah, blah…not leaving again," before I clear my throat and ask, "Shouldn't you go and call your girl-friend, let her know that you landed safely?"

The look he gives me is murderous, which does nothing but make me smile at him. He lays her hand down and walks out without another word to either of us.

"Well, that went well, huh? Reggie said there had been a 'moment.' You want to tell me about it?" Mav asks, his eye-brows raised.

"Not really, though I will say it's a good thing that you made me promise not to go to blows before you left."

I'm not sure why I expect him to be surprised by that, but he isn't.

"I'm not a dumbass, Deac. I see you, brother. I see how you're barely hanging on to your sanity as it is and then he shows up. You're a minute away from detonation, and it'd take a whole lot less than Cristiano to set you off right now."

He must see the pissed off look on my face because he quickly says, "Nobody blames you for being on edge, Deacon. Hell, we're all riding the fence right now. We're just not as vol-atile as you are."

He says the last part on a chuckle to lessen the blow a bit. He's right, I know it, and clearly so does everyone else.

LONG AFTER MAV leaves, I'm still sitting here just watching her, willing her to wake up. I sigh loudly and pull my chair closer to the bed, taking her hand in mine and brushing the hair off her forehead, careful not to touch any of her wounds. Her mouth is pulled down in a frown, which is not the norm for my girl when she's awake, but it reminds me of a time when we were younger.

"Hey, Frankie, you remember that time in high school that tool, Nick, asked you out? He came to your dad's to pick you up and my brothers and I made sure that we were there to answer the door?" Smiling as I recall his face, I continue, "He was so scared, Princess. Stuttering and shit. It was so hard for us not to laugh at him. Fuck, you were so pissed." I laugh softly. Gently, I take her hand and place a kiss to my spot, exhaling against her wrist and say quietly, "Even then, I knew, Frankie. Even then, when I was too young to appreciate you, when I was doing my best to keep the guys away from you, pretending like I was doing it to protect you like some kind of big brother. Even then, I knew that I loved you and not just like the pain in the ass little sister that Mav and Sonny treated you like. I loved you, but I wasn't ready for you. I hadn't earned the right for you to love me back yet."

Chapter
SEVEN

I'M NOT SURE what time it is or what has woken me up. Slowly I open my eyes and take in the dimly lit room without actually moving my head, since my neck feels like one big knot. "Without You" is still playing. I'd been feeling the weight of missing Frankie in a big way yesterday and had put it on repeat…guess I fell asleep before turning it off.

I'm sitting in my usual chair with one of my hands tucked underneath Frankie's thigh, my head resting practically in her lap and my other hand loosely holding hers, which is how I find myself waking up most days. Any way that I can touch her, even in sleep, I'm taking it. If I weren't so damn big and afraid of hurting her, I'd climb into the bed next to her.

I take a deep breath and let my eyes start to drift shut again, when I feel a soft touch like fingers running through my hair. I slowly raise my head, not willing to believe after ten long days that she might actually be awake, and turn to look at the head of the bed. My girl is there, blue eyes open, the most beautiful fucking sight I have ever seen. I squeeze my eyes shut and put my head back down in her lap as the guttural sob rips through me, tears that I hadn't allowed myself to cry streaming down my face and onto the blanket, my shoulders shaking. I feel her soothing me with her gentle touch on my head. My body still trembling beneath the weight of my emotions, I start to gather

her and everything on the bed into me, bringing the Princess closer, but stop myself before I can hurt her or dislodge anything.

It all came crashing down on me at once the moment I saw those blues, the ones I'd been afraid I would never see again. All of the rage that had been consuming me, the absolute terror at the possibility that she might not come back to me. It was all coming to the surface and spilling over. It takes everything I have to pull it together and look at her again, to accept the reality that she's here. My girl is awake and she is taking care of me while she lies in the ICU. Typical.

Taking a deep breath, I face Frankie and take her in. Her bruises have faded to angry shades of purple and green with some yellow and blue thrown in for good measure. The cuts all over her body are finally starting to heal, although a plastic surgeon did have to stitch a few closed because of how deep they were. For once I have no idea what to say to her. I'm so relieved I'm literally speechless.

"Princess—" My voice cracks, my chin hits my chest, as I take in another shaky breath. "You're beautiful, you know that? Fucking hell, I can't tell you how fucking happy I am to see those beautiful blues eyes, baby. So fucking happy."

The tears are forming again but there is nothing I can do about it. I shake my head and bring her hand up to my mouth and kiss my spot on the inside of her wrist. She reaches out and touches my still beat-up face and split brow, concern in her eyes. Frankie opens her mouth to speak but nothing comes out. She struggles to swallow past what I'm sure is the worst case of cotton mouth ever. I reach past her to grab the pitcher of water on the tray table and pour her some, still not letting go of her.

Bringing the straw to her mouth I tell her, "Slow, small sips. I'm not sure if you should even have any of this right now. I need to call for the nurse."

She nods her understanding as she takes a small sip and

finally speaks.

"How long have I been here? How long have you been here?"

Her voice is even raspier than usual, but it doesn't matter as long as she's talking. I grab for the call button hanging from the bed and press it, summoning the nurse.

Instead of answering her question, I ask one of my own.

"Do you know who I am, Frankie?"

I don't know why that is so important to me right now, but it's something that I have worried about. You see it in the movies all of the fucking time. Person gets in accident, wakes up from coma, has no fucking clue who the poor asshole crying at their bedside is, no idea that it's actually their person. And whether she knows it or not, or is ready for this, for us, I am her person and she is mine.

She gives a little rusty laugh, "Like I could ever forget who you are, Deacon."

Her voice sounds so weak, it makes me nervous.

"I know that's right."

I wink at her and squeeze her hand, not letting my worry show.

"I—

Whatever she is about to say is interrupted by the nurse rushing in.

"Oh! Look who's awake! Why, hello there, pretty girl. I'm Pam, your nurse for the next little while at least. Mary will be here soon and she is going to be thrilled to see that you have joined us. This one here has been giving her a hard time." She tilts her head in my direction.

"I don't doubt that for a minute. He can be a bit of a bully sometimes," Frankie says while trying to smile at me. I can see that interacting is really starting to take its toll and that she won't be awake for much longer.

"Only when it comes to my girl, Frankie. Gotta take care

of you."

"How cute is he? Now get out of here so that I can check out my patient. I'll page Dr. Ashley now, and if it's ok with Francesca, you can come back in when he gets here."

Locking eyes with Frankie, I smile reassuringly, "I'll be in the hall calling everyone. Your Pop and Indie will probably want up here."

"Not tonight, Mr. Love. You can tell them she's awake and that I'll be able to let them up here no sooner than 7 a.m."

I'm about to argue when she starts talking again.

"Mary lets you stay because you're not coming and going during off hours. She would have to get clearance to let anyone up here in the middle of the night. I wouldn't push my luck with her or she might revoke your slumber party rights."

The nurse is talking to me, but I'm not paying much attention, instead I'm watching her work on Frankie. I catch a flinch of pain, which puts me on edge and causes that muscle in my jaw to start dancing.

"Careful with her, Nurse Ratchet," I say in as playful a voice as I can, because I'm really not fucking playing.

With closed eyes, nearly asleep, Frankie says, "Get out of here, Deac, and let her be. She's being very gentle." I can barely hear her now, Frankie's voice is so low.

"I'm going. I'll be right outside the door here waiting for Dr. Ashley and making my calls."

As I'm leaving, I look back just as the nurse is pulling the curtain to give her privacy, and the look on my girl's face about does me in. She looks sad and lost, tired and scared, just broken inside and out, and I hate it.

She is so strong and confident in everything she does, and to see her like this makes my fucking heart hurt.

"Hey, Princess!"

Frankie's eyes open slowly, her brows raised in question.

"I'm here, okay? Everything is going to be all right. I got

you, Frankie. Always."

She gives me a watery smile and nods her head in agreement, the braids and barrette that Indie put in her hair making her look incredibly young, which only add to her air of vulnerability.

Chapter EIGHT

"DETECTIVES." I NOD at Flores—I still don't like that cagey prick—as I reach across to shake Detective Adams' hand.

Her I like, and not because she's a woman either. I'm not sure what it is about her, but I feel like she has my girl's best interests at heart. Frankie isn't just another case to her; she actually matters.

"Frankie is having some tests done. I'm not sure when she'll be back or if she'll be up to talking with you today. It's already been a clusterfuck of a day for her."

Adams nods her head in understanding. "I promise not to push her, Mr. Love. It's just better to do this as soon as possible so that things are fresh, and she's already been out for so long. We don't want whoever did this to get away with it."

I grunt my agreement. I know who fucking did it, they just need to find his sorry ass.

"We'll be back in a bit," Adams says, smiling reassuringly at me.

"Sounds good, I'll be here," I tell them, heading back into Frankie's room as they walk away.

About an hour later, she's rolled into the room. The nurse locks the bed and goes about hanging up fluid bags and messing with the rest of the shit Frankie is still hooked to. My girl looks exhausted, mentally and physically. She turns her head toward me and gives me a small smile.

"Hey, Princess, how did it go?" I ask her while reaching for her hand, kissing my spot.

"I slept through most of it," she tells me in a quiet voice.

"That's good. You need your rest, baby. Listen, the detectives were here and they want to ask you some questions about that night. I told them that you may not feel up to it, so just say the word and I'll have them come back another day," I tell her as I brush the hair off of her forehead.

"Will you stay with me, Deac? I don't want anyone else in here though. Not my dad or Indie, only you."

Her tone is pleading, which hurts me. I'm glad that she trusts me though, that she asked, because there is no way that I'm not going to be here. I need to know what actually happened that night. I haven't had the time to talk to her about it yet.

"Of course I'll stay."

Giving her a reassuring smile I turn to her nurse.

"Can you make sure that everyone stays in the waiting room when the detectives are in here, please? Blame it on me if you have to; I don't mind being the bad guy. I usually am anyway." I give her a wink to further convince her that she should do my bidding.

"No problem. I'll keep them out and send the detectives in once I'm finished here," she tells us, patting Frankie's leg.

I turn my eyes back to Frankie and notice that her eyes are closed, her breathing slow. She's out. Chuckling, I let her sleep. I'll wake her when they come in to grill her.

Francesca

I FEEL SOMEONE gently nudging me, trying to wake me. Opening my eyes, I see Deac smiling from what I've noticed is his usual spot next to my bed. I feel bad that he has been sleeping in the horribly uncomfortable looking chair, but also relieved that he's there.

"There's my girl. The detectives are here to talk to you. You feeling okay?" he asks while stroking his hand over my hair. Deacon is a toucher, always has been.

Struggling to sit up, I clear my throat and nod. Every muscle in my body aches. The already throbbing joints scream out when I shift, but it's nothing compared to the emotional agony I'm about to be in. I've played that night over and over in my head, but so many parts are fuzzy. It frustrates me. Makes me anxious.

I glance warily at the detectives standing just inside the room. One is a tall, striking woman; the other, a bulky, stone-faced man. The woman steps forward, coming closer to my bed, hand extended.

"Hello, Miss De Rosa. My name is Detective Adams. I'm happy to see you awake. You gave everyone quite a scare." Her smile eases my nerves a bit.

I release Deacon's hand to shake the one she has offered.

Detective Adams motions in the man's direction, "That's my partner, Detective Flores. We're just here to ask you a few questions about the night you were assaulted. Do you think you're up to it?" Still with that gentle smile on her face, she releases my hand.

Giving her a small nod, she grabs the chair from across the room and pulls it over to my bedside.

"If at any time you need a break just let us know," Detective Adams says with empathy laced in her voice.

"Okay." I look at her partner who standing there and I tense up.

Detective Adams doesn't miss my reaction and she places her hand next to mine, drawing my attention back to her. "If you like, I can have the boys leave and we can just chat. Do you mind if I call you Francesca?"

My hand automatically finds Deacon's and I grip it tightly.

I shake my head no and draw a deep breath. "No, I don't mind. I'm tired, but I would like to get this over with, so we can do it now."

"Remember, Francesca, any details will help us find who did this to you. Nothing is too big or small. So just take your time and walk us through anything you remember." Detective Adams makes sure that I understand what she is saying. "Okay? Whenever you're ready...."

I nod again, apparently it's all I am capable of. I glance over at Deacon, his hair pulled back in a messy man bun. He squeezes my hand reassuringly and leans forward closer to me, which calms me. I'm a little uneasy and unsure about how he's going to react—you can never tell with him—but I know it's not going to be good. It's selfish for me to ask him to stay, but I need him to be able to get through this.

Ready to just get this over with, I sit a second, trying to rein in my galloping heart. I look one more time at Deacon, who is looking down at our joined hands, and then back to Detective Adams, bracing myself for the task at hand of reliving the nightmare of that day and fighting my own mind for the details.

Glancing at the clock one more time, I debate whether I should just leave a note for Andrew or if that's the chickenshit way out. Going into our bedroom, I grab the two pieces of luggage that I've packed and roll them to the front door. Just as I make my way back into the kitchen, I hear him in the garage. This is it; it's now or never. He knows that something is off—we talked briefly about how we were growing apart, and he of course blamed Deacon, which is a big part of it, even if I haven't spoken to him in months.

I don't have much more time to think about it when I hear the mud-room door squeak open. "I was about to give up on you," I call out, trying to keep the mood light.

Just as I'm turning to flip the light on and greet him properly, brave face firmly in place, I'm bashed in the head with something solid. I see nothing but stars as I fall to the floor, reaching for him. Once I hit the ground, I have no time to get my bearings before he grabs me by the arm, yanking me upright and pushing me against the counter. I try to focus but the room is spinning. His hands wrap around my throat, tightening as he slams my head against the cabinet.

"I didn't think you would be here, Francesca? Where the fuck is he?" he hisses at me, his cherry and tobacco scented breath hot against my lips. He must have been at the cigar bar with a client, that's the only time he smokes. I wish he would've stayed, I think in a haze.

"Wh—who? Deacon? He's not here, I swear, nobody is here," I sob.

"Where. Is. He?" With each angry word, his grip gets tighter. I can't speak. The pressure he's applying is cutting off my air, causing a tight burning in my chest. I can't even shake my head to tell him no because of his iron tight hold and the throbbing behind my eyes making everything fuzzy. He makes a low frustrated noise in his throat.

My hands are wrapped around his wrist, nails digging into his flesh, trying to get him to loosen his hold. "Where is it?" he asks and I don't respond. I have absolutely no clue what he's talking about. What is "it"? Deacon?

He bangs my head against the kitchen cabinets once, twice, three times. Each time harder than the last. Causing pain to shoot from my skull to my shoulders with each jarring thud. The metallic smell of blood makes bile rise to the back of my throat as it trickles from the gash in my head, down my face, obscuring my view. All I can see are his dark brown eyes which are absolutely wild and filled with disgust. He starts reaching for his belt with the hand not secured around my throat. "I bet I can make you talk. How about if I fuck the truth from you while I choke the life out of you for being a lying bitch," he snarls at me, hatred dripping off of every word. I don't even recognize his voice, it's filled with such malice.

Up until that point, I had been frozen in fear, but the thought of him forcing himself on me spurs me into action and my fight or flight response finally kicks in. My throat on fire from lack of oxygen, still dazed from him banging my already injured head, I manage to raise my arm and swing wildly at him, clipping his temple with my closed fist.

"You fucking bitch! You wanna fight, sweetheart?" he asks with a demonic smile on his face, the only thing visible the flash of his white teeth. I question myself repeatedly... Why? Why would he do this? What is he talking about? What truth? These question swirl around as I try to keep from passing out. The shooting pain in my head is making me so tired and weak. I just want to close my eyes for a little bit.

Abandoning my throat, he wraps a fist in my loose hair while I struggle to pull in great big gulps of air. He wrenches my head backwards, dragging me toward the bedroom. I stumble, struggling against his brutal hold on my hair, when he jerks me forward again, and as I start to go down, he yanks me upright and backhands me. The pain explodes across my cheekbone, the skin splitting. I cry out and he does it again, this time catching me in the mouth, the coppery tang of blood against my tongue instantaneous.

I fall to my knees in agony. When I reach out to try and catch myself, I sprawl forward, upsetting the dining chair and toppling the table. I'm once again snatched by my hair and dragged while I scramble to crab walk behind him. Once in the bedroom, he flings me toward the bed, the forward momentum sending me flying into the nightstand, breaking the bedside lamp and I take a hit from the mattress directly in the abdomen, knocking the wind right out of me. All the while I can smell the sulfur from the candle I had blown out earlier and the tobacco and cherry scent clinging to his clothes and hands. Sobbing in earnest, I crumple to the floor, my stomach muscles clenching from the lack of air. As I struggle to breathe, he kicks me hard in the ribs, screaming obscenities at me.

"Tell me where!" he demands with such venom.

He kicks me again, and this time I'm sure that he has cracked a *rib, and what little breath I had managed to take in is stolen from me. I swallow back the bile brought on by the onslaught of pain and try to focus on getting air into my lungs. Curled up into the fetal position, I put my arms in front of my face to shield any other blows that might be coming. He's completely unhinged, obviously set on causing me as much pain as he can possibly inflict. I don't know this man. He's become someone dark and terrifying, nothing like the man I once loved.*

He keeps kicking me, and I moan when an especially hard kick catches me in the temple, completely stunning me. My vision had been going in and out with each hit, and now my ears are ringing to the point that I can barely understand what he is saying to me.

He grabs me roughly by my arm and pulls me to my feet, my ribs screaming in agony, my legs jelly from the pain. I can feel the blood trickling down my face into my eyes, my split lip swollen, my arms and head throbbing in protest. With one hand, he squeezes my face in a steely grip, the other holding me upright by the arm as I hang weakly at his mercy. Crying in fear and defeat, my heart no longer beats rapidly in terror, but instead slowly thumps in a dispirited tempo.

He's going to kill me.

"Such a beautiful name, a gorgeous face, and it's all a fucking lie. You're a dirty plaything for a vile, white trash, piece of shit. Do you know that? He thinks he's so smart, that he can fuck with me. It's a shame you'll have to suffer the lesson I must teach him. Such a shame he doesn't value you the way that he should. Doesn't recognize your worth, the way that I can see your worth." I can feel him leaning in, smell the sweet tang of cherry on his fingertips. It's unfamiliar. I can't place the scent any more than I can the man I thought I knew.

His hand is like a vice, and I'm terrified that he's going to dislocate my jaw any second. I almost wish he would, maybe then I would black out and this nightmare would come to an end. Somehow I don't think this is going to stop until he kills me though. He swipes the back of his hand over my mouth, clearing it of blood, spit, and snot. I would cry out if I could, but there's not enough air or energy left in me as he kisses me roughly before hurling me toward the bathroom.

"One last chance. Tell me where." I'm not able to focus long enough to form a coherent thought through the debilitating haze of pain and terror that has washed over me, let alone answer his questions. "No? Then I will take what's mine out of you for now. Not when you look like this. You'll wash all of his filth off of you before I touch you."

He's not making any sense. I shake my head no, ready to beg him, but he rears back and lets his fists fly. That simple refusal clearly annihilating whatever thread of control he had been hanging on to.

I put my arms up again to protect myself as best I can, but he lands blow after bone rattling blow, forcing me farther and farther into the bathroom. Startled by his new found strength and the force behind every hit, I start to fall backwards, my arms windmilling furiously to catch my balance, but he doesn't allow it. With another punishing kick to my stomach, I fold at the waist and feel yet another rib give way. I don't even see the fist coming at me that sends me sprawling through the shower doors and slamming hard into the glass shelf on the opposite wall of the enclosure. I am barely able to raise my arms as glass rains down on me and I finally feel the blackness taking me under, stopping the excruciating pain I'm in. Who is this monster?

I'm brought back from my thoughts when I feel Deacon squeezing my hand almost to the point of pain. I hadn't even realized that I'm crying, my body trembling from the onslaught of emotions. "Deac?"

He glances up and I can see the anguish written all over his face before he schools his features and loosens his grip. "Sorry." One word as he bends his head and places a kiss to my wrist, leaving his lips there for a moment.

"Francesca, do you know what time this was?" Adams asks thoughtfully.

I close my eyes, trying to picture as much as I can about that day.

"It was dark...I couldn't see much and I had just blown out the candle. I was going to turn the lamp on when I heard the garage door. I don't recall the time, only that it was dark out and that Andrew was late, he said that he would be home before five."

Gradually I open my eyes, unable to recall anything else from the memory. Not able to look at Deacon, I pull a breath into my too tight chest and dash the tears still flowing.

"Francesca, can you tell me what he was wearing? You said that you thought that he had been at the cigar bar...do you know the name of it?" she asks gently.

Hands wrapped around Deacon's, I narrow my eyes, willing myself to remember. "I think, I think it was blue. I remember him wearing blue that morning...no, brown." Rubbing my forehead I look up at her. "I can't remember."

"It's okay, we'll circle back to that. Do you know the name of the cigar bar?"

"He likes to go to The Redhead on Ontario," I tell her confidently. I know that answer.

"Did he say that he was going there on his way home?"

I shake my head no.

"Then what made you think that that's where he had been?" she questions gently.

"The smell. It wasn't his cologne, it was cherries and tobacco. He doesn't smoke other than the occasional cigar." I shrug, "It's the only thing that I could think to explain it. The only thing that made sense."

"Okay." The soft lilt of her voice doesn't help soothe the tension or ease the adrenaline causing my heart to race and then stutter as I try to remember details of that night that seem just out of reach. I can smell it all and feel every punishing blow, every ounce of hurt, hear the sound of my own cries, but I can't fill in the missing pieces.

Slowly I shake my head to rid myself of the images of that night. My tongue darts to the corner of my mouth and the salty tears clinging there. A broken sob makes its way past my lips when I look over at Deacon. He has one hand thrust into his hair gripping so tight I'm afraid he'll rip it out. His leg bounces furiously and the muscle in his jaw ticks violently. I squeeze the hand still holding mine until he looks at me. The tortured look in his beautiful, hazel eyes wrecks me. I shouldn't have asked him to stay and sit through that. I know the type of man that he is, and that had to be so incredibly hard for him to hear.

"Francesca, I know that was extremely difficult for you, but if you can just bear with me for a few minutes more, we'll leave you be, okay?" the detective says in her soothing voice. "Did he seem like he had been drinking?" She pauses waiting for me to answer but I just shrug. "Was he alone?" I nod yes, my brows pulled in concentration, tugging at my stitches uncomfortably. "Who else did he think was there?"

I huff out a frustrated breath. Reaching and grasping for the answers, but not able to grab a hold of them. "I don't think he had been drinking but maybe. He always has a scotch with his cigar, but I don't think he was drunk. Then again, he wasn't acting like himself, so I guess he could've been." Running my fingers over my tender scalp, I can feel the tears gathering and falling faster and faster as I try to massage the information free, but I just can't find it. "I don't know. I just don't know!" The anguished sound that escapes me startles us all as I shout, "I can't remember! It hurts to think about it! It physically and emotionally hurts." My cries get louder, the floodgates now completely open. "Please, I—I d-don't know," I stutter brokenly, closing my eyes to shut them out.

Clearing his throat, Deacon brings my wrist to his lips and places a kiss in his spot, his lips trembling slightly, his stubble scratching familiarly. He talks softly against my skin. Doing his best to soothe me. Standing, he looks down at me, devastation written all over him.

"I have to take a minute, Princess. I think we could all use one. I just need to get my shit straight, okay?"

He doesn't wait for me to answer, just kisses his spot again and strides to the door. I press my lips together tightly, biting them to keep the plea from escaping, that he can't leave me alone with them right now. Once across the room, he opens the door wide, and says in a monotone, "Detectives, I think that's all that she can handle for one day. She's still recovering and I don't think that we should push her anymore today."

They glance at each other and then both stand to leave. Detective Adams steps closer and grips my hand. "You did well, Francesca. Here's my card. If you remember anything about what he was wearing, what he may have been looking for or who, call me."

They nod their goodbyes to me before heading past Deacon. He closes the door behind them and comes back over to me. I watch him as he nears. And I can see every emotion on his face, in his movements, and they all chip away at my already fragile soul.

Once at my side, he doesn't say anything at first, just sits, eyes roaming my tear-stained face as he wipes them away with his callused fingers. Our gazes meet, he takes a deep breath, screwing his eyes shut, and brings my wrist back to his mouth. The beating of my heart is like a deafening roar in the silence of the room, and I can barely hear him whisper brokenly, "I'm sorry. I'm so fucking sorry."

I just broke the strongest man I know.

Chapter NINE

DEACON

FINALLY! AFTER NEARLY two weeks, they're springing my girl today, and I couldn't be happier. I think that in order for her to heal properly we need to get her the hell out of the hospital. Away from the reminder of who put her here. I fought and fought for her to stay with me, but she refuses. She's so damn stubborn. We all agree that with Guy's schedule it would be best for her to stay with Indie.

The elevator doors open, I wave hello to the nurses as I walk to Frankie's room, stopping dead in my tracks when I see Cristiano standing in the hall with a bouquet of flowers.

"What are you doing here?" I ask as I reach him.

He eyes me warily. "I've come to see Francesca. The detectives are in there with her though, so I am waiting."

Not saying another word to him, I turn to her room and enter without knocking. She's with the detectives, not the doctors, so she doesn't need any privacy. I can hear Flashdance huffing and puffing about it, and see him stalk off as the door closes.

Three sets of eyes land on me the second the door closes, but there's only one pair of fiery blues I care about.

"Hey, Deacon. I was just getting ready to call you," Frankie says with a tired smile.

"Speak of the devil and all that, right, Princess?" Winking I turn to Detective Adams and offer my hand, and nod at Flores hovering in the corner, which seems to be the norm.

"Have you found any leads on Andrew?"

Adams glances at Frankie for permission before turning back to me and answering. "Not yet, Mr. Love, but we are doing our absolute best to find whoever did this."

I believe her. She seems to really be invested in finding Frankie justice. I wonder if she knows that the Feds are involved and if she's said anything to Frankie about it.

I take a seat on the bed, taking Frankie's hand as I do, placing a kiss in my spot.

"So what brings you guys here then?" looking between the pair for answers. They haven't been here since the day after she woke up.

"We just wanted to touch base with Miss De Rosa, make sure we had a phone number and address where she can be reached," Adams says.

"Will you have patrols on Indie's house until Andrew is caught or what?" If they don't, I will. There's no way that I am leaving her anywhere unprotected while his crazy ass is on the loose.

"We will do all we can to keep Ms. De Rosa safe, but you have to understand that there is only so much that the CPD can do in a situation like this," Flores says from his side of the room.

Fair enough. "I'll have someone with her at all times, regardless."

"Do you really think that's necessary?" Frankie replies with the fire in her voice that I've missed. "And what about Indie, huh?" Her lips purse and I can't stop the smile taking over my face. All right then, she wants to argue.

"This isn't negotiable." I stand my ground waiting for her

next move.

"I doubt she wants your goons hanging around the house all the time." Even beat down, my girl is a fighter. I smirk. She thinks that she can win this one. She can't.

Adams stands, interrupting our discussion. "We're going to go, but we'll be in touch soon. I'm glad you're feeling well enough to go home, Miss De Rosa." We thank her as they leave.

"Listen, it's necessary, and Indie will just have to deal." I give her hand a squeeze. "If you're worried about Indie feeling put out though, we can always move you into your room at my place," I tell her smugly.

Her mind is working it all over—I can see it in her heavy-lidded eyes. "I want to stay with Indie, and if it becomes a problem, I can figure something else out," she says reluctantly before turning her blues on me again. "Can it be Reggie though? I feel more comfortable with him and...safer, honestly."

"Anyone you want, baby," I agree.

"DEACON, YOU ARE being ridiculous," Frankie cries out. "You are not sleeping here. It's bad enough that you are making Reggie stay. You can't stay too," she says, but her tone is questioning as if she's not entirely sure that's true. It's not.

"I can and will do whatever I want, Princess. Don't you forget it." I tap her nose and stride over to the couch flopping down. "Jones!" I yell. "Bring me some food, woman!"

Poking her bandana covered head out of the kitchen, she flips me off and says, "You must have lost your motherfucking mind. Get it yourself and get your feet off of my furniture while you're at it, you animal."

I look over at a smiling and exhausted Frankie. "Come sit next to me. You look like you're about to drop." As she makes her way slowly over, I notice the lines of pain bracketing her mouth, the way she has an arm wrapped around her torso to hold her ribs. "Would it help if I carried you?" I ask in all seriousness.

Startled, she looks up at me and I can see that there are tears in her eyes from the hurt she's suffering, and it kills me. "I think that might make it worse, if that's even possible, but thanks, Deac. You know, I'm just going to go and lie down in my room instead. I'm really tired and I'm afraid that once I land somewhere, that's going to be my spot until tomorrow. Might as well make that spot be my bed." She laughs tightly and maneuvers around the coffee table, heading to her room.

Her suffering is the hardest thing for me to watch. I just want to make everything better, and not being able to is about to do my ass in. Unfolding myself from the couch, I go over and take her arm gently. I'm not sure where to touch her that won't hurt. She still has little cuts all over her, on top of the broken ribs and lingering concussion. I don't want to make it worse, but I need to help her. For me.

Once in the room, I rush forward and pull the blanket down on the new bed I ordered. One of those mechanical things so that she can be comfortable. I hand over the remote which allows her to lower the bed, making it easier to get in. As she sits on the edge of the bed, I help her to scoot back, then squat to take her shoes off. "You want to keep your socks on or do you still hate sleeping with them?" I ask, tossing the shoes behind me.

When she doesn't answer, I look up and see that the tears are really flowing now. Not just tears because she's in pain, these are different. These are fear, anguish, exhaustion, and defeat. All things I can't bear to see on her. My thumb swipes at them. "Hey, what's this?" I ask quietly. She struggles to suck in a breath, her taped ribs making it hard. Gingerly lowering myself onto the bed next to her, I tuck her into my side as gently as possible.

Once we're settled, I lift her wrist for a kiss. "Shhhh, I'm here now, baby. I swear to you, I will never let him put hands on you again. I'll never let *anyone* put hands on you again."

Shoulders shaking, she turns her face into my chest, her sadness soaking through the thin cotton of my shirt, burning my skin. I make a promise to myself right then that if I find him before the cops do, he won't survive me. Not a chance in hell would I let him get away with breaking Frankie.

After a few minutes of me whispering soothing words and stroking a hand over her head and back, I can tell by her breathing that she's asleep. Carefully I lay her down, pulling the blanket up. I watch as she sleeps, her tear-stained face the most beautiful thing I've ever seen. She's making me soft. I turn away from her before I have the urge to read her a damn bedtime story or some shit and go to the window checking the locks. Satisfied that she is locked in tight, I hit the lights and close the door behind me.

EVERYONE IS STILL asleep. I'm in the kitchen waiting on the coffee when I hear shuffling and a hiss. I turn just in time to see Frankie grab the doorframe in pain. "Damn it, Princess. Did you take your pain meds before getting out of bed?"

She hits me with a vicious glare—the lady is definitely not a good patient. "No, I didn't, because they're in here on the counter."

I'm a little afraid of this Frankie. Fairly certain that any minute now her head is going to start spinning. "Okay. Well, let's get you in a chair and I'll bring you everything you need, baby." A smile and a wink get me nothing, so I concentrate on settling her at the table and collecting the pain meds and a glass of water. As she takes her pills, I pray that they kick in quickly for both our sakes. Reaching into the cabinet, I bring down mugs for our coffee, chuckling when I read that one says: "Caution! Very hot. Blow Me." Maybe that will get a smile out of her. A shit ton of cream and sugar later, I hand Frankie a coffee and sit across from her with my "Blow Me" mug. "Isn't this nice? Just you and I sitting around drinking our coffee. We could be doing this in my kitchen so that I wouldn't have to sleep on Indie's uncomfortable ass couch, but whatever."

Her eyes meet mine over the rim of her cup and I don't like what I see there. My smile slips away. Slowly she puts her coffee down. "Deacon, thank you. Thank you for everything. I'm sorry that you had to forfeit fights to sit by and babysit me. Th—"

"I wasn't babysitting you. You were hurt. Fuck, we could've lost you!" I'm not sure where she's going with this, but I can feel myself getting angry. I don't want to lose my cool in front of her after everything that she's been through. Rolling my lips in over my teeth, I shake my head. "I'm sorry. I didn't mean to raise my voice."

"It's okay," she reassures me. "I just want you to know that I appreciate it and you. But—this can't—we can't..." Exasperated she huffs out, "I'm just not ready to get into what we talked about at my party and I don't want you to get the wrong idea." Not meeting my eyes she goes on "I don't know how this works or where we go from here, how to navigate us now that everything is out in the open." She trails off bringing her eyes to mine.

That anger I was trying to beat down is fighting its way to the surface, turning into frustration. Scratching at the stubble covering my chin, I weigh out my words. "So, what you're saying is you're scared. I get that. Don't you think I get that?" I can hear the desperation and exasperation in my voice.

"I am scared. I'm tired. I'm hurt. I only want to thank you because I know that you didn't have to be there. Not many people would've been." Frankie sighs wearily and continues, "But as grateful as I am, it still doesn't change anything with us. I don't want to…" Again, her voice trails off like she can't bring herself to finish the sentence.

Slowly I stand and place my mug down with a heavy thud, making her flinch. My feelings are completely unreasonable right now but I can't help them. I can't fight the frustration, anger or the guilt that I feel. It's not her fault. None of it is. I struggle to get my emotions in check and do my damnedest to let her know that I understand. I get that me staying by her side doesn't make us a couple. I just need to be sure that she knows that's not why I'm there. Why I'm still here. Her doubting my motives in the slightest kills me.

"Tell me one time I haven't been there when you needed me, Princess. One time that I haven't dropped everything to be by your side, whether it was a dance, a plumbing problem, a broken heart." My voice is controlled now, but breaks when I say, "Except for this one crucial time, I've always been your go-to guy. I couldn't save you from him that night, but I'm doing my best to save you from him now. I'm not here because I think it's going to get me into your pants quicker." I'm disgusted with this whole conversation. I place my palms on the table and lean toward her, forcing her to see me. "I'm here because I love you. But I've always loved you. That hasn't changed. Only the way I love you has."

She holds my gaze for a beat before glancing down at the hands gripping her mug, "Please, I just need time to figure out what I want. If this—" she moves her hand in between us, "is what I want." Our eyes meet. I can see the affliction in hers and I need out.

I straighten abruptly from the sting of her words and nod, letting her know I hear her. Turning I stride out of the kitchen before I give myself the chance to hurt either of us any more than I already have.

Chapter
TEN

THE PRINCESS HAS been home from the hospital for a couple months now, back at the gym for one, and it is both heaven and hell. I have either Reggie or Trent with her at all times because they still haven't found that douche bag, Drew.

Things between her and I have been a little strained ever since that morning in Indie's kitchen. I know that a lot of that has been the fear talking, and add to that the physical pain that she's in, and it's a fucking miracle we still talk at all, no matter how stilted.

I lashed out at her when I shouldn't have and I know a lot of that was because I feel partly to blame for everything that went down with Drew. Although deep down, I know that's ridiculous, I can't stop it. In my mind I let my girl down, wasn't there to protect her because I was too busy getting my dick sucked by some chick whose name I don't even know. All because my feelings were hurt. Hell, thinking about all I'd done over those last couple weeks when we hadn't been speaking made me want to kick my own ass! I know that we weren't together, but it still feels all wrong. If I'm honest with myself, it hadn't felt right while I was doing it either. I had just needed something to take away the hurt I felt from her rejection. Her refusing to take my calls, not calling me for two long ass months was exactly that:

rejection. It fucked with my head, pissed me off, and I'm not at my best when I get like that. That was one of those times.

Frankie's busy getting back to her normal routine, or as normal as she can. She's still pretty banged up and it's slowing her down, which pisses her off to no end. We still haven't talked about us, and I blame that on that prick Cristiano still hanging around. She was really excited to see him. Too fucking excited. He decided that he needs to stick around and help her with her classes and whatever else he can do when it comes to her dance studio. Don't think I don't know what the fuck he's doing. I make sure to bring up his girlfriend every chance I get. I'm tempted to fly her ass here for a little surprise visit. I miss my girl, and not just the one I want wrapped around my cock, but my friend as well.

Walking into the gym used to bring me such a sense of peace, but lately I'm pretty sure it's doing the exact opposite, which in turn is pissing me off on top of being pissed off.

My brothers are blowing me shit about it because it's fucking with my training, and I can't afford that shit right now. I bowed out of the season, taking forfeit after forfeit in order to be with Frankie in the hospital and even after because I wasn't ready to go on the road and leave her. So now I'm busting ass to try to make up points and get back in the standings for the championship.

I avoid looking over at her studio knowing that she and Flashdance will be in there together doing whatever the fuck they do, and instead make my way to my brothers who are talking over by the mats. I almost reach them when I hear Jay-Z and Linkin Park talking about 99 problems coming from my pocket. I pull my phone out and see a picture of Indie flipping me off on my screen. Why do these chicks insist on fucking with my phone?

"Now's not the time, Jones. I'm not in the mood for any of your shit today," I say in way of greeting.

"Well, hello to you too, Deacon. I see you're doing fanfuck-ingtastic so I won't bother asking. Listen, asshat, you need to step up your game with Frankie. I mean, now that Cristiano is hanging around so much, all of this giving her space BS is going to blow up in your face. Don't get me wrong, I really like him. Seriously, what's not to like? He's a little too refined for me, but he's still sweet and sexy, and then there's that fucking accent. Mmm...did I men-"

"INDIANA! Do you have a fucking point besides trying to make me lose my shit?" I yell, pulling the phone away from my ear and talking into it like a walkie talkie just in case she's still going on about the asshole. "Plus I thought you were into chicks." Smirking even though I'm frustrated, I wait for her to blast me. I know damn well she swings both ways, I just like to give her hell.

"Shut up! You know I play for both teams, asshole. Don't be jealous that Frankie is sleeping in my bed and not yours," she teases mockingly.

"I'm hanging up," I snap.

"God, you're touchy today," she huffs. "Deac, I've known you forever and I've tolerated your man-whoring and your all around douchebaggery because of Frankie. She has always seen the good in you, though I don't know why, and I know that you would never hurt her on purpose...so I've decided to try and help you."

"Help me? Help me what?"

"With Frankie dumbass!" she scolds.

"Indie, as touching as your words are," I roll my eyes at that, "I don't need your help. I'm giving her space for now, but if you think for one fucking minute that I am gonna let Rico Suave have my girl, you're even crazier than I thought. Frankie is mine. I'm just giving her some time to get used to the fact that there will be no more pretty boys for her," I say with way more confidence than I feel at the moment.

"Do you feel better now? Do you need to beat your chest a little like the caveman that you clearly are? Just do me a favor and try not to piss all over my friend while you're marking your territory, ass," she grumbles right before she hangs up on me.

What-the-fuck-ever. The women in my life are driving me out of my fucking mind and I'm not even fucking any of them! Hell, I'm not fucking anybody. Maybe that's my problem—I need to be balls deep in some stranger. It's been way too long. Definitely not my first choice, but I'm pretty sure I won't be able to talk Frankie into a little friends-with-benefits action right now, especially with Cristiano around.

My mind made up, I feel a little of the tension drain from my body. I meet my brothers on the mat and slap Sonny's back hard enough to make him stumble a bit. "Let's go out tonight—I need to get laid."

Chapter ELEVEN

THAT NIGHT AS we're walking into our usual stomping grounds, Hawkey Time, I feel the weight of my plan kicking my ass. I haven't fucked around with anyone since the night I got that phone call and not because I haven't had it offered, because I have, repeatedly and often. I've been on a dry spell because the only one I want is Frankie, and for once I don't feel the need to get lost in some meaningless ass. I talk a big game most of the time, but I know what I want and what I want is her, and there isn't a chick in here that is going to compare. Project "Get Some" just turned into a boys' night out with my brothers and Trent. Most likely ending with me stroking my own cock when I get home. When did I become this fucking guy?

We've been here for two hours just drinking, dicking around, and turning down advances from women left and right when shit gets real.

"Ohhhhh fuuuuuuck," Sonny says under his breath.

I'm more drunk than I've been in a long time, so I'm a little slow on the uptake when I see the Princess headed our way with Flashdance right behind her, a hand on her back to guide her. Reggie follows them, shrugging his shoulders apologetically. You have got to be fucking kidding me, right? I mean, who the fuck keeps testing me like this, and how much can I take before I go off?

I glance briefly at Sonny and Mav and they both look a little worried. At least those two haven't had more than a beer each…someone's going to need to have a clear head for this.

"My Loves! What are you guys doing here?" she asks in that voice that hits me straight in the dick every time.

"Just blowing off some steam. Deac's been training hard… we've got some big fights coming up," Mav tells her as he gives her a hug and a small wave in Cristiano's direction.

She pecks Sonny on the cheek and waves to Trent and then turns to me.

"I'm surprised that you're drinking. You normally don't allow yourself when you're training." She tilts her head a little baffled.

I know that if I open my mouth, something hateful is going to come out because of Cristiano standing with his hand on her like he has every right to, so I just shrug and ignore the hurt look that crosses her face. I don't even greet her; I can't bring myself to touch her in the slightest way right now. I am too drunk, too on edge, and I don't trust myself.

"You guys want to join us? There's plenty of room," Sonny, ever the nice guy, asks them.

As Frankie is answering yes, Cristiano is saying no, and I don't know whether to be pissed off or happy about that. She glances over at him.

"Oh, did you want to sit somewhere else?"

"No, no, mi amor. This is fine, I just wasn't sure that there would be room for all of us once Indie shows up."

"My love?" Really? Fuck him.

She laughs. "There's always room for Indie…don't you worry about her!"

That gets a laugh out of everybody at the table—well, everyone but my moody ass.

There is one chair open next to me and one on the other side of Mav. It's clear that I'm not moving, so while Cristiano is helping Frankie off with her coat, Sonny moves around the table to the empty seat next to Mav so that Cristiano and Frankie can sit together. Why the fuck they need to sit together is beyond me. Just as she's sitting in the chair to my right, she leans in and brushes a kiss across my cheek. It feels like white hot heat shoots throughout my body, and all I can do is lean into her kiss and inhale her scent. A scent that I know so well, a scent that I could pick out of a room full of heavily perfumed women. I'm instantly hard and have to adjust myself as she settles into her chair. She sits and crosses her legs, the skirt of her cream-colored sweater dress rising up revealing her garter belt tattoo. My eyes are riveted to the spot, and all I can think about is how I want to lick it, bite at her inner thigh where the ink wraps around, kiss and suck the lace that I know is so close to the crease of her ass. I'm so focused on my own lust-filled thoughts that I flinch when I see a tan finger begin tracing the delicate edges of the garter. The tick in my jaw is instantaneous, the grip on my beer nearly enough to shatter the amber bottle.

"This is new, no? I would have remembered seeing this," Cristiano says to her in a voice full of heat that makes me see red.

Frankie turns to me, effectively shifting out from under his wandering fingers that I want nothing more than to break.

"Not really. I think about a year and a half, right, Deac?"

I nod and murmur, "Sounds about right," before downing the rest of my beer and signaling the waitress for another round.

Mav leans in close so that I am the only one that can hear him, "You sure you want another round, brother? We can go if you're ready."

He sounds so hopeful that I almost agree until I hear the next words out of Flashdance's mouth.

"I can't wait to see the new tattoo you got. All the mystery has me so intrigued."

My blood goes cold at the words "new tattoo." I'm not sure

what emotion to tap into first—the anger or the hurt. Before I can decide, Indie plops into the seat opposite me and gives me what can only be described as the stink eye.

"What's with the face, Deac? You look like someone just pissed on you."

She says it with a nasty little smirk. She knows that I'll remember her telling me not to piss on Frankie when we spoke earlier, right before she hung up on me.

"Nothing at all, Jones, nothing at all." I turn to my girl and I'm sure that she is afraid to see the hurt in my eyes and that's why she won't quite meet them.

"You got new ink, Princess…without me?" I try to sound as nonchalant as possible, though I'm not sure if I succeed.

"It wasn't like that, Deacon," she all but whispers.

"Oh, for the love—calm down, you beast. You can shake the sand out of your vagina right now. I took her to a girl that has done some work for me because it's in a…'sensitive' area," Indie says, laughing at my reaction.

I still haven't looked away from Frankie and notice her wince at Indie's words.

"Oh, now I am *very* intrigued to see this 'sensitive area,' mi amor. Very intrigued," Cristiano says in that stupid accent of his.

She laughs him off but still hasn't met my eyes. What is it, and more importantly, where is it?

"You guys are all ridiculous," she huffs. "Now, if you'll excuse me, I am going to the washroom. Indie, grab me a drink when she comes back around please?" she throws over her shoulder as she walks away from the table.

I look down at my hands holding on to a fresh beer that I don't even remember the girl bringing. My mind is on Frankie and her new ink and the things I want to do to her old ink. Tipping back in my chair, I peer through the crowd in the direction that she went.

"Fuck it," leaves my mouth, too low for anyone to hear, about two seconds before I stand up and walk in the direction that Frankie disappeared to. I don't give a shit if everyone knows where I'm going.

By the time I make it to the back of the bar where the ladies' room is situated, I've been groped by more hands than I can count and I'm pretty sure I was slipped at least two phone numbers and what felt like a key card for a hotel room. MMA is becoming more and more popular with the ladies, and it seems like I'm being recognized way more often.

Frankie is just walking out of the bathroom when I grab her by the wrist and pull her into an alcove that has an ancient looking payphone and nothing else except really dim lighting.

"Deacon!" she yelps when I push her gently against the wall.

"Show me," I whisper against her ear, pressing into her, molding her softness into the hard lines of my body. I don't pull away; I just keep my lips to the shell of her ear, waiting for her response.

"Show you what?" she breathes against my neck.

"Don't play with me, Princess, I'm all out of control for the night. I used every last bit of it when I watched Rico Suave put his hands on you. Show. Me," I growl.

"Rico Suave?" she asks with an almost exasperated giggle. "Deac, there is no way in hell that I am showing you, especially in a bar, you ass!" Her voice says that she's angry with me, but her hands at my back clutching my shirt, pressing me closer to her, say something different.

"Where is it? On that perfect ass of yours?" I ask as I bring my hand from the wall and slide it over her waist, over the swell of her hip, then behind her to cup one rounded cheek.

She shakes her head that I'm wrong, eyes wide at the path my hand just took, no doubt.

"Tell me that you didn't put it right above your pretty, little pussy, Frankie." I nip her ear and groan into her hair when she gasps and presses tighter into my chest. The hand that isn't on her ass cradles the back of her head, my fingers tangling into her hair, tilting her head a bit to give me better access to her neck and the pulse that I can see there. I lower my head and place a kiss on that rapidly beating spot and then swipe my tongue across it, eliciting yet another sound out of her that is part moan, part plea.

"Deacon, we cannot do this here. What the hell is with you and walls anyway?" she asks in a somewhat amused voice.

"I don't know what it is. I just need to feel you—all of you—and this seems to be what happens when I reach a point where I can't deny myself anymore. Stop making me deny myself, Frankie. I don't like it."

The last part leaves my mouth without me even realizing what I'm saying. Not that I don't mean it, I'm just not sure that I want her to know how much power she actually has over me. I shake the thought off—I've had too much to drink to analyze those kinds of things right now. I go back to trailing kisses across her jaw, ending at her ear, where I again nip the lobe.

"Are you gonna show me, baby, or should I keep guessing?" I ask her softly.

She manages to get her hands in between us and gives a little shove to my chest. "No, Deac, I am most definitely not going to show you," Frankie tells me, her tone firm.

"Okay, you don't have to show me, but I'll tell you right now, I find out that you showed your 'sensitive areas' to Cristiano or anyone else, I'm gonna knock heads, Princess."

She snorts at me, and it does nothing but make me harder.

"I'll show my sensitive areas to whomever I want, Deac. I don't belong to you!" she huffs out in that raspy voice of hers. I can hear the lie in her words though. I hope that she can too.

"That's where you're wrong, Frankie," I tell her, and mean it.

"Oh yeah? Why don't you tell that to Veronica then!" she accuses, lip curled in a face that makes her look like she tastes something foul.

I laugh. "Veronica? I haven't been with Veronica in a while. Jealousy looks really, really good on you though. Hot as hell," smirking at her frown.

It's true I haven't been with Veronica or anyone else. Blow jobs don't count, right? I'm going with no, no, they don't.

"Why don't you help me forget all about her? It won't be hard. Well, something will be hard, but not the forgetting," I say trying not to let the threatening laugh escape.

"Just what I want—to be used to fuck some other girl out of your system," she says, her frown turning into a scowl.

I nudge her with my hips and my rock hard cock, which gets her attention if the shiver that races up her spine is any indication.

"Let's get a couple things straight. One: I'd never use you for anything. *Anything*." I bend to make eye contact. "And two: the only one in my system is you, and trust me when I say, nobody is going to be able to fuck you out," I utter with complete and total sincerity.

"Lovely, Deacon. I can see now why they call you the *Hitman*, you ass," she says, a little exasperated and a whole lot turned on. I can see it in her fiery blue eyes, in her rapidly beating pulse.

The Princess wants me.

She pushes against my chest making me take a step back and slides past me. I let her go, for now. Watching her ass sway in that fuzzy dress that hugs every one of her perfect curves. Lace socks peeking over the top of her calf high boots, making me want to fuck her wearing nothing but them.

Jesus fuck, I want her. I have to figure out a way to get her to stop walking the hell away from me! Shaking my head and giving myself a second to get my raging hard on under control,

I hit the men's room before I go back out to our table. Soon as I get there, I'm pissed all over again when I see her and Cristiano sitting next to each other, his arm draped on the back of her chair and her laughing at something he's saying. At least he isn't feeling her up this time. I'm not sure I'd stop myself from hurting him right now.

The scowl on my face firmly in place, I sit in my chair, leaning back on two legs trying not to pay any attention to them. I bullshit with my brothers who seem to be working overtime to keep me engaged, poke fun at Indie some, but when he starts whispering in Frankie's ear and kissing her jaw, her allowing him to, it all stops. I don't think, I just act. I look over at the bar, see some chick that's been throwing "fuck me" eyes all night and say screw it. Guess my original mission is back on. My chair slams down hard, I reach for my wallet in my back pocket and throw down two hundred dollar bills.

"It's been fun, guys, but I've had about all I can take for one night. I'm out of here," I say pointedly.

Trent stands up to follow me but I stop him.

"You stay with her, big man. Go with Reggie, make sure the Princess gets home safely. I won't need you tonight," I tell him inclining my head toward the woman at the bar.

I can feel my brother's eyes boring into me, willing me not to be a dumbass, but I'm determined. I make the mistake of glancing at Indie who is shooting daggers at me, shaking her head in disgust.

"Deacon, you sure you don't want us to head out with you? We have an early gym time tomorrow anyways, brother," Sonny tries.

"Nope, you guys stay and have fun. I'll make sure I make it home in time for the gym." I clap him on the back and turn to leave when I catch the look on Frankie's face. She is trying to hide it, but I know my girl—she's hurt. Her eyes are glassy, like she's trying not to cry, but I can see her bottom lip trembling, sure that she wants to. She refuses to look at me, and that kills me. I don't want to take anyone home but her, so why the fuck can't I? Why is this so goddamned difficult? Why is *she* so difficult?

I lean down and put my lips to her ear, pushing Cristiano's arm off of her chair, not caring that he isn't happy about it.

"Come with me, come home with me and…come. Over and over." I'm not sure if anyone else at the table hears me, and I don't really give a fuck. All I know is that I want this, want her so bad I can't think straight, and if she doesn't come with me, I know I won't be leaving with anyone else. This woman has got me so twisted.

She hasn't moved or said anything, and if it weren't for her erratic little puffs of breath, I wouldn't have thought she heard me. She finally pulls away enough to look at me. She's searching my face, my eyes, for what, I don't know.

"Why?" she breathes, her voice cracking a bit on that one word.

I lean in again trying to control the impulse to just yank her out of her seat and drag her out of there.

"You know why. Do you really want me to get into it here with all of them listening, because you know they are, right?"

I see her eyes dart around the table and chuckle a little while I do the same. They're all pretending not to listen well, except for Cristiano. He's openly trying to hear what we're saying. I smirk at him and go back to whispering in her ear.

"I'll tell you what—I'll leave, by myself, and give you some time to follow and say goodbye. Have Reggie bring you to my place. I'll be waiting for you, but Frankie, don't make me wait long, yeah? I'm through with all that shit. I need to be inside of you. It's time that I show you how good we can be together."

I don't give her a chance to answer, I just scoop up her hand and lay a kiss to my spot, whistling as I amble out, straight past the bar and the hot, little Spanish chick who thought she was coming home with me.

Chapter
TWELVE

Francesca

I WATCH HIM leave and I'm not gonna lie, when he walks by the girl at the bar, who just minutes ago I was sure he was going to leave with, my heart does a little happy dance. The look on her face thrilling me even more. I try to pay attention to what Cristiano is saying to me, but all I can think about is Deacon and how he is relentless, trying to convince me that we should be together. Could I do it? Do I want to take that chance? What would everyone think? We have been friends, best friends, inseparable friends for the majority of our lives. Would they accept us being together? Do I even fucking care? I'm lost in my thoughts and on fire from his words. Crossing and uncrossing my legs in an attempt to ease the ache that he caused, when she walks in.

Mav groans and mutters something under his breath that I can't hear over the raucous bar noise and the sound of Kings Of Leon's song "Your Sex is on Fire," which couldn't be any more fitting really. She obviously notices us all sitting here, because Veronica makes a beeline toward our table like she's on a mission. This should be interesting, since she has always disliked the shit out of me, and I, for damn sure, don't like her.

As Veronica nears the table, I look over at Indie, who rolls her eyes and mouths "cunt," making me burst out laughing. Needless to say, Veronica isn't our favorite person.

Finally making it to our table, Veronica flips her long, mahogany colored hair over her shoulder and looks down her nose at me.

"Should you be out, Francesca? I thought you were hurt and that's why Deacon had to throw all his fights."

"Well, not that it's any of your business, but I'm recuperating just fine. Thank you so much for your concern though." My voice is saccharine sweet, my smile condescending as all hell. If she thinks she's gonna shake me by being a bitch, she's dead wrong. This is the first time that I've gone anywhere other than the studio, and I'm not going to let her make me feel guilty.

"Whatever, I was more worried about Deac and his standings than you breaking a nail," she retorts snidely.

I am just about to let loose a string of filthy words when Sonny speaks up.

"Watch it, Veronica. You're talking about shit you know nothing about and it won't fly here."

"Oh, Sonny, I'm just messing with the Princess." She says "Princess" with such disdain it's almost comical.

"Where's Deacon? He told me to meet him here."

"Uh, you sure about that?" Mav asks dubiously.

"Yes, Maverick, my boyfriend wanted me to come out and have a good time with him and his friends," she says while aiming her fake ass smile at me.

Indie barks out a laugh.

"Bitch, you are delusional!" Shaking her head at Veronica she continues to laugh.

"Cute, Indiana. This bar isn't really Rockabilly. I'm surprised that they let you in," Veronica says snarkily.

"Oh, clearly, they're not real picky about who they let

through the door." Indie eyes her pointedly.

Huffing out a bored breath, Veronica zeroes in on Cristiano, her look and body language instantly changing. Looking at Indie, I just laugh. This must be skank mode that I'm witnessing. Before she can go in for the kill, Mav speaks up.

"He left a little while ago; he has an early gym time." He's clearly trying to discourage her.

"Perfect, I'll just head over there then and make sure he's not too tense for the morning," she says glancing at me.

I swear she's trying to get a rise out of me by rubbing it in that she knows him intimately. Get in line, sweetheart, there's not many who don't. The boyfriend jab hurt a little, as did her saying he wanted her here. Maybe he did, he hadn't known that I was going to be here. I've never known Deacon to lie though. Not to me especially. If he said that he hadn't been with her in a while, then he hadn't.

Right?

Shaking my head I give her a doubtful look. "Funny, he never mentioned that you were coming."

She throws me a wicked grin as she turns away from our table heading toward the door. "That's because I'm not...yet," finger waving before she disappears.

Well, fuck. I guess she made the decision for me. There is no way that I'm going over there now. I hadn't been sure that I was going to begin with—no, that's a lie. I had every intention of going, even if I had been trying to deny it. He had me too worked up with a few dirty words not to. Even if it was only to talk about whatever this thing was with us. He had a lot to drink tonight and as convincing as he can be, drunk sex with him isn't what I'm looking for. Well, my body is, but not my mind.

The guys look around the table in apprehension.

"Should we text him and give him a heads up, Sonny?" Mav asks.

"Already did, brother. There's no way he invited her ass

here and he for damn sure doesn't want her at his house. He's been dodging her calls for weeks, dude!" Sonny tells him.

I stand and grab my coat. "This has been lovely, but I'm going to head home."

I want to believe what he's saying, what they're saying. I'm just not sure that I can. I know Deacon too well and the lines are slightly blurred between reality and what I hope is the truth. He's the guy with a different girl in his bed, on his arm, every night. The thought that I might be different is almost too much for me to accept. Veronica shook my faith in him and I hated her for it. After what I've been through, trusting people isn't as easy as it used to be, but I never thought that would carry over to Deacon.

Leaning in, I give Sonny a kiss on the cheek and then do the same to Mav before making my way over to Indie.

"Don't let that bitch get to you, Frankie. You know where Deac stands; it's all on you now," my best friend whispers to me. She knows me so well.

Reggie and Trent stand to follow me out when Cristiano stops, telling them that he can see me home safely. I nod my head letting them know it's okay and say my goodbyes. Not believing for a second that they won't be right behind us.

Cristiano takes my hand and leads me outside to hail a cab. Unfortunately Veronica is also curbside waiting for one. I stand with the wind blowing, whistling through the tall buildings around us. My mind once again wanders to Deacon and my feelings for him, which are becoming more and more apparent to me. Obvious, yet still I tamp them down as best as I can. He is breaking me though. One by one I can feel my defenses crumbling. I try to not think about her being at Deacon's house with him. He's expecting me; will she be an adequate replacement though? I've never felt uncertain when it came to Deacon, but we're on a completely different playing field now and I'm not sure that I like it. It leaves me feeling unsettled mostly because I am trying to separate the kind of guy that I know Deacon to be and the man I want him to be for me. My mind is at war with my heart…and with Veronica on her way to him, my mind is regrettably looking like the victor.

Doing my best to ignore Veronica and her destination, I stuff my hands into my pockets against the chill in the air, when suddenly on a gust of wind I smell *him*. Cherry and tobacco. Whipping around, breaking the hold Cristiano has on my arm, I search the darkened street for a glimpse of him. That smell. God, is my mind playing tricks on me? My gaze darts over the many faces crowding the entrance of the bar, smoking, laughing, under the heaters.

The smell of cigarettes wafting, replacing the sweet but sinister smell that reminds me of that night, I can feel myself begin to tremble as the panic and fear bubble up to near hysteria. Cristiano, sensing that something is wrong, takes hold of my elbow and leans down peering at me. "What is it? What's the matter, mi amor?"

Shaking my head, I grip onto his arms, my fingernails digging into his biceps through his coat. "Do you smell that? Cherries and tobacco?" I ask him in a voice radiating alarm.

He glances around. "The cigarettes?" he questions, baffled by my reaction.

"No, no, it's different, sweet and smoky, but…not smoke." I struggle to explain what I mean, frustrated because I still can't put all of the pieces together, details eluding me. This fear holding my mind hostage causes me to quake in dread, overcome with terror and anxiety. I curse the feelings and my lack of control as the tears start to fall. Cristiano pulls me into his warmth, his scent the one now surrounding me. Safely wrapped in his arms, he strokes a hand over my head.

"Shhh, shh, it's okay. I don't smell anything, Francesca. Whatever you thought, it's not. You're all right." He whispers to me in Spanish, the words washing over me making me feel slightly crazy and embarrassed but no less fearful. I bury my face into his sweater and will the anxiety and trembling to subside.

Finally we're ducking into the back of a taxi, Veronica a thing from the past, though I can feel her eyes on us as she gets into her own cab.

Cristiano slides all the way over so that our thighs are touching and puts his muscular arm around my shoulders. His woodsy, slightly spicy scent fills the car and I settle into his side, still uneasy and with tears sliding down my face, dropping from my chin in rapid descent. I know I shouldn't, that he wants us to pick up where we left off years ago, but right now I just need to feel comforted. I need Deacon, but clearly that isn't going to happen.

After a few moments, I've calmed down and my eyes, though sore, and I'm sure red rimmed, are dry.

"You okay?" Cristiano asks softly as he runs his nose across my cheek.

Nodding I pull back to look at him. "I'm good now, I think. Tired and ready for bed."

He smiles his sexy smile. The one that used to get him into my panties without a word. "Would you like some company? We can just hold each other, or if you like, I can remind you of how well I know this beautiful body of yours."

His voice is hypnotic, his accent like a caress. He continues stroking my arm looking at me with hooded eyes. It would be so easy to forget about everything and just let myself be taken care of by him right now. This vulnerable, needy person is so not me. The attack has left me completely raw, inside and out. It's left its mark on me physically and emotionally.

"Cristiano, you have a girlfriend. I'm sure that she would not appreciate your reminder," I say lightly, trying to break the trance he has me in.

Thankfully, it works because there is no way I'll be the *other* woman for him or anyone.

Cupping my cheek, he leans in until our lips are almost touching. "Ahhh, mi amor, that's where you're wrong. Our relationship was over the moment I stepped into your hospital room. She just doesn't know it yet because I dread hurting her over the phone." Brushing his thumb over my bottom lip, he says softly, "Say the word, *princessa*, and I'll call her right now no matter what time it is in Spain."

Looking into his eyes, I see that he's serious, but is that what I want? Not twenty minutes ago I was contemplating going home with Deacon. Who is probably showing Veronica a good time as we speak. So she gets him and Cristiano will break up with his girlfriend, but only if I give the word to? Where do I fall with either of them? The reality is I have no clue and I'm not sure that I want to know. I'm still trying to come to terms with the life changing fact that I was attacked in my home and left for dead. I do *not* need this added confusion on top of it all.

Sighing, I pull away from him and lean my forehead against the cool glass of the window, watching the lights of the city pass by in a blur. When did my life fall to pieces and become total chaos? It's so exhausting.

Melancholy, I turn my head so that I'm looking at him again.

"As flattering as that is and as much as I appreciate you being there for me just now, I'll be going to bed alone. Thank you."

And just like that, I choose Deacon no matter what my mind is screaming at me.

Chapter THIRTEEN

DEACON

THE CABBIE MAKES it to my place in record time. Jumping out, I enter the gate code and leave it open so that I don't have to worry about letting him back through when he leaves. After paying him and autographing a napkin that he shoves at me, I head inside and deactivate the alarm. Overzealous fucker that I am, I decide I may need some mood music to soothe Frankie's nerves once she gets here. I scroll through until I find a John Legend song. Chicks love John, right? And another one that talks about being a better man. I've never in my life had to resort to mood music, but Frankie is different and these songs remind me of the time I'm gonna have to put in to reassure her that I am in this. She's not just a quick fuck; I know it, now I need for her to. I quickly flick through and pick a few more songs I want to use to convey my message, setting the list to repeat. My girl speaks music, and this will mean more to her than any lines I can come up with. No matter how true they would be.

Going into the kitchen, I debate grabbing one of the bottles of wine that she has here from the chiller or if that's pushing it. No, I don't need any more to drink tonight. I'm hoping to sober up a bit before she gets here. I haven't been this drunk in a long while. Jesus fuck, what is the matter with me? I'm over-thinking this whole thing. I need to calm down and not lose my shit before Frankie even walks through the door.

As I turn to head up the stairs to my room, the doorbell chimes. Why the hell is she ringing the bell? She has a key. May-be she's as nervous as I am. Chuckling, I throw open the door.

"Where are your ke—" I'm cut short by the unwanted vis-itor I find on my doorstep.

"Veronica, what the fuck are you doing here?"

I glance behind her, seeing the taillights of the taxi heading down my drive. I step past her out the door and whistle trying to get the driver's attention to take her ass home. This cannot be fucking happening right now.

"Deacon, is that any way to greet your guest?" she pouts.

Whipping around, I point an angry finger at her. "I have company coming, and you cannot stay here."

Huffing, she spins on her heel and heads into my home like she has every fucking right to be there. I have got to get her the fuck out of here. Frankie shows up and sees her here and I'm done.

"Veronica, I'm serious, you need to leave. How did you get through the gate anyway? I never gave you the code."

Arms crossed over her chest, pushing her fake tits up high enough for her to rest her chin on, she looks at me through narrowed eyes.

"It was open, Deacon. If you'd just give me the stupid code, it wouldn't even be an issue, you know?"

I laugh at her like she's fucking crazy. She must be if she thinks for even one second I would ever give her such easy ac-cess to me and my home.

"Never gonna happen."

Rolling her eyes at me she says, "Whatever, Deacon, who are you waiting for? It's late and your brother said you had an early gym time."

My eyes go all slitty.

"When did you speak to my brother?"

"I saw them all at the bar just now and he told me. Speaking of which, who is the hottie that Francesca's with now? Sure didn't take her long to move on, did it?" she says in a snide tone.

I don't even want to hear this shit.

"What are you talking about? Frankie isn't with anybody."

"Well, that's not what it looked like to me. They were all over each other getting into the back of a cab. I wouldn't be surprised if they ended up fucking in the backseat," Veronica says, laughing like what she says is even remotely fucking funny.

Shaking my head in denial, I tell her, "There's no way. Flashdance has a girlfriend anyway."

Not that that shit matters to him, but I know it does to the Princess. She wouldn't allow that noise, would she? I hate the fucking doubt that's creeping in, but my mind is all over the place when it comes to her and him lately. On top of that, I'm still lit from all that I drank at the bar and it's clouding my judgment in a big fucking way. Jealousy, pure red hot fucking jealousy is coursing through me and my alcohol fucked brain.

"That doesn't explain what you're doing here."

I'm leaning against the wall right next to the main speaker and the panel that controls the sound system watching her, hands stuffed in my front pockets.

Looking at me coyly, she uncrosses her arms and walks over to me. Running her long, blood red fingernail down the buttons on my shirt, Veronica looks up at me through her eyelashes, licking her lips seductively.

"I'm here to help relieve some of this tension, Deacon. I know how to help you relax. You're wound so tight, baby," she says, reaching up on her tiptoes, nipping my jaw as her fingers trail further over my belt buckle and onto my now hardening cock. Fucking thing has a mind of its own and right now it wants sucked. Trying to remind myself that I need to not do this if I ever want to prove to Frankie that she means more to me than the rest of them, but all that I can think about are the words *"I wouldn't be surprised if they ended up fucking in the backseat."* I hear them over and over and it does nothing but make me feel out of fucking control, feeding my anger and need to lash out.

I know that I've lost this battle when she slides down onto her knees and pops the buttons on my fly. When the hell did she even get my belt undone? Thumping my head back against the wall in defeat, I screw my eyes closed and will myself not to think about what Frankie and Cristiano could be doing at that very moment. Just the thought pisses me off all over again. Before I have time to let the thoughts fester even more, my cock is hitting the back of Veronica's throat making her gag. I refuse to even touch her. My dick might be enjoying the hell out of this, but I know as soon as it's over I'm gonna regret it. Hell, I already regret it even as mad as I am. She's giving it her all though, and the girl can fucking suck, but all I can think about is running my fingers through silky strands of blonde hair, not the stiff brown covering the head bobbing on my cock.

Gritting my teeth, I try to get my head in the game, but fuck if I know which game I'm trying to be in. Frustrated, I slap my hand over the system to silence the stereo from taunting me with a song I chose for the Princess. I'm about to say fuck it and push Veronica off me, when she does that thing with her finger by my taint. She knows it makes me blow every goddamn time.

Groaning, my hips jerk, pushing me farther down her throat while she swallows my load. Once she's licked me clean, she stands up wiping the corner of her mouth. With a satisfied smile, she starts to shimmy out of her jeans. My head spinning, I know I need to put a stop to this shit right now.

"My turn," she purrs, her pants nearly to the ground before I get my head straight.

Tucking myself back into my pants, I can feel a trickle of

sweat slipping down my spine. I know I fucked up. Frankie can't find out about this—together or not, Cristiano, whatever. This shit should not have happened. She won't forgive me for this totally "Deacon" goddamn move.

"Fuck! Fuck. You gotta go. Fuck!" I yell, the sound echoing in the entryway that we never even made it out of.

Veronica looks at me like I've lost my mind, eyes bugging out of her overly made up face, just gaping at me, stunned.

"You're kidding me right, Deacon? You are not kicking my ass out after I just gave you the best head of your life."

The best head? Really? It was good, but the best? Shaking off that thought I look at her.

"Veronica, I'm dead ass serious, you need to get the fuck out of my house," I say through gritted teeth. I have never hit a woman, but fuck me, if I don't want to shake the shit out of one right now. I know this clusterfuck isn't really her fault, but she's the one I want to place the blame on at the moment. Anything to make myself feel better, right? Fucking hell.

She still hasn't moved when my phone starts ringing. Thank fuck it isn't Frankie, not that Sonny calling is gonna be a good time.

Pointing toward the door indicating that I still want her to leave, I swipe my finger across the screen.

"What?" I snap.

"I've been fucking texting you for the last thirty minutes, dude. Where the hell have you been?" He's pissed and shit's only gonna get worse. Sonny knows how I feel about the Princess, and he's been on my ass about not being a douche and proving to her that I deserve her. This is definitely not what he's been talking about.

"Jameson, let me call you back."

"She's there isn't she? You let her in, Deacon? Are you kidding me?" he shouts.

My silence is answer enough for him.

"You dumb motherfucker. Did you fuck her?" he yells loud enough for her to hear him, causing Veronica's eyebrows to shoot up her forehead.

Closing my eyes against the throbbing headache that's beginning at the base of my skull, I sigh loudly.

"No, Sonn—"

"Not yet, Sonny, but I did suck his dick," she calls out, leaning in toward the phone in my hand so that he can hear her.

"Get the fuck out now, Veronica. I'm not fucking you now or ever. This was a slip of the dick that won't happen again. I can promise you that," I seethe. I can hear Sonny cursing me out, but I can't make out what he's saying because I'm too busy trying not to put my foot in this bitch's ass. Opening the door, I tell her one more time, "Out. Now."

"Where do you want me to go, Deacon? I don't have my fucking car here."

"Fucking fuck. This shit cannot be happening," I mutter when I finally hear what Sonny is saying.

"I'm at the gate now. Tell her to wait outside. Trent and Reggie can take her ass home."

"What? Why aren't they with Frankie, Sonny?"

"Really, Deac? You wanna do this shit now? I don't think so, brother. We'll talk when we get in the house."

With that he ends our call leaving me standing in the open doorway, chest tight, breathing ragged in anger, knowing that my brothers are about to hand me my ass and that I deserve every bit of it.

I watch as Sonny and Mav climb from the Range Rover and Veronica stomps down the steps toward them. She turns back to say something to me, but I go inside before she has the chance to fuck up my night any more than I have already allowed.

Taking the moment I have to myself, I contemplate texting Frankie, but can't bring myself to do it. The guilt I feel is eating away at me, sobering me even further. The decision is made for me when Sonny and Mav slam into the house making their way to where I sit in the kitchen. With no preamble whatsoever Sonny starts in on me.

"One time, just one fucking time, can you not let your dick control you, Deacon?"

Mav crosses his arms over his chest and stands shaking his head at me.

"You fucked up, brother. Hard to prove that she's different if you're not willing to change for her. Whatever though. It's probably for the best that it happened now instead of after you've put all the work in. Cut your losses quick and salvage your friendship, ya know?"

I look at him like he has lost his motherfucking mind.

"Are you drunk, Mav? There's no way in hell I'm cutting shit. I fucked up. I know I did, but she won't find out. I'll just make sure it doesn't happen again," I say, shrugging like it's that easy, knowing it's not.

Glancing up, I see that both of my dumbass brothers are now looking at me like I'm the one who has lost his fucking mind.

Sonny shakes his head at me, absolute incredulity written all over his face.

"Are you that stupid, Deac, or just in complete denial? Do you for one minute believe that she won't find out? That Veronica's conniving ass won't run and tell her the first chance she gets?"

He blows out an exasperated breath.

"Do you know why it was Veronica here tonight instead of the Princess? Don't think I don't know what the fuck you were doing at the bar by the way. You're not as smooth as you think, brother," he says pointing an accusing finger at me.

"She came into the bar and taunted Frankie, but only after she blew her shit for being out and clearly not as hurt as the

Princess made us all believe," he tells me in disgust. "Then she made sure Frankie and everyone else at the table knew that you invited her, and since you weren't there, she would just come here to fuck you. And you know what? She did!"

Spinning around to leave, Sonny turns back and gets in one last shot.

"I thought out of anyone, you deserved her most because you've loved her for so long and so hard. Even if you couldn't see it, I did." Shaking his head sadly, he continues, "You're my brother and I love you, but I think I was wrong. This isn't the Deacon she needs. Mav's right; cut your losses now because you're just gonna hurt her in the end and we might not love her the same way you do, but we don't love her any less and I refuse to let Frankie get fucked over by you, brother or not."

Head down, I listen as Sonny storms out, shaking because I'm so pissed at myself, at Veronica, at Sonny for being so fucking right. Veronica did fuck me, but I fucked myself by letting it happen. I wanted to deserve Frankie, but maybe Sonny was right about that too. Just because I love her doesn't mean I'm man enough to not hurt her.

I don't look up when Mav walks over and squeezes my shoulder.

"Don't let him shake you, bro, he doesn't believe half the shit that comes out of his own mouth," he says, chuckling a little.

In a more serious tone he goes on, "He is right about one thing though, and that's that we won't let you hurt her. You're the fighter in the family, but there's two of us besides, yeah? Just keep it in your pants, baby brother, and we might let you live."

Slapping me on the back, he walks out after Sonny leaving me wondering if my two older brothers can actually still take me, because that was one thing my punk ass really does deserve.

Chapter
FOURTEEN

I'M NOT SURE who is avoiding who, but I haven't seen the Princess in days. It's killing me. I've seen the shit out of that fucker Cristiano though. Always in her studio whether she's here or not. I cannot wait for his ass to go back to Spain. He's gotten a little too comfortable here though. If they're together now, heads are gonna roll.

A shooting pain down my arm and across my shoulder brings me back to the present and the fucking armbar I've just allowed my sparring partner to put me in.

"Let him go before he lets you break it, Jax. His head is obviously up his ass. Again," I hear Sonny call out.

Fuck! I have a fight in less than a week and I just got laid out by Jax for the third time this morning. I can't get Frankie out of my mind. I still feel guilty as hell over the goddamn Veronica thing, and she's not making it easy on me either, calling all the damn time and shit. Jax releases his hold and I jump up slapping him on the back, walking toward Sonny and my dad standing off to the side, identical scowls on their faces, arms crossed over their barrel chests.

"He's getting better with that damn arm bar," I try to joke but neither of them is amused.

"What the hell has you losing focus before such an important fight, son?" my dad asks. "You've got to be all in or you're going to get yourself hurt. Get your head on straight or sit the fuck out, Deacon. Those are your only two options."

"I'm in it, Pop. Just have some shit on my mind, but I'm in it," I reassure him, not quite believing it myself.

"There's no time to fuck around, brother. I won't take it easy on you so that you can shake your shitty ass mood. It's go time," Sonny says, the smirk on his face letting me know that shit just got real and the rest of the day is going to be torture. He is still punishing me on behalf of the Princess, and I'm pretty sure he's getting off on it, the fucker.

Sighing, I turn toward the showers and throw over my shoulder, "I hear you guys. Just let me rinse off and clear my head and then you can use and abuse me."

I hear Sonny yell out, "Me love you long time!" and him and my father laughing their asses off as I walk into the locker room.

Yep, I am officially fucked.

After six hours of hitting it hard, my sadistic fuck of a brother finally calls it a day.

"That's it, Deac. We're done for now. Tomorrow we need to take it to the mats again though. Maybe you'll be able to figure out how to get out of Jax's armbar," he says, his eyebrows raised, taunting me.

"Fuck off, Sonny," I laugh, catching the towel and the bottle of Gatorade he tosses my way.

"I forgot to tell you, you're on your own for the game tonight. Pop and I need to watch some tape of Tamasino. Your fight is coming up quick, and we need to be better prepared than we are. I need you to get focused—this is no joke. Tam is big time; you lose and it's all over. You were undefeated before everything went down with the Princess, so the two fights you forfeited didn't hurt you too badly, but if you want the title match, then you have to win the next three fights."

Swallowing the last of the Gatorade, he hands me another.

"I know it, Sonny. I won't lose. I can't lose—it's not an option. Get off my ass, yeah?" Rubbing at the sweat running down my torso, I shake my head in apology.

"I'm sorry. I know I'm being a dick. Do you and Pop want me to watch with you?"

"Nah, let us work it out tonight and then we can break it down for you in the morning."

"Okay. So just me and Mav for the game then?"

"Mav isn't going. He's got an out of town '*date*,'" he says, air quoting "date."

"What the fuck does that even mean?" I ask him, confused.

"Dude, I have no fucking idea. That's how the dumbass said it, so either it's a real date or he's going out for a piece," he says to me as he heads toward the stairs leading to our dad's place.

"Without a wingman? No way. It must be serious if he's flying solo *and* leaving town for it."

Shrugging he just says, "Maybe," as he disappears into the stairwell.

Wow, Mav with a chick? He's as bad as me when it comes to relationships, though he's a lot more selective about who he hooks up with. I can't wait to bust his balls about it when he gets back.

Chuckling to myself, I glance into Frankie's dance studio as I walk by, but don't see anyone except Cristiano pacing while he talks on the phone. Opening the door to ask what he's doing here, I hear him in his rapid-fire Spanish telling whoever is on the other end of the line that he isn't coming back to Spain. I'm not able to understand anything more than that though. Before he can see me, I close the door, going to my locker for my phone. Fuck, he's staying? I'm thinking it's time for Frankie and me to stop avoiding each other. I can only hope she'd love to catch the Hawks game with me.

Phone in hand, I grab the jersey I brought with me today

and dial her number.

Finally on the fourth ring, she picks up sounding out of breath.

"Hey, Deac, I haven't heard from you in a few days. What's going on?" Her enthusiasm sounds a little forced, but I'm not going to let it deter me.

"Hey, Princess. Yeah, sorry, I've been training hard with the Tamasino match coming up."

It's true, but I know it's not really why I've been out of touch.

"Tam's a beast—you ready?" she asks, real interest evident in her tone.

"Worried about me?" I ask, smiling at the thought.

She's always been worried about me when I fight, but for whatever reason, the thought of her being worried now, after everything that's happened between us, has me grinning like a teenage girl at a One Direction concert.

Sighing she says, "Of course I am, Deac. You lock yourself in a cage with big ass men who want to kill you. Somebody has to worry about you."

"I guess somebody does."

Smiling wider now, I crank the cold water in the shower— all of this worrying is making me hard.

"So the boys and my pop have ditched me for the game tonight. You wanna go? I can scoop you from Indie's place in about an hour?"

Radio silence.

"Princess? You there?" I laugh.

"Umm, just us, huh?" she asks warily.

"Uh, yeah, just us, Frankie. Just like a million times before. So get dressed. I'll be there in a few, woman." I end the call before she can say anything else.

Chapter FIFTEEN

FORTY-FIVE MINUTES LATER, I'm double parked in front of Indie's Bucktown brownstone. Putting the flashers on, I get out and jog up to the door, rapping it with my knuckles. Stuffing my hands in my pockets to keep them warm and from fidgeting too much, I wait for one of the girls to answer. I'm about to knock again when the door is thrown open by Indie.

"What's up, asshat? Haven't seen you in a hot minute. Who you been hidin' in?" she cracks, leaning against the doorframe.

"Yo mama! Now let me the fuck in – it's cold out here, Jones!"

Pushing past her, I notice a rolling carryon bag in the foyer.
"You going somewhere?"

"Yeah, I have a wedding that I got roped into planning for a friend. I'll only be gone over night though," she says, leading me into her kitchen.

"So that means Frankie will be here alone?" I hate the idea of her here by herself with Andrew still off the grid.

"Yeah, I know. I don't like it either. What are you guys doing tonight? Just the game? Can you take her home with you?" Indie asks, handing me a beer.

"I'm going to have to—there's no way I'm letting her stay here on her own."

"That's what I was banking on. I was going to call you to

figure it out, but she said you were picking her up, so I figured we could work it out then."

"Work what out?" Frankie walks in and I stop, bottle halfway to my mouth and stare.

How the fuck did I forget how beautiful my girl is in the few days that I haven't seen her? She's got her hair pulled back in a ponytail, what I call her hooker hoop earrings in, and the new necklace I got her for her birthday. Her jeans—fuck me—her jeans, they're soft and worn looking, nearly white in places and I'm pretty sure they were painted on. As if her jeans aren't hard on inducing enough, she has on black and red stilettos that have these corset-looking laces tied into a bow up the back.

They are probably the hottest fucking things I've ever seen in my life—ever.

Placing the bottle down on the island, I adjust my now-hard cock behind my zipper before I walk over to where she's standing next to Indie sharing a beer. Her question forgotten in her quest for a drink, thank fuck.

"Nice shirt there, Tits McGee," I say, gesturing with my chin at her jersey-style Blackhawks shirt and impressive cleavage.

Taking her hand and flipping it palm side up so that I can kiss my spot, I can't help but inhale her scent and smile against the delicate skin of her wrist when her breath catches.

Pulling her hand out of mine, she reaches for Indie's beer and takes a sip, licking a lingering drop from her bottom lip, causing my already rigid cock to harden further.

"Shut up, Deac, you know I hate when you call me that." Laughing, she turns her attention to Indie. "Don't worry about waiting up. It's going to be a late night and I know you're on deadline."

"Doll, I'm leaving for the night, remember?" Indie reminds, pulling the ends tight on the purple bandana holding her hair in place and adjusting her glasses.

With a small frown, Frankie nods. "That's right, Cara's wedding, I forgot. Okay, well, then I guess I'll see you tomorrow then."

She gives her a hug and says goodbye. Over Indie's shoulder, I see Frankie biting the inside of her lip, her mind clearly working, and decide that instead of hashing this out with her here and now, I'll just take her to my place after the game and deal then.

"All right, Jones, we're outta here. Have fun and drive safe, yeah?" I wink and give her a small nod.

"Have a good time, you crazy kids. Take care of our girl, Deacon," Indie says as we head for the door.

Helping Frankie on with her coat, I nod and wave one more time as I usher her out the door and into my illegally parked and thankfully not towed Range Rover. Closing her door, I make it around to my side and slide in.

"You ready for some hockey, Princess?"

"Hell, yes, and some nachos."

Shaking my head and laughing at her, I put the truck in gear and head to the UC.

"That's my girl."

WE MAKE IT through the throngs of people to our level with about thirty minutes to spare. I hand the two tickets my brothers or dad won't be using over to Frankie once they've been scanned.

"You heading to standing room only with these?"

"Yep. You going to grab beer?" she asks, walking backwards toward the stairs that will take her up to the third level.

"Of course."

"Don't forget my nachos. Jalapenos and extra, extra cheese.

Oh, and popcorn!" Frankie yells over the crowd.

"I know what to get." Smiling at her, I turn to get into one of the long ass lines when a thought occurs to me.

"Frankie!"

I whistle loudly, getting her attention and that of a few dozen other people. Smooth move, dumbass. Leaving the line, I jog over to where she's waiting on the stairs.

"You shouldn't go up there alone. I'll go with you and we can grab our food when you're done doing your thing."

"Deacon, it's fine. You would never let anything happen to me and there are over twenty thousand people here. I'll be okay. Andrew hates hockey anyway," she tells me, trying to lighten things up, even though I can see a trace of worry in her eyes. "I'll probably beat you to our seat. I promise to stay put."

I nod my head in agreement, even though I don't like it. "All right, just be careful, yeah? I'll see you in a few."

Blowing me a kiss, she goes on her usual mission of giving away two seats on the first level against the glass to someone up in the nosebleed section. She does it every time we have extra tickets. I usually just hand them off to the first dad I see with his kid or a couple of hot chicks. That little move has gotten me more ass than I care to admit. Not my girl though—she likes to go search someone out.

About a minute before the anthem starts, which is just as big a deal as the actual game in the Mad House, I make my way to our seats loaded down with all of our shit. Lifting my chin in greeting to the other season ticket holders that sit around us, I can't help but laugh at who Frankie is sitting with. She managed to find a couple decked out in head to toe Hawks gear. I mean, Head. To. Toe. I wouldn't be surprised if they were wearing matching underwear. The man even has his face painted black and red.

We have prime seats—center ice on the glass and the first four seats in the row, which means I can sit on the aisle and not worry about my long ass legs being too cramped.

"Hey, Princess, who're your friends?" I ask, handing her the nachos and popcorn so that I can sit down without spilling our beers and other goodies.

"Deacon, this is Paula and her husband, Steven. They've never been to a game before," she says, beaming at me.

She loves this and I love her for it.

Reaching out my hand, I shake theirs in turn. That's all we have time for before Jim Cornelison is being announced to begin singing and the roar of the crowd drowns out everything else.

Two periods fly by. The game is fast paced, straight up "old school" hockey. Seconds before intermission, the Hawks score, and "Chelsea Dagger" fills the arena, bringing everyone to their feet, high fives all around. Paula and Steven are jumping up and down, making Frankie smile even brighter. Turning my way, she gives me a wink, and just that has me fighting the urge to scoop her up and kiss the hell out of my girl right here in front of the whole damn place.

After turning down the offer to "shoot the puck," a little intermission time killer they do with local celebrities and athletes, I settle in next to Frankie and throw my arm over the back of her chair, leaning in to talk to her.

"I missed this," I tell her, my lips against her ear so that I can be heard over the crowd.

Frankie dips her head slightly, her hair falling over one shoulder, nodding before looking at me.

I can see that she is going to say something, so I lean down, tucking my loose hair behind my ear, putting her mouth only inches from the side of my face.

"Me too, Deac. I feel like we haven't seen each other at all lately." Her warm breath fans over my face.

I'm just about to say something in return, when I feel someone nudging me in the back and pointing over my shoulder toward the ceiling, yelling something that I can't make out. Looking to where he is pointing, I see that Frankie and I have been captured by the Kiss Cam and we're on the Jumbotron. I bump her leg with mine to bring her attention to the screen and raise my eyebrows at her suggestively, a smirk lifting my lip waiting for her answer to my silent invitation. She shakes her head no, laughing the whole while, but when the crowd starts to chant "KISS HIM! KISS HIM!" she has no choice but to kiss me. I turn my face offering her my cheek, tapping the stubble roughened area right above my jaw, then at the very last second I pull the man move and turn my head quickly, catching her lips with mine in what starts out as a very innocent kiss. The moment our mouths meet, I know I've fucked up. There is no way this little peck will be enough and without a moment's hesitation I deepen the kiss, slanting my mouth over hers, my hand fisting in her ponytail, using it to guide her. I lick at her bottom lip tasting the salt from the popcorn, begging for entrance, and I would've gotten it too, had the twenty-two thousand other people in the room not exploded into loud catcalls and whistles. Cockblocks, all of them. I allow her to pull back and hide her face, while I throw my head back, laughing at her embarrassment, adjusting in my seat to try and alleviate the rock solid hard on one kiss has caused.

Midway through the third period as she's explaining a penalty to Paula, I take hold of her hand, placing a kiss to my spot and then settling it on my thigh. I can feel her eyes on me, but I never take my gaze from the game. If it makes her uncomfortable, she doesn't say and doesn't remove her hand until the Hawks score again and we all jump to our feet in excitement. Steven leans over, raising his hand for a high-five over Frankie's head. She smiles up at me and throws me a little hip bump, mouthing thank you. I bend down and cover her lips briefly with mine, startling her with the quick kiss. I feel the need to throw her off balance, just as she's done to me without even

trying.

THE CAR RIDE back to my place is quiet, not exactly awkward but close enough. I'm waiting for her to notice that we aren't heading back to Bucktown and Indie's place, but she hasn't yet, so I leave it be. Turning the radio up, she says, "Ooh, I love this song, we'll have to check them out when they're in town next."

"Who is it?"

"It's Neon Trees, 'Everybody Talks.' It's one of my favorite songs on their album. This one and this one," she says, grabbing my phone from the cup holder. Cranking the volume, she starts dancing in her seat to the song she queued up and then stops abruptly as the song's lyrics fill the cab.

"'Sleeping with a friend,' huh?" I throw her a cocky smile enjoying her embarrassment for the second time that night. "Great choice, I think this might be my new favorite song." Winking at her, I turn the volume up even higher and drum along with the beat. Probably not smart to get her fired up since she's going to be plenty pissed when she finds out I'm not taking her home. I can't help it though -- it's too much fun making her blush.

Chapter
SIXTEEN

Francesca

LOST IN MY thoughts about that kiss at the game—hell, kisses—I don't even realize that we've been heading away from Indie's until we pull up to the gates at Deacon's place. Whipping my head in his direction I ask, "Why are we here?" completely confused.

He bites at the corner of his bottom lip and scrunches up his face, which tells me that I'm not going to like his answer.

"Ummm, can we talk about it once I get this jersey off? It's really starting to itch," he says, trying to distract from the fact that we are pulling into his garage and not in front of Indie's brownstone.

"Deacon, I know that we did not come all the way the hell over here so that you can change before taking me home, so cut your bullshit," I demand, slamming the door on the Rover a little harder than necessary and smiling at the way it makes him wince.

Walking through the mudroom, I toss my coat on the bench there and stop at the alarm on the wall in the kitchen. I punch in the code and immediately turn the music system on.

His house is too damn big and echoes— I need the noise. The soulful sound of Alabama Shakes fills the void but doesn't stop me from spinning at the sound of him coming into the room.

I suck in a breath at the sight of his naked chest and bare feet. Where the fuck did his shirt go so quickly? Deacon is a sight to behold clothed…shirtless though? He is stunning. His chest and arms the canvas to some of the most beautiful ink that I have ever seen. All of his tattoos are gorgeous, but his chest piece and arms are my favorite as is the script across his ribs. I stare at the wings that stretch from shoulder to shoulder, meeting in the middle at a barbed heart with the words "LOVE HURTS" scrawled across the top just under his collarbones and my name etched into the tattered heart. My name? When the hell? I open my mouth to ask him when he added my name and why, just as he starts explaining my reason for being here instead of in my own bed.

"Indie isn't coming home until sometime tomorrow and we didn't think that you should be alone there tonight. I had already given Trent and Reggie the night off, so I brought you here," he tells me unapologetically.

"We? Who the hell is 'we'?" I ask, my eyes narrowed into slits, my hands planted firmly on my hips.

Clearing his throat, he has the decency to look sheepish.

"Jones and I. She was worried. I was worried."

"You have no right to make decisions for me, Deacon. Neither of you do!" I am on the verge of a serious hissy fit I'm so pissed at them, but mostly with him because this overbearing bullshit has to stop. I don't know if I'm coming or going with him lately, and I'm over it.

Pointing a finger at him, I lay it out for his too-beautiful-for-words, frustrating ass.

"I am going to say this one more time, Deac, and you're going to fucking listen. I do not belong to you. I am not yours to—"

"Every fucking time you say that it makes me crazy and that much more determined to show you that you *are* mine, Frankie," he interrupts, planting himself directly in front of me, but not invading the space I obviously need to keep between us.

Taking a deep breath, I look into his hazel eyes, taking in the lush lashes that frame them, and the way he tucks his hair behind his ears so that it doesn't catch in the scruff bordering on a beard covering his chin.

"What do you want from me, Deacon? Do you even know anymore? Because I have no idea," I ask him, defeat evident in my softly spoken words.

Never releasing my gaze, he shrugs and says simply, "Nothing, everything—you." His eyes bore into mine, the words as unmistakable in the mossy depths as they are hanging in the air between us. I can feel their truth, and it scares me on so many levels.

Rapidly blinking back the tears of frustration and confusion, I shake my head and admit, "Deacon, I'm scared," in a near whisper. "I don't want our friendship to change. I need you, Deac. Aside from my dad, you're the most important man in my life—you always have been." I glance away to keep myself from getting swallowed up by the intensity staring back at me, but whip my head back so quickly at his next words, I'm sure I've done some damage to my poor neck.

"Frankie, lock that shit up. Our friendship changed the moment you wrapped those sexy, fucking legs around me and rubbed that sweet, little pussy against my cock when I had you up against the wall in my office," Deacon says with an all-consuming confidence. Clearly he's not going to let me get away with easing into this conversation.

I gasp partly in shock at him for being so crude, although I'm not sure why. Deacon is bold, raw, and just *Deacon*. I've never been on the other end of all that in-your-face alpha though. No, I gasp mostly because the reminder and the feral heat in his tone are hot as hell and have my panties instantly wet.

He gives me a knowing look, his mouth kicked up in that smirk of his—the one that says *"I'll take you. I'll take you any way I want, anywhere I want, and you'll not only let me, you'll fucking love it."*

I am so screwed. I don't know how to fight *this* Deacon, or if I even want to.

Huffing out a defeated breath, he shoves his hands into his pockets. "I won't share you with Cristiano anymore. I don't play nice with others, and throw having to share *you* into the mix and it's gonna get ugly."

I look up at him and gone is that sexy smirk. Now all I see is vulnerability, and I don't know what to do with that. Deacon doesn't do vulnerable; he is always confident, overly cocky even.

"Actually 'won't' isn't right...I CAN'T share you, I'm completely incapable of it. I cannot share you with him or any other man. Please don't ask me to, Frankie," he implores in earnest.

It's the "please" that has me quickly blinking back the tears that are once again threatening. That one word hits me straight in the heart, leaving me a little more breathless, a little less capable of fighting him on this for much longer. I have never heard him ask for anything, plead for a chance. If he wants something, he takes it, earns it, fights to achieve it. That he is pleading for me, for us, undoes me. Makes me weak. And that scares the hell out of me, putting me on the defensive.

"Deacon, I'm not asking you to share me! I'm just confused," I say exasperated, beginning to pace with that admission.

My hands tugging at my hair, heels clicking on the wood floor in front of where he leans against the counter, his long denim encased legs crossed at the ankles, him looking calm and relaxed when I am anything but. How can he not see what this could do to our friendship, our family? The Loves are my family! This wouldn't last. Deacon doesn't do relationships or girlfriends. He fucks who he wants, when he wants, and lets no one hold him down. Veronica is the closest thing to a girlfriend I've ever seen and I know that he never stopped messing around while they were doing…whatever. But how can I walk away? I know in my heart that I would always wonder, always regret it. I can lie to myself all I want, but I know the truth in my heart.

"What are you confused about, Frankie?" he all but shouts, blowing that calm and relaxed façade to shit. "Are you confused about his feelings, your feelings, mine? Do you need me to tell you again exactly what I feel for you?"

I know I wouldn't be able to handle that right now. My emotions are all over the place as it is. Add to that him standing there barefoot and shirtless, my name inked into his skin, that deep V that disappears into the top of his jeans, the tattoos along his cuts following, and I am completely overwhelmed. He can't throw his feelings at me right now. He can NOT. I bite my lip so hard I can taste the coppery tang of blood, and with downcast eyes I shake my head no.

"No? You don't want to hear how just the sight of those little white teeth of yours sunk into your lip has me hard?"

He punctuates that statement by putting a hand to that hardness and squeezing. It takes everything I have to swallow my moan.

"Or how about that you're all I think about? So much so that I'm getting my ass handed to me on the mats by sparring partners. Sparring partners, Frankie!" He shakes his head. "Not that either, huh? Then how about how all I want is to be inside you right now? Under you, over you, behind you, I really don't fucking care as long as I'm inside you," he growls, "Because I need to show you that you're mine, that he can't have you, and that I fucking love you."

He slaps a hand to his chest, over his heart. "I fucking love you, Princess."

My pacing had stopped the moment that he'd raised his voice, but as soon as that last sentence leaves his mouth, I spin around trying to catch my breath and begin pacing again. Continuing the torture on my poor lip, willing my heart to slow its frantic beating. He says that he loves me, but does he *love* me love me? We tell each other "I love you" all the time. This feels different though. My mind is screaming at me to run, run far and fast because in the end, he'll burn me. It's what he does, even though it's not what he sets out to do. My heart though, my heart is swelling, weeping, and singing all at the same time. I'm not sure which to listen to and it has me completely spun.

I sense him coming toward me, can feel the heat rolling off of him as he stands at my back, not nearly close enough, making me realize that I am holding still, waiting for his next move. My body craves his touch no matter what my mind is trying to convince me of.

"Look at me, Frankie," he says roughly.

He waits for me to make eye contact with him before speaking. He must know that I am all out of fight by the look in my eyes because he says dominantly, "When I fuck you, it won't be as your good buddy Deacon, you feel me? When I finally get you to choose this, choose me, I am going to show you what it's like to belong to a man. To be taken and completely owned by him, by me. I don't even want to think about you with anyone else, but I can promise you that whatever you've been doing with them," he pauses and I hold my breath waiting to see what filthy thing he'll say next, "Isn't even close to what you and I will be doing," he finishes with absolute confidence.

My heart is beating so hard in my chest I don't see how he can't hear it. Maybe if I weren't gasping to get air into my lungs, he would have.

This is the Deacon that I have always wanted, I just hadn't been aware of it until recently. I watched women be consumed by him, go completely stupid and set on fire with little more than a touch or a look, and I didn't understand it then because no one had ever affected me in that way, but I knew that I

wanted to understand it. I wanted to feel on the verge of losing
control because of a man and now I am. I am affected and it
both scares the hell out of me and excites me beyond reason. I
swallow slowly.

"What is it that you think we'll be doing, Deacon?"

He gives me that smirk of his again.

"I don't think, Princess—I *know*. I'll have you up against the
wall with your legs wrapped around me like they were on your
birthday. I'll have you right here in the kitchen on the counter."

With every word, he is stalking toward me, backing me into
the island at my back, but not touching me yet, which is killing
me, and I'm pretty sure that he knows it. He has me trapped
between his rock hard body and the island now, my ass resting
on the edge so that I have to lean back to look up into his eyes.
Eyes that I can't even put a color to right now, but I can see the
need in them, and it causes a little shiver to run down my spine,
which has his wicked grin turning into a knowing smile.

"I'll have you in my bed, in yours, in the shower, and anywhere else I want to take you, Frankie, because once I've had
you, I'll own you, and you'll be begging me for more. I will fuck
you the way you need to be fucked, the way you want to be
fucked, even though you don't know it yet, and I won't stop until
you come over and over again. On my cock, when I'm buried so
deep in that perfect, little pussy, on my tongue while I suck on
your clit, and on my fingers as you ride my hand."

My chest is heaving now, I'm so turned on. Eyes completely glazed over and he hasn't laid a hand on me yet. He is
standing with his long legs on either side of mine, arms caging
me in, his scent surrounding me, lips nearly grazing my ear with
every dirty word he whispers. He goes on in that same husky
voice so full of promise, "Then when I'm finished fucking you,
I'll make love to you, slow and soft. It will be a first for me, but
I'll take care of you. I'll make sure that you know what it means
to be mine, Frankie. It's something that I should have showed

you long before now. I have a lot of time to make up for, but we'll call the last few years foreplay. All of that anticipation—mmmm, I bet I can make you come without even getting you naked first."

He says the last bit with a smile in his voice, as if he's just issued himself a dare and it pleases him.

I can't form a coherent thought let alone words right now. I am still struggling to breathe, staring at his chest and wondering how long I have to wait before he shows me, because I'm pretty damn sure his challenge isn't going to be that difficult. I'm ready to come right now, fully clothed and without him even physically touching me.

My mind is made up for me by the need coursing through my veins. I'm afraid that this might be awkward since we've been friends for so long, but he's right, he isn't my buddy Deac anymore. He is the man making my pussy wetter than anyone ever has with nothing more than his words. He is the man who has me trembling from head to toe, incinerated by need from the slightest ghosting of his lips over my ear.

Deacon has always been the person in my life who allows me to just be me and I know that this won't be any different. He'll let me reveal my deepest fantasies—no, he'll insist that I tell him—and then he'd help me make them into reality. I have never been brave or secure enough in any of my relationships to let anyone in and see what I really crave. I've settled for vanilla when what I really wanted was *more*. I'm not sure exactly what that means, only that it's what I need, and Deacon would give me more. I have no doubt he'd give me more and then some. Just the thought of the possibilities raises goose bumps along my arms.

Watching the rise and fall of his chest, the steady throbbing of his pulse in his throat as he stands there and just lets me take him in. My eyes roam over every hard plane of his body, my gaze caresses every inch of beautifully inked skin and taut muscles. Down the ridges of his abs until I come to the very obvious bulge in his pants. My jaw goes slack, and for the first time in my life, I want a man's dick in my mouth for my pleasure, not just his. My tongue sweeps over my bottom lip, my teeth sinking into the wetness I've left behind. Would he let me? I've only done it twice before, but fuck me, I wanted to do it now, so bad. "You keep looking at me like that and you'll be on your knees to get the edge off before I get you on your back and I'm tryi—"

"YES." The word falls from my mouth on a hushed breath interrupting whatever noble thing he was going to try to force on me. Just one word—that's all I can get out. His arm snakes out, wrapping around my waist, pulling me in tight, chest-to-chest with no space in between, his large hand splayed wide across my back, the other gripping the edge of the countertop.

"Say it again, Frankie. Tell me that you want my cock in your mouth, but I'm warning you, if you say it, you better fucking mean it, because I'm way past turning back now. I want to go slow with you, baby, but you on your knees is something I've thought about for years. After though, I'm going to have to take you how I want, my way."

Chapter SEVENTEEN

DEACON

STANDING THERE LOOKING down as I hold her tight to me, I take Frankie in. She has this beautiful flush across her chest and climbing up her exposed throat to her cheeks, giving away just how hot our talk has made her. I try to tamp down the urge to lay her out right here on the kitchen floor. I want inside of her so fucking bad. My mind is a riotous clusterfuck of want and need. I know that I should be gentle with the Princess and show her what I feel by making this special, but fuck me if I know what that looks like. I've never done sweet, never made love to anyone. I've only ever loved one woman, and she is standing in front of me offering all of her, and me being me, I just want to take everything she's willing to give.

Reaching out to sweep back the hair that's fallen across her forehead, I tuck it behind her ear. Slowly I let my fingers graze over the shell and then down her neck, resting my palm against the base, my fingers lightly encircling her throat, feeling her heart thundering against them.

"Frankie, you deserve special. I want to give you special, but that's something you might have to teach me. I know fucking, and right now, that's what I'm gonna teach you, baby. There's nothing wrong with dirty—in fact, I'm going to love showing you how good it can be. I want you to know that everything I do, every touch, every word, it's different because it's you. You're different, you always have been. You feel me?"

She looks up at me shaking her head, a small smile playing over her lips, lips that I can't wait to see wrapped around my cock.

"That, right there, Deacon, is how you make it special."

I smile down into her upturned face and nod, thankful that she can't read my mind at that moment. Feeling a little more in control of my emotions, but not the raging hard on demanding attention, I kiss Frankie one last time, releasing my hold on her to take her hand and pull her behind me up the stairs to my room. She stops in the doorway and looks a little apprehensive, biting at her bottom lip and then the pad of her thumb.

"Princess?"

Her eyes shoot to mine.

"Sorry. Do you maybe want to go to my room?" she asks in a rush, indicating with her head the room down the hall that she uses when she stays here.

I'm so fucking confused right now, probably because all of my blood is pooled in my cock.

"Why would we go in there?" I ask squinting at her trying to figure out what it is that I'm missing.

And then, like a motherfucking lightning bolt to my ass, I get it.

Pulling her into my room and over to the bed, I lightly push her so that she's sitting, and then lean in placing my hands on either side of her until she's forced to lie down and scoot back, feet dangling as I climb over top of her, keeping my weight on my forearms.

"Frankie, you are the only woman that has ever been in this bed. EVER," I tell her. Never breaking eye contact so she knows I'm not bullshitting. "In fact, you are the only woman who has ever even been in my room." Lowering myself by my arms so that I'm doing a pushup over her, I nip her bottom lip. "I told you, baby, every little thing is different with you." Straightening my arms so that our bodies aren't touching anymore, I look down into those blues that make me feel lost and found all at once. Bending my arms again so that my mouth is hovering over hers, I ask, "We good now?"

Instead of answering me, she grabs the back of my neck and pulls, closing the distance between us. Our mouths fused together, I yank the rubber band from her hair as gently as I can and then tangle my fingers in the cool, silky strands, letting them slide through my fingers. Tightening my hands into loose fists, I bring her even closer, swiping my tongue against her full bottom lip at the same time as I press my solid cock against the seam of her jeans. Swallowing her moan, I smile and rock against her again. I need to quit that shit though. I'm so fucking close I might blow before I even get inside of her just from teasing her.

Breaking our kiss, I sit up, bringing her with me, not stopping until we are both standing. I take a second to just look at her. She's so fucking beautiful, every bit of her perfect and I've waited for so long I don't want to rush, but fuck me, I just want in so, so bad. Hands trembling like a kid about to get his dick wet for the first time, I reach for the hem of her shirt, her arms raised giving me the permission I didn't realize I was asking for. I let my hands skim over every inch of skin I expose. My knuckles brush over the sides of her breasts causing her to suck in a breath between her teeth. I finally get the top off and fling it across the room. Inhaling slowly I run my fingertip along the edge of the lace barely covering the most perfect set of tits I've ever seen.

"As hot as this is, it's coming off," I tell her as I reach behind her with one hand and release the clasp.

As the straps start to slide down her arms she lifts her hands and holds the cups to her, stopping them from falling away.

"No way, Frankie, those are my tits and I want to see them. I want them wet from my mouth, nipples hard little points because I've got you so worked up," I rasp a little rougher than I intended.

Grabbing her wrists, I pull her hands away and watch as the black lace falls to the floor, leaving her naked from the waist up with nothing but that same pink flush covering her chest. My eyes roaming over every part of her, I'm mesmerized by the sight of her hand skimming over her taut belly to the button on her jeans, releasing it along with a long breathy sigh.

"You want these off too, Deacon? Is this yours to make wet as well?" she asks, as she shimmies out of her pants, in that fucking voice of hers. It's pure sex.

Holy shit. There's no way this is gonna last. Frankie talking dirty is by far the sexiest fucking thing I've ever heard. Snapping out of it just as she's about to take her shoes off, I growl, "The shoes stay. I've thought about fucking you in those all goddamn night. They're staying. I can't wait to feel them digging in to my back."

Breathing through her mouth, she nods and slips the red and black heels back on so that she's standing there completely fucking naked except for those corset shoes that are gonna be the death of me.

Taking in every gorgeous inch of her, eyes lingering over the tattoo wrapped around her thigh and then centering on her very bare pussy, I reach out with one long digit and dip into the heat in between her legs, groaning at the wetness there. She shudders as she throws her head back, mewling low in her throat.

"Deacon, God, mmmmmm."

"You're so wet for me, Frankie. Do you know what it does to me to know that I did this to you? It makes me so fucking hard, baby. So. Fucking. Hard," I tell her, punctuating each word with a bend of the finger buried in her, hooking it, pressing against her G-spot.

I can feel her legs trembling against my palm moving against her thigh as I thrust into her. Dragging my fingers out slowly, I bring my hand up and paint her tight, rose-colored nipples with her juices, smiling as she moans, her nails digging into my shoulders where she latches on to keep herself upright.

Lowering my head, I swipe my tongue over one, the taste of her bursting against my tongue, driving me insane. Switching to the other, I show it the same attention before cupping them both in my hands and squeezing, bringing them together as I simultaneously bite at her nipples, and then immediately soothe the sting by sucking as much of her in my mouth as I can. I pull away from her with a little pop, "Mmmmm, tastes like pussy." I smirk at the way her eyes go all fiery hearing that before I put my mouth on her fevered skin again.

"Deacon, please, I'm going to come. I need you inside of me," she begs which is totally my undoing.

Releasing one of her tits, I reach down and unfasten my belt one handed and then yank on the button fly relieving the pressure on my cock. Taking her hands from my shoulders, she pushes my pants down, the belt buckle clanking loudly as it hits the wood floor. As Frankie reaches for my boxer briefs, she brushes against the head of my dick which is escaping over the waistband, no longer able to be contained. The tip is glistening with precum that I can feel on her fingers now as she slides them to my hips, hooking into the sides of my briefs and pulling down, leaving a wet trail and causing me to hiss out a breath as I kick my pants away.

"Princess, this first time—" I don't get to finish before she drops to her knees.

"You said I could do this first, Deacon. Please let me." Looking up at me with those goddamn eyes, I can't even think straight, let alone argue with her. Not that I would.

Running my palm over her hair, I gather it in one hand, bending down, my other hand disappears between her legs and rubs slowly into her pussy. Gathering some of that wetness, I straighten, rubbing it over the head of my cock and down the shaft. Pressing on the back of her head as I do.

"I want you to taste both of us, Frankie. I want you to know how fucking sweet your pussy tastes. Now be a good girl and open your mouth," I growl in a nearly feral tone.

Blinking slowly up at me, she nods.

"Holy fuck," she breathes across my dick causing it to twitch.

My lip quirks up in a smile as I grab the base and guide my cock past her lips, moaning the second her hot, little mouth closes around it. I know I'm a lot bigger than average, so I'm fighting the urge to push all the way in in one swift motion to test her gag reflexes. Fisting her hair again, I hold her still for a second while I try to keep from spraying the back of my girl's throat. She hums in appreciation, causing my balls to tighten up even further.

Eyes screwed closed, "Ahhhhhh. Fuck it," I mumble to myself.

There will be plenty of time for going slow later. Letting go of my dick, I cup her jaw and draw her further down, guiding her with the hand in her hair.

"Fuck, Frankie, your mouth. Your hot, wet, motherfucking mouth. This is gonna be over fast, but I promise, next time—I promise," I vow on a moan as she swirls her tongue over the crown and then flattens it as I glide even further into heaven.

My head falls back on my shoulders as I let out a string of curses mixed in with praise and other incoherent filthy shit. Slowly opening my eyes, I force myself to look down at her and watch as she swallows me almost entirely, causing her to gag a little before she licks her way back to the tip.

"Jesus fuck, baby," I say under my breath. "I need inside

you. Now." Pulling her gently off of my cock and onto her feet, I sweep her up and lay her on the bed.

Brushing her hands across my chest, she lets them trail down my sides, around to my back until she has my ass in a firm grip, urging me forward.

"Please, Deac, I want you deep," she says against my neck as she licks at the tendons straining there.

I try my damnedest to reel my shit in and slow down, but I can't with her saying things like that.

Growling, I sit up on my knees and press her thighs wide, opening her to me.

"Look at how pretty that is." Running my thumb over her clit, I press lower, entering her before pulling back out and circling it around again.

Writhing beneath me, head thrown and back arched, I reach and encircle her throat with my hand before sliding it down the center of her chest, stopping right at her pussy, holding her still.

"Let me see those blues, baby," I say as I guide my cock forward, pushing just the tip past her lips and holding there until she focuses on my eyes.

"I'm not covering up. I'm sick of shit being between us. I wanna feel it when you come all over my cock. I've never gone bare before so we're good." I look at her expectantly through hooded eyes.

Nodding her head in acceptance, she says in a dazed, husky voice, "Okay, Deac."

That's all I need before I thrust home. The room instantly fills with our moans. Pulling her legs tight, I wrap them around my waist, those sexy-as-fuck shoes digging into my ass. Hands spanning her tiny waist, I drag her closer still, pressing her clit against me as I slide out almost completely and then thrust back in hard and deep. Her back comes off the bed pushing her tits up into the air and her head against the pillow.

"Mmmmmm, Frankie, you have no fucking clue how hot you look wrapped around me like this," I tell her as I pull back and press back in even deeper, watching as I disappear inside of her.

"Oh fuck. Oh, Deacon. Please. Again please," she begs as she reaches up and plucks at her nipples, rolling them in between her fingers.

"You want more, Frankie? Tell me you want my cock, baby. Tell me and I'll give it to you." My balls rest against her ass I'm so deep. I roll my hips, rubbing her clit with the base of my cock as the head bottoms out.

Panting and rocking against me now, I watch as she comes apart beneath me, my balls tightening at the thought of her coming and the vice grip her pussy has on my cock right now.

"No, Deacon, please don't stop. Please. I want it. I want your cock. I want to come all over it," she says in a husky voice.

Fuck me sideways, that's all it takes.

"You don't come again until I tell you to, Frankie, you hear me?"

Thrashing her head back and forth she chants, "Please let me come," over and over, completely causing the tiny thread of control I have to snap.

Slamming forward, I flex and roll my hips before pulling out and doing it again, and on the third thrust I know I'm not going to be able to hold back any longer. With the way her pussy is sucking at my cock, I know she's there too, thank fuck.

"Come for me, baby. Right now, come for me," I grit out as I slam harder and faster. The sound of our skin slapping together driving me.

She's so tight around my swelling cock that it's almost painful. Stemming from that pain and the pulsing that I feel with every slide home is pleasure so fucking intense I start to see stars as she screams my name and digs her heels deeper into my ass, triggering my own release. Gritting my teeth, my head falls back, exposing my throat as a guttural roar escapes past my lips along with her name.

Breathing heavily, I look down at her and take in her sated posture, heavy lids, and the soft smile playing over her lips. Lowering myself so that we're chest to chest, I kiss my girl tenderly, letting the love I have for her be felt in every brush of our mouths, every shared breath, and hope that it's enough.

After raiding the fridge downstairs and a little countertop loving, Frankie and I end up back in bed completely relaxed and worn the fuck out.

"What do you want to watch?" I ask, pulling her into my side, tucking her under my arm as I flip through the channels, landing on one of the music stations while I pull up the guide.

"I don't care, Deac, whatever is fine. As long as it's not any of your zombie shit," she says, her nose crinkled in distaste.

"Zombie shit? Woman, I'll have you know that by watching that shit I will be ready for the zombie apocalypse and you'll be thanking my ass when we survive it in one piece."

"Oh my God, you're so dumb." Laughing at me she snuggles in closer, her hands drawing circles over the tattoo covering my chest, then tracing her name that I'd had added to the heart one drunken night while she wasn't speaking to me.

I can tell that she's getting ready to ask me about it I don't want to ruin the moment by telling Frankie how I came to acquire it, so I switch gears and bring her attention to the very first tattoo that I got for her.

"Do you remember how surprised you were when I got this?" I ask, lifting my arm, turning it so that the ink is facing us.

When I'd told Frankie that I had enlisted, she was upset and worried. She went out and got us a Mizpah charm—not that I had any fucking clue what that was—and chains so we could each wear our half of the coin. Whole, it read, *"The Lord watch between me and thee while we are absent from one another."*

The day before I left, I had Cage tattoo my half of the coin and chain on my forearm so that even when I wouldn't be able to physically wear the charm, that I'd always have my half of the coin with me. Inked into my skin is a jagged half of a heart with the words *"watch and thee are absent om another,"* the words not making much sense unless put together with her half. Fitting really, since I don't make a whole lot of fucking sense without the Princess—she's the other half of me.

Frankie smiles and reaches out. Grazing over my forearm and wrist. Fingers dancing over the tattoo there.

"I was so scared for you," she breathes out. "I was also pissed that you were leaving me." Laughing she gazes up at me under her lashes. "I missed you so much, Deacon. I felt a little lost for a while, even though I had the rest of my Loves. It's always been me and you, ya know?" she asks softly.

"Yeah, baby, I know. It always will be too, Princess, no matter what," I reassure her.

I return her smile and raise Frankie's arm, the one with her charm bracelet, and hold it against my tattoo, lining them up so that the message is complete. I had her half added to her bracelet when the chain broke a couple years ago. Kissing the inside of her wrist, I lower her arm, pulling her in even closer when I hear the song that's playing on the TV.

"I played this song over and over when you were in the hospital. I never let the room go silent, always had something on, but I found myself hitting repeat all the time when this one would come on."

I'm glad that she can't see me—I'm embarrassed by my admission, but hearing "Without You" brings me back to those days, almost making me feel weak.

"I love this one. I think I remember the music, but I'm not sure. I can't separate what was real or what was a dream during that time." Her brows are drawn low in concentration.

I don't want to talk about this shit. It makes me absofuckinglutely crazy to think about Andrew putting hands on her, and I just want to enjoy this time with Frankie without feeling the need to kill someone. I don't want to bring that ugliness to our bed.

"Yeah, well, I played all kinds of your shit music too because I'm a nice fucking guy."

That makes her giggle just as I'd hoped it would.

Reaching over her, I grab my phone and set my alarm. Setting it back in the dock, I switch off the lamp and pull the blanket over us. Kissing her wrist one more time, and then her shoulder, I whisper, "Night, Princess, love you and your shitty music."

Waking up with Frankie lying across my chest, her soft, silky thigh thrown over my much harder one, I know there's no way in hell that I'm making my gym time. She's dreaming, making small little whimpering noises, her face twisted as if she's in pain and then smoothing out as soon as I run a finger along her puckered brow. Tucking her hair behind her ear so that I can get an unobstructed view of her face, I can't help the smile just looking at her causes. Jesus fuck, she's so beautiful. She wiggles closer, causing my morning wood to jump against the leg that's hitched over my waist. Moving as slowly and carefully as I can, I slide out from under her to go call Sonny and tell him I'm not coming in until later. Just as my feet touch the floor, she rolls over flat on her back, throwing her arms over her head, the sheet pooled around her waist, leaving her perfect tits completely bare and begging for my attention. Allowing my eyes to roam, I take in her golden skin and every dip and indentation that make up my gorgeous girl. I stop at the "sensitive area" ink that she got with Indie. Right under her breast, following the curve of her body to her side are the words, *"And though she be but little, she is fierce,"* in an elegant script that I traced my tongue over last night. It's fucking sexy as hell and describes my Princess perfectly. The thought of her showing this one to Cristiano makes me want to piece that motherfucker out.

Shaking my head, I let my gaze dip down over her belly to her long, toned legs and that pretty, little pussy in between them. Yeah, I'm definitely not making my gym time; my brothers can kick my ass later.

Pulling the sheet the rest of the way off of her, I ease back onto the bed, lying flat on my stomach, eye level with my breakfast. Inhaling deeply, I take in her scent and wish to hell I could just fucking live inside of her. Settling myself in as comfortably as I can with my painfully hard cock, I place a soft kiss to her inner thigh before sweeping my tongue right through her center, stopping to nibble lightly at her clit. Leaning back, I look at her now glistening slit and hum in appreciation. I could eat her all fucking day. She tastes so sweet and I can still smell the sex on her from the night before. It's so goddamned hot. Putting my mouth back on her, I take my time laving and kissing, biting and blowing. It doesn't take long before I can feel Frankie writhing beneath me. Clit pulled in between my lips, I glance up and see her gorgeous blues watching me. Smiling, I release her with a little pop.

"Good morning. I got tired of waiting for you to wake up, so I decided to start breakfast without you."

"Mmmm. Well, don't let me stop you then, baby. I know the kind of appetite you fighters work up," she says sassily in her raspy voice, spreading her legs even wider in invitation.

Looking back down at all that she's offering, I run a finger over her lips and into her wet heat.

"This pussy was made for me, Frankie. It was made for me to worship," I breathe out over her sensitive flesh before sliding one digit in deep while I flick my tongue over her.

She reaches down, raking her fingers over my scalp and through my long hair, pressing me tighter to her at the same time she lifts her hips up to my mouth.

"Oh God, Deacon, I swear, you could make me come with that filthy mouth of yours," she moans out.

Backing away from my greedy girl, I hook my finger, pressing forward.

"That's kinda the point, baby," I tell her before taking another taste.

Panting now she says, "Your dirty talk…nobody, ooooohhhhh." She stops talking and goes completely still to concentrate on what I'm doing for a second. "I love the things you say to me. Nobody else ever has…ahhhh, right fucking there, Deac." Gripping my hair tighter, she grinds herself against my face, riding my tongue, exploding into my mouth.

I don't have time to think about what she just said—I need to be inside of her before I blow my fucking load all over myself. Not giving her any time to come down from her orgasm, I drag my lips along her thigh, up to her mouth, transferring her wetness in the process. As soon as my hips meet hers, I slam home hard until my balls are resting against her ass, thrusting deeply three times without pulling out even an inch, making her slide up the bed.

"Fucking fuck, Princess, you're so fucking tight. So. Fucking. Tight." I punctuate the words by sliding out slowly before plunging back in hard and fast.

"This pussy is mine, Frankie. I own it, just like it owns me." Gritting my teeth, I press my hands to her thighs, opening her wider, making her impossibly tight pussy even tighter.

"You came all over my tongue, now it's time to come all over my cock, baby." Growling out the words in between clenched teeth, I reach down and pinch her clit lightly as I enter her again.

Gasping in pleasure, Frankie arches her back, all of her seeking my touch. I can feel as she pulses underneath the thumb pressed against her clit. Breaths coming out in bursts past her swollen lips before catching when I slide high and deep, clearly hitting her sweet spot.

"That's it, baby, that's the spot, huh? Come for me, I wanna feel it all over my cock while I'm buried inside of you."

Body bowed taut, head thrown back, she whimpers, "Deacon, I'm so close, so fucking close. You make me feel so good. I need you to fuck me, please. Fuck me like you mean it."

Motherfucker! Frankie talking dirty is something I don't think I'll ever get used to. Her words go straight to my cock and I lose all control. I'm lucky that she's so close because one more word past those fucking lips and I'm done.

"You want dirty? You want me to fuck you so good that even when we're done, you'll still feel me deep in your tight, wet, beautiful pussy? Hmmm, is that what you want, baby? I'll make sure that every time you move, you'll be reminded that I was inside of you. Making you feel out of control, to the point that my classy as fuck girl was begging me to fuck her dirty." My whole body is on fire, aching with the need to finish.

Removing my thumb from her clit, I bring it up, pressing it into her mouth, groaning as she wraps her lips around it, skimming the roughened pad with her teeth before I remove it on a tortured hiss.

Pulling out of her, I place my hands on her waist, stopping her from following my cock with her greedy, little pussy.

"Roll over, Princess. I want that ass up in the air," I command roughly as I take a firm hold of my cock, pumping it as I watch her maneuver to her knees. I will never get enough of her, enough of this.

As soon as she is on all fours, she looks back at me over her shoulder, wiggling her ass from side to side.

"Like this, Deac?" she asks, her voice husky with need.

"Yeah, baby, just like that."

Moving into position behind her, I glide my hands up the backs of her thighs, over the perfectly rounded globes of her ass, squeezing once before continuing across her back and the delicate lines of her ink until I reach her shoulders, pushing down on them until her chest is flat against the bed. Brushing the hair off of her face, I place one hand at Frankie's nape holding her there as I lean over, running my nose along her jaw, causing her breathing to come out in little, excited puffs. Making my way to her ear, I nip her lobe.

"I'm taking it. It's mine to dirty up; no one else's," I growl low in my throat. "No one fucking else's," I say again as I sit up straight and align myself with her opening.

Entering her just enough to tease us both, I stop,

"Tell me, Frankie. Give me what I need to hear," I rough out, feeling my control slipping as she pulses around the head of my cock.

"It's yours, Deacon, I'm yours. You've completely wrecked m—""

I can't even let her finish, her words have me so fucking twisted. Flexing my fingers against the soft skin of Frankie's nape, I bring my other hand around to her clit, effectively holding her in place while I slam into her. Setting a punishing pace that I know is going to leave her sore, I circle her nub just as quickly until I feel her tighten like a vice around me, her legs trembling violently before they give out, giving me the approval I need to dirty her up just like I promised.

Chapter EIGHTEEN

SLOWLY I RELEASE my hold on her neck to bring myself down over her, resting my weight on my arms. I kiss her shoulder and smile as she shudders letting out a soft, satisfied sigh. Out of breath from our climax and with me still buried deep inside, I affect her with a simple kiss. I can't put words to how that affects me.

Kissing her one last time, I roll away from her reluctantly, just as my phone starts ringing. It's gotta be one of my brothers wondering where the fuck I am. I snag it off the nightstand and swipe my finger over Mav's goofy looking face at the same time I hook an arm around Frankie, dragging her close to me. I know that our time alone is coming to an end, and I just want to enjoy the feel of her against me for a little longer.

"I know, Mav, I'll be there soon," I say in way of greeting.

"Soon? Motherfucker you were supposed to be here thirty minutes ago," he barks at me.

I knew I was going to catch hell, but smelling the sex lingering in the room, on the two of us, I couldn't really give a shit less. I can't say any of that to Mav though. I'm not sure how the Princess wants to out us. Then I'm pulled back to the conversation that my brother has just now realized he is having with himself.

"Yo, Deacon! You there, bro? I said that Sonny and Pop

are about to lose their shit. You know you have weigh-in today, right?"

Sighing deeply "Yes, Maverick, I know. Tell them I'm jumping in the shower now and I'll be there."

"Yeah, do that. You come in here smelling like cheap perfume and pussy and Pop is gonna have your ass," he warns. Laughing even though I know he's one hundred percent correct, I can't help but cave just a little and tell him smugly,

"Ain't nothing cheap about it, brother." Before disconnecting and leaving him wondering.

Looking down, I see that she has fallen asleep again curled into my side. I would give anything to be able to stay in bed all day with her but I know there's no way. Brushing the hair from her forehead, I put my lips to the skin I've exposed, murmuring her name in between light kisses trying to wake her.

Groaning in displeasure, she opens her eyes and glares up at me.

"I prefer the other way you have of waking me much better," she pouts.

"Trust me, baby, I do too but I missed gym time and I'm pretty sure that if I don't get my ass in gear, Sonny will be breaking down the door."

"Ooooh, you're going to be in so much trouble!" she jokes.

And then it hits her that it's not just *any* gym time. We're the day before the fight. Sitting up straight, almost head-butting me in the process, "Deacon, please tell me that you did not miss your fucking weigh-in? They'll kill you!" She's a bit panicked now, which is cute.

Not even for her would I miss a weigh-in. It's disrespectful to your opponent and to the Commission.

"Come on now, Princess, you know better than that," I tease while openly staring at her tits.

Snapping her fingers in front of my nose, "What time is the weigh-in?"

Folding my arms behind my head, I go back to ogling her fuck hot body, noticing the patches of beard burn I've left behind on her sensitive skin. My cock is literally still wet from being inside of her and I'm ready to go again. She has no clue what she does to me. None. How in the fuck did I go this long without being with her like this? There is no turning back for me. She's my forever, my motherfucking end game. I'm done. The Princess owns me, and pussy that I am, I couldn't be happier about it. I feel invincible right now.

"I have to be at the Convention Center by four, I think, and then the press conference right after."

Glancing at the time on the cable box, I groan.

"Fuck. I have to jump in the shower and get my ass to the gym or Sonny really is going to come for me."

Smiling down at me, she places a soft kiss on my lips, pulling back just enough to look me in the eyes. Hers are so fucking blue they're almost white.

"I would offer to wash your back, but we'd never get out of here. I'm going to use my bathroom." Kissing me once more, she hops out of bed completely naked and sashays her sweet ass out of the room.

Grabbing a hold of my cock, stroking over it once, I contemplate following her until my phone starts ringing again, making the choice for me. Ignoring the call, I go straight for my shower.

I'm tugging a shirt over my head when she enters my room wearing the jeans from last night and a Deacon "The Hitman" Love shirt, the collar ripped out of it so that it hangs off her shoulder, exposing the swirling ink there and her black bra strap. Fuck, she's so beautiful.

Leaning against the door frame, arms crossed under her tits causing my name to pull tight across them, she snorts as delicately as one can while snorting, and shakes her head at me, gesturing in my direction with her chin.

"Nice shirt, Deac. You ass." She's laughing now.

Brushing a hand down the front of my black t-shirt that reads "Just The Tip, I Promise…" in vintage barbershop letters, I feign hurt.

"You don't like it? I bought it just for you."

I give her a knowing smirk and watch as the heat my words cause creeps across her skin. I love making her blush. It's not just her cheeks that go all pink, it's her whole body and it's sexy as hell.

Before she can say anything more, her phone starts playing some weird ass song from where it sits on my dresser. Watching her walk over to it, I raise a curious brow that she's either pretending she doesn't see or she just isn't going to indulge my ass. Slipping my feet into my chucks and grabbing a hoodie from my closet, I try not to eavesdrop but can't help the rush of jealousy when I hear her say, "Goodbye, Cristiano."

"What did he want, Frankie?" I bite out.

I know that I need to reel my shit in because she's not gonna put up with me barking shit at her because I'm all ass hurt that he called.

Now she's the one with the raised eyebrows.

"I have a class that he can't teach and he just wanted to make sure that I didn't forget about it. Usually I'm there whether he's helping out or not, but clearly this morning I'm not. He was concerned." She's talking to me like one would a bratty kid, which I probably deserve.

Concerned, my ass. Fucker is keeping tabs and getting a little too used to having her around all the time. Why is he staying? As far as I can tell, Frankie is at full strength and doesn't need him anymore. Unless she's not telling me something.

"You feeling okay? Your ribs still bothering you, your head?"

Shit, did I hurt her? I never even thought about her still being sore.

"Nope. I'm good." Smiling reassuringly, she comes over and loops her arms around my neck, going up on her tiptoes. I meet her halfway and let her kiss away my concern.

Before things get too heated, she pulls away, gazing up at me through her lashes, looking as dazed by the power behind our kiss as I feel. She drops back down to her heels, "Come on, baby, we gotta go before I beg you to do filthy things to me again." The need for those filthy things coming through in her husky voice.

Groaning up at the ceiling in frustration, "Keep saying shit like that and you're gonna get fucked, Princess."

STANDING OFF TO the side of the stage waiting for them to call my name, I search the crowd for Frankie. She's here with Guy somewhere. Knowing him, they're in the front row or close to it. Finally spotting them, I just watch and wait for her to feel me looking at her. I hadn't been sure if she was going to be here tonight, since I didn't see her after we got to the gym this morning. She had her class and I had my asshole brothers riding my ass for being late. I'd meant to ask her, but I'm so used to Frankie just being at these things anyways it slipped my mind. This relationship shit is fucking tricky. I've never been in one, so she has a lot to teach my slow ass. Letting my eyes travel over her, I can feel my cock getting heavy. Great, just what I fucking need before I drop trou in front of thousands of people. Wouldn't be the first time I've been semi hard getting weighed in, but if I'm not careful, I'll be sporting full wood. Adjusting myself in my track pants, I just stare at my girl. She's changed out of her "Hitman" shirt. Her hair is down and wavy, the lights in the auditorium casting a halo over the long, platinum strands. She has on this low-cut, white top that I'm pretty sure is lace underneath a black blazer with the sleeves rolled up revealing her delicate wrists covered in bracelets. I can see that she has on jeans, but I can't tell what she has on her feet, but I know I'm gonna want to fuck her in nothing but whatever they are later. All of a sudden I've developed a fucking shoe fetish. This train of thought isn't helping with my hard on even a little bit. Making my way back up to her face, our eyes meet. I mouth, "You look hot as fuck," winking at her.

The smile that spreads across her face is contagious, and before I know it, I'm standing there like an asshole, hand on my cock and a dopey fucking smile on my face. Shaking my head at myself, I chuckle and give her my, "You're so getting fucked later" smirk before turning away to listen to what my pop and Sonny are saying to me.

When the emcee calls my name, the room explodes into applause, catcalls, and screaming. Smiling and waving as I step onto the stage with Mav, I nod at the men waiting to weigh me in and pose me with Tamasino for the pictures, completely ignoring the bikini-clad chicks lining the wall. I've fucked too many of the ring girls here to feel comfortable even making eye contact with any of them knowing Frankie's in the same room. Standing to the side of the scale, I toe off my shoes and bend to yank off my socks, handing them to Mav before giving him my hat and "Just the Tip" shirt, leaving my pants for last since I'm still more than semi hard. Once I'm down to nothing but my black boxer briefs, my hard on, and my ink, I take a deep breath and step onto the scale. Being a heavyweight fighter, I have to stay under 265, which isn't a problem for me, but it's all still pretty nerve wracking.

"Two hundred and forty pounds," the guy manning the scale announces.

Flexing once for the cameras, I hop off the scale and go over to where Mav is holding my clothes to wait on Tam to get weighed. Leaving my shirt off for the pictures with Tamasino, I look over to see Mav looking at me in amusement.

"What?"

"Way to rock out with your cock out, Deac."

Shrugging, I take the coconut water that he offers me since I hadn't been able to drink anything before the weigh in and it's important to stay hydrated for tomorrow. Handing it back to him, I watch as Tam gets on the scale, a fierce looking scowl on his ugly mug.

Shaking hands with Derek Elliott, the President and founder of the Elite Warriors Federation, I lean in so that I'm able to hear him when he starts speaking, welcoming me back and wishing me luck. Thanking him, I turn and wait for "The Devil" to get his bitch ass dressed. Finally he comes over to where we're standing and he's still got his tough guy face on. Laughing at him, I give him my sexy smile, the one I reserve for the ladies and guys who think they're scary, and raise my fists for the picture.

"Tam, my man, what's the matter?"

I get nothing, just a deeper frown.

Shaking my head, I clap him on the back and turn toward the cameraman for one last shot before Tamasino is stalking off the stage.

I look over at Mav, taking my shirt from him, and we just shrug our shoulders at his douchebaggery.

"Sand in his vagina, brother?" I ask Mav, not able to hold back the shit eating grin.

I love how pissed these guys get, like it's gonna fucking matter one way or another once we get in the cage. Heading off the stage, I hear someone calling my name, a female someone, a not-Frankie female someone, so I ignore it and keep moving. Once we hit the bottom step where Sonny, Pop, and Reggie are waiting, I look to where Guy and Frankie had been sitting. They're talking with Derek, Trent standing close by, so I turn my attention to my brothers and dad.

"I'm heading over to the press room now to go over the

questions a final time. I'll see you in there in five minutes, Deacon." Mav turns and walks off toward the front of the convention center.

"Pop and I are going to talk to Derek, and then we'll meet you in there," Sonny says raising his hand for a high-five.

Signaling for my brother to go on without him, he starts in on me, "Now, Deac, the questions are bound to get personal no matter how well Mav does fielding them. You took time out during the middle of a season—people want to know why. It's not their business. Try to keep your cool and stick with the answers that you and your brother went over, okay?" Cupping the back of my neck, he gives me a stern look. "That shirt is not cute either, you fucking hooligan."

Smirking at my dad, I try not to laugh.

"'Hooligan,' Pop, really?"

He shakes his head like he's exasperated with me, although we both know he expects nothing less, and leaves to join the conversation with Derek who is still speaking with Guy and the Princess. I love how she's so comfortable in my world. I know it's because of her dad, but still, it makes me happy and life a little bit easier. I look over at Reggie to tell him that we're heading out when I feel a small hand on my back. Looking over my shoulder, I groan inwardly. Fuck me. No good can come of this shit.

"Hey, D. I'm so glad that you're back. I've missed you. Not sure if Veronica is here tonight, but we could call her—or not," Sylvia says in what she must consider her seductive voice, running her talon-like fingernails over my arm and curling them around my bicep.

Cringing, I pull my arm out of her grasp. Not only is she a friend of Veronica's, she's also a friend who doesn't mind sharing, and the three of us have *shared* a few times.

"Not gonna happen, Sylvia. No fucking way." As I turn to walk away, I'm stopped dead in my tracks when I see Frankie standing right behind me.

"Oh my God, what are you doing here? I thought you were like dead or something."

Snapping my head in Sylvia's direction, I can only stare at her in fucking amazement. Did she seriously just say that shit? Before I can even recover from my shock, Frankie blows out a deep breath.

"Charming," she says in a bored tone, rolling her eyes. Dismissing Sylvia she focuses on me. "You ready to go, Deac, or do you want me to head in with Reggie?" I can hear the edge in her voice, the hint of pissed off simmering just below the surface. My girl is jealous. Fuck, that's hot.

"Ummm, we were talking, Franny," Sylvia says nastily.

"It's 'Frankie,' and why don't you do us all a favor and go put some clothes on?"

She's looking at me expectantly for an answer, but I can't even remember the question.

I've seen Frankie get into a couple catfights before—talk about hot—but this, this is because she's jealous. Over me. I'm hard; I can't help it.

"Don't be jealous—I'm sure you'll grow a pair like these someday too," Sylvia says, cupping her barely covered and very paid-for tits.

Scoffing, Frankie flicks an icy gaze at her in amusement.

"If by 'grow' you mean go into the nearest alley and have some fakey plastic surgeon you found on Craig's List implant them, I think I'm good. You might want to get a refund though, those things look lumpy."

Gasping loudly, Sylvia hisses at a cool and collected Frankie as Reggie and I stare in absolute wonder.

"Fuck you, you ratchet bitch!" she yells before pushing past us.

"Classy, doll. Real classy," Frankie calls after her before pinning those glacial eyes on me.

"Really, Deacon? Sylvia Cortez? You know what, don't fucking answer that. Can we go now or are there more of your girls to deal with?" Eyebrow raised, lips pursed in aggravation.

All I can think to say is "You're my girl, Princess. And you're stupid fucking hot when you get jealous." Scooping her up and kissing her pouty mouth before she can argue with me, I smile against her lips. "Would you have hit her?"

Shoving against my chest forcing me to release her, she huffs out an exasperated breath and stomps off in the direction that the press conference will be held.

I follow behind her, watching her bubble ass sway as she walks. A quick glance over at Reggie and I catch him looking at her ass too. I can't even be mad—it's fucking perfection.

Sitting at the long table in the front of the room, I take my seat at the microphone in between my two brothers. Normally both fighters would be here, but seeing as this is my first fight back, it's kind of a big deal and so I'm the only fighter being interviewed. I already did a spot for the EWF last month that has been running for the last two weeks, so this is purely for the press. All of the big name magazines, newspapers, and sports stations are crammed in here. Derek Elliott, the president, enters the room and makes his way to where we are sitting. I stand to shake his hand once again as cameras click and whir. Once he takes his seat, the questions begin.

After twenty minutes, I'm over this shit. Everything has gone pretty well so far. The reporters have kept the questions away from my private life and why I forfeited the fights that I did. That is until Rick "I'm a dick" Withers sneaks one in.

"I was told by a source extremely close to you that there wasn't anything necessarily important that you took time off for, only that you needed a break from the Octagon. Did you think that because you had already accumulated so many points that you would be able to jump right back into the game even if you bowed out of a few fights? Are you worried how other fighters, your peers, might perceive that bold move?" Rick asks conde-scendingly

Trying to keep my cool even though I want to come across this table and hand him his ass, I manage to say as evenly as possible, "I didn't realize Extreme Fighter ran a gossip column now. Next time tell them to send their sports reporter not Anne fucking Landers, yeah?"

Looking away, dismissing him, I scan the reporters in the room so I can take the next question. I'm still heated, the mus-cle in my jaw ticking. I know that I'm going to get fined by the EWF for the f-bomb I just let fly, but I really don't even fucking care, I knew as soon as I saw his face and his smug fucking grin that he was going to be trouble. Just like his sister. Fuck me. What the hell was I thinking, fucking around with Veronica? Clearly the whole family is a bunch of assholes.

Chapter NINETEEN

FIGHT NIGHT:
Deacon "The Hitman" Love vs. Bruno "The Devil" Tamasino

SITTING ON THE table in the dressing room I look down at my girl standing in between my legs wrapping my hands and wrists like she's done a thousand times before. She has her hair down tonight, a little braid in the front keeping it out of her face. Hot pink heels that match the lettering on my shorts perfectly put her head even with my chin, allowing me to take in the coconut smell of her hair. She has on this black strapless one piece shorts thing that is beyond sexy. It leaves her shoulders completely naked except for her ink and a light dusting of freckles, and her tanned legs smooth and bare. Who cares that it's cold as fuck outside? Not me...my cock is about to break through my fucking cup I'm so hard. Plus I love that she always makes sure that she's wearing the gym's colors, my colors. What a fucking pussy I am.

Lips pursed in concentration, I let the sure and steady movements of her hands hypnotize me and concentrate on not having a goddamn hard on right now. I'm not one of those fighters who gets anxious, throws up, or paces liked a caged animal before a fight. I don't need to be talked down or massaged to loosen up. Before stepping into the cage, a sense of calm takes over my body. It's one of the only times I feel completely at peace and then when the door slams closed leaving me standing in that Octagon, I'm home. My mind and body go into warrior mode, my training kicks in. This is what I was built for. I shut out the outside world and go hard.

Glancing at the guy in the corner sent in by the Federation to make sure there's nothing against the rules going on, Frankie asks, "Blue or red?"

"Red tonight, Miss De Rosa."

Nodding, she takes the roll of red tape and tosses it to Sonny. When we get out there, my taped up hands, mouth guard, and gloves will be checked. Once I get the okay, I can put my gloves on and the red tape will then be wrapped around my wrists over my gloves, indicating that I am the fighter in the red corner.

Looking up at me, I can see that she's nervous in the way that she keeps biting at her lip and the tight smile that doesn't reach her eyes.

"What's wrong? You worried about the crowd? Reggie and Trent are both with you, tonight. You're safe here, baby—this is my house," I tell her, raising my arms to encompass the room and wink at her.

Laughing at me, she shakes her head.

"Shut up, you dumbass. I'm nervous because this is your first fight in a while and Tam is no fucking joke! He's mean and I don't like him," she says, crossing her arms over her chest and pouting a little.

Now it's my turn to laugh at her.

"He's *mean*? Really? That's all you got, huh? Okay, I'll give you that. He *is* mean, but I'm better than he is in every way that counts."

Not caring who is in the room with us, I pull her in closer, forcing her to drop her arms, and whisper in her ear, "Bet you sex in the cage that I beat him by the second round." Smiling at her gasp, I nip her ear and pull back.

Her face is tinged pink with both embarrassment and lust. I need to get out of here before I forfeit this bout too just to be inside of her.

She doesn't get a chance to snap out of her stunned silence before Mav walks in with my dad.

"It's go time, boys," my pop says, smiling at Frankie.

He doesn't know what's going on between us, but her being here like this is the norm so nobody thinks twice about it.

"You too, Princess. Guy is already out there schmoozing."

Giggling, she says, "Sounds about right."

Turning back to me, she takes both of my hands in hers and with a serious look crossing her face, flips them palm side up and places a kiss on each of my wrists, leaving soft pink lipstick stamps on the white surgical tape.

"Take him out, Deac, and don't let up until he's out. If he gets you on the ground, don't let him get you on your back. Go for his legs, and he'll submit – just make him do it before he gets too mean."

I nod my head and she squeezes my hands, dropping them, and goes to the door where Reggie and Trent are standing.

"Hey Frankie?" I call as she's walking through the door.

Shooting me a questioning look over her shoulder, she stops in the doorway. I just smirk and hold up two fingers, reminding her of our bet. Shaking her head, she tries for a reprimanding glare that falls flat when her lips twitch into a flirty smile. Reggie gives me a nod as he shuts the door behind the three of them, leaving me alone with my dad and brothers and our chaperone over in the corner.

"She's right—if you go for the submission, do it before he starts to get mean. He has weak legs. Don't let him take you to the ground though, Deacon, because once you let him have control, he'll wear your ass out." Sonny is in trainer mode now, gone is my brother. This guy is all business.

"If you don't think that you can get him to tap out, let him up and stay on your feet—do not let him take you to your back. Go hard at his upper body and take the KO."

My dad and Mav stand quietly and let Sonny and I go over the war plan. Rolling my head on my neck, I feel the pops and pulls, allowing them to loosen me up. Sonny lets me down from the table, and I stand twisting at the waist and stretching my arms and shoulders. This is our ritual—my brothers and dad let me do my thing while they watch. Bouncing on the balls of my feet, I feel the adrenaline course through my veins. Closing my eyes and breathing deeply I chant my mantra silently to myself, *"That's my cage. I'm a warrior. I dominate because this is who I am. I will win. There is no other option. I am a warrior."*

Opening my eyes, I clap my hands together,

"Let's go boys…OORAH!" I yell.

Leaving the room with my entourage, we head down the hallway toward the tunnel that leads into the arena. As we are passing, the door to my right opens and Tamasino steps into the doorway.

"Nice shorts, you fucking pussy," he shouts, snickering.

Looking back over my shoulder, I smirk, which throws him off.

"I'm always in the *pink*, motherfucker." I continue toward the opening, a smile on my face. It's fucking good to be back.

Chapter TWENTY

Francesca

MAKING MY WAY down the aisle toward my seat, I'm flanked on either side by Reggie and Trent having to hold crazed and screaming fans back until they realize that I'm not one of the fighters coming out of the tunnel. Flashing my ticket and all access pass to the usher, he leads me to the first row behind the commentators. Thanking him, I look around the crowded arena for my dad but don't spot him.

"You guys go on and walk with Deac; I'll be fine," I yell to the boys.

Leaning in so that I can hear him, Reggie asks, "Are you sure you don't want us to at least wait until Guy makes it over?"

Shaking my head no, "I'm fine, Reg, really."

Scanning our surroundings for what, I don't know—it's not like Andrew is going to come after me here—he finally agrees and jerks his head, indicating for Trent to follow him. Watching them stride quickly back the way we came, I take out my phone to check the time and see a text from Cristiano.

Cristiano: Just thinking about you, preciosa.

Groaning I ignore the text and shove the phone back into my purse just as my father slips into the chair next to me. He hugs me and presses a kiss to the side of my head before releasing me to shake the hands of the commentators as they turn to greet him. My father is treated with much respect in this world of tight-knit men. He and Joe Love both. They have trained many talented fighters, making a name for themselves and the gyms that they own. Waving to me, they jump into action when the sounds of Imagine Dragons "Radioactive" starts playing, signaling that Deacon is making his way to the Octagon. His intro song is drowned out by the roar of the crowd chanting his name over and over, louder and louder the closer he gets. I can feel their excitement; the energy is a living thing rolling off of each and every spectator. They've missed him and I don't blame them. That he is able to make his comeback in his hometown could not be any more perfect. Chicago loves him and they are not shy about letting him know.

Deacon is all fluid grace and rugged strength. Every move precise and calculated, nothing wasted. He is one of the best fighters in the organization, his style all his own. Never taking my eyes from him, I think back to something that he once told me.

"There are fighters that actually love to fight, Frankie. It feels as natural to them as breathing. It's the only time they feel completely free, free to be who they really are. There aren't any pretenses or prejudices in the cage. A fighter can be just that—a fighter—and he's championed for it. I'm one of those fighters, Princess. That's who I am through and through and I'll never apologize for it."

This is where Deac shines the brightest and although I am more nervous than usual, I need to remember that. I'm not sure why tonight is so much more nerve wracking than the hundreds of other fights I've watched, but it is. I'm a hot mess, on the verge of chewing my nails off as I watch him stand at the bottom of the platform having his hair, hands, gloves, and mouth piece inspected before he's allowed into the cage.

I let my eyes rake over him. I think he is literally the most beautiful man on the planet. Standing in all of his inked glory, wearing his black boardshorts with the hot pink writing across the ass and front. I marvel, not for the first time, at a man secure enough to wear pink in an arena such as this. He never even thought twice about it. I said that I wanted bright pink and black as the gym's colors so that I could incorporate my dance studio and he said okay. So there he stands, sporting neon pink and owning it.

Once he's cleared, he hops up the two steps and holds still so the cut man can swipe Vaseline over his eyebrows, nose, and cheekbones to help prevent them from breaking open. Hair pulled back in a tight man bun, mouth piece in place, he's finally let into the cage where he does a sweep of the arena, arms open wide. His cocky-as-hell smirk in place, I know that he's trying to spot me. I also know with the lights and my height, he won't be able to until everyone is sitting. He stands there listening to his dad and Sonny as he sways and bounces on the balls of his feet, completely immune to the fact that Tamasino's intro music has started and that the crowd again is going wild, though there's a lot more booing coming from loyal Deacon fans. As Bruno "The Devil" Tamasino finally makes his way into the cage, Deacon turns around and smiles at him.

As the announcer rattles off their stats, I can hear the commentators discussing Deacon's comeback and what they feel the outcome of this fight will be. They're split down the middle, but I'm with the one who thinks Deacon is going to take it early.

Watching the men meet in the center with the referee and stare each other down has chills of anticipation running down my spine. Anticipation for the fight, and if I'm honest, for what's to come after. Looking at that sexier-than-should-be-legal smirk,

I'm reminded of all the wicked things I let him do to me and the things I want him to do again. Brushing away those less than pure thoughts, I turn my focus back to the Octagon just as I hear the ring of the bell indicating the start of round one.

Deacon moves around the cage and I can see him assessing Tam, reading him to see what his best course of action is going to be, and then BOOM he strikes! I don't see it coming, and by the way The Devil flies back into the cage from the beautiful push kick that Deac got him with tells me he sure as hell didn't see it coming either. Once up against the fence, Deacon goes to town on Tamasino's upper body, throwing jab after jab, showing no mercy and not slowing enough to give the other man time to do anything but cover his guard as best he can.

Finally able to break away from Deacon's assault, Tam tries to sweep Deac's legs, but has no luck, so instead dives for his waist, hoping to take him to his back. My father places his hand on my bouncing leg to try and calm me, but it's no use. Chuckling, he just pats my knee and takes his hand away, allowing me to resume my nervous bouncing. Not wanting to take my eyes off of the fight, I glance quickly at the clock to see how much time is left in the round. Less than a minute remains, thankfully, because the last four minutes seemed like an eternity. Counting down in my head now, I shoot to my feet excitedly when Tam hits the ground hard after another well placed kick from Deacon.

When the bell rings signaling the end of the round, Deacon's fans are on their feet screaming his name, encouragement, and of course, the random offering of sexual favors. I'm able to laugh it all off, releasing the breath I've been holding and look over at my dad.

"I think he took that round, don't you?" I ask him excitedly.

He smiles down at me and I can see the love for this sport, for our fighter, shining in his eyes. Smiling back at him, I lace my arm through his and squeeze. He bends to my ear and starts speaking to me in Italian.

"I've missed seeing him like this. Fighting again and happy. I was very afraid for him when you were hurt," he says solemnly.

Pulling back slightly to look up at him, "Afraid that they wouldn't let him come back? I thought it was only two or three fights that he missed, Daddy?" I ask, confused, feeling the guilt of him forfeiting any fights at all wash over me once again.

"No, not afraid of that, afraid for HIM. He had so much anger and hate in him, it seeped through his skin, out of every pore. Sitting there by your side it festered—I was afraid it would consume him. We all were." Shaking his head as though clearing the image, his voice becomes animated.

"The thing that makes Deacon such a skilled fighter is that there is no rage inside of him. No demons he is battling that make him angry."

At my raised eyebrows he continues.

"Yes, he has a quick temper and oftentimes reacts before thinking, but that is outside of the cage. In there, he's not at war with anything. That's where he finds his peace. His fighting is pure artistry. He reminds me of you very much in that aspect. You're both artists in your own way."

Hearing him say that makes me think that he was reading my mind just a moment ago.

"Watching him fight is no less beautiful than watching you dance. You're both made to do it, *cara bella*," he tells me tenderly. "He's like a feather floating on a breeze, weightlessly riding the wind, until that air starts to swirl around him violently and the lightness of the feather no longer matters, because now in the tempest, it is a deadly, living thing. That's our Deacon. Pain is his art and he's incredibly adept at it."

My father is old school Italian. He has a way with words that always paints such a vivid picture. A picture that has a way of invading every piece of me. Soaking in the simple beauty and truth of my father's words, I let my eyes find Deacon.

Taking in all that he is, all that he stands for, I finally admit to myself that he's *it*. He's my forever. He always has been. I don't love him because he's Deacon. I love him despite it. I love him simply because I'm *in* love with him. It seems ridiculous to just now realize something that I'm pretty sure I've always known.

Deacon asked me if I'm confused about my feelings for Cristiano. I'm not.

He's thought that Cristiano and I have been reconnecting and I hate that. I think that we've moved past all of that for the most part, but still, it bothers me that he felt he couldn't come to me and just ask. I would have told him that, yes, Cristiano has been trying to convince me that we are better together than I remember and that we could be that way again, but that I know the truth now.

The truth is, Cristiano lost his shine all those years ago the minute Deacon came home from the service. Cristiano had been my first in many ways, and to an extent, I might even regret that a little. Looking back now, I realize that he had just been filler. I had loved him, true, but I missed Deacon so much that I allowed myself to get swept up in Cristiano and all of his mystery and newness. He lavished me in attention and affection, and with Deacon gone, I took every bit of what he offered. We had so much in common, and he was hot, sexy, and totally different from Deacon. Added up, it all made it easy to do.

Cristiano was never *it* for me, he could never be *it* for me, because whether I had realized it or not, that had always been Deacon. I don't want to fight Deacon or my feelings anymore. I love him and I need to tell him. I also need to figure out if I am prepared to be with him, if I can handle all that it entails. There are so many *Sylvias* in Deacon's not-so-distant past. I know it will be something that I have to overcome. I've always been a little jealous of the women that were with him, no matter how briefly, because whether I realized the depth of my feelings or not, he's mine. He always has been. Am I strong enough to handle them? Him?

I'm pulled out of my musings by my father nudging me and pointing to the cage and Deacon standing over in his corner waiting for the bell to start the next five-minute round. Now that everyone in the arena is sitting in their seats, we have a clear view of one another. He raises his hand and wiggles two fingers at me to remind me of our talk earlier. It's so unlike him—he's usually so focused—but nonetheless, I smile at him, shrugging my shoulders, mouthing, "We'll see."

He smirks that beautiful, confident, Deacon smirk and nods in acceptance before turning his attention back to Sonny and whatever he's saying.

Exactly sixteen seconds into the second round, Deacon takes out Tamasino with a Superman Punch that stuns him stupid and has him flat on his back. Once they are able to get The Devil up onto his feet, the men are brought to the center of the ring where Deacon, being the gracious fighter that he is, shakes Tam's hand and says something in the other man's ear. The referee raises Deac's arm in the air, a smile splitting his slightly battered face, softening him, as the announcer proclaims him to be the winner of the night's bout by way of a knockout.

Standing on my chair so that I don't lose sight of him as the arena explodes into thunderous applause around me, I'm able to catch his eye. I give him two thumbs up and a little fist pump that makes him smile even wider before I hold up two fingers and wink.

Chapter
TWENTY-ONE

DEACON

I LOOK UP when I hear my name from across the gym. Even raised to be heard over the noise on the floor, her voice is sexy, smooth, and hits me straight in the dick every damn time. A smile takes over my face as I watch Frankie walk toward the ring where I've been working on some boxing moves with Mav and Sonny. Her lips tilted up in an irresistible grin, eyes on me—all over me actually—as they sweep down my body before landing back on my face. My girl is checking me out. I glance away when I hear some fucking asshole let out a wolf whistle. I scan the gym floor to see whose ass I'm kicking. Or I guess whose ass I'm kicking first, since most of the eyes in the gym are on her. The sway of her hips under the little black skirt she has on is sexy as sin. The clicking of her heels on the wooden makeshift steps brings my attention back to her.

"Hello, my Loves," she says before leaning against the ropes and pinning me with her blues. "Deacon, do you have a minute? I need you."

I can't help the wicked grin as I saunter over to her.

"Oh yeah, you need me, Princess? I thought I took care of you this morning," I tease in a suggestive tone. "I'm more than happy to do it again, especially if you do that thing ag—"

"Deacon!" Exasperated and pink with embarrassment, she just shakes her head and starts to walk away.

My brothers try to cover up their laughter and groans as I duck in between the ropes and shoot them a smug smile.

"Frankie, I was playing, wait up!" I yell as I jog to catch her.

I'm able to snag her around the waist and swing her into me before she makes it too far. Pulling her close, I smile as her hands automatically land on my chest and glide up to rest on my shoulders. I've embarrassed her, but I'm not sure if she's pissy about it or what, so I wait her out. I have my answer when she slaps my bare skin hard enough to leave a mark.

"I don't want your brothers knowing about what we're doing in the bedroom, you ass! It's awkward," she says, her nose scrunched up in mild disgust.

All I can do is smile at how fucking silly she's being. Especially when she's pissy. Leaning down to whisper in her ear, my smile only gets bigger, along with my cock, when I feel her shiver as my lips graze over the delicate shell.

"Awww, Princess, no worries, yeah? They won't say anything. Besides, we weren't in the bedroom this morning when I was making you come all over my face, were we?" Nipping her lobe I straighten. Slapping her ass, I lean back so that my now rock hard cock is pressed into her softness. I can see into her flushed faced, eyes cloudy with desire instead of the aggravation of a moment ago.

"Now tell me what you need, baby, and it's yours."

Clearing her throat, she looks at me a little dazed.

"I need your help with a routine. Cristiano isn't here this afternoon and the couple will be here so that I can teach it to them for their wedding."

Jaw set at the mention of that fucking asshole, I just nod and follow her as she turns into her studio. Going over to the cabinet in the corner, I pull out a Frankie's Place T-shirt and pull it on as she messes with the music. Once she finds what she's looking for, Frankie walks to the other side of the room to where her duffel bag sits.

"Okay, so the couple has chosen to not do any specific style of dance, so I've been winging it, but it's kind of hard to do by myself," she says laughing as she rummages through her bag.

I walk over and lean against the wall next to her, watching as she slips out of one pair of fuck-me heels pulling out an even sexier pair. Indicating with a lift of my chin, I ask, "So what's with the wardrobe change? Not that I'm complaining. You know how I love your fucking shoes, especially when that's all you're wearing." She lets out a little laugh when I just smile and wink.

Dropping down to one knee and pulling her foot onto my thigh, I give her the nude heel that she took off, take the black strappy one that she hands me, and slip it on her. When I'm finished, I lean forward and place a kiss on the inside of her knee. The sight and feel of her tiny feet on me are doing nothing for my raging hard on straining to be freed. I set her foot down and reach for the other. Her soft sigh and half moan as I drag my palm down to cup her heel aren't helping either. Once that shoe is on, I run my hands up the backs of her legs over her thighs and under her skirt until I have a handful of perfect fucking ass. I give her cheeks a firm squeeze as I pull her closer almost causing her to fall into me.

I ask again, "Why the different shoes?" Kneading her flesh, struggling with my need to lay her out right here and turn her ass pink, I concentrate on her face instead, only to realize that it isn't any less of a distraction than her ass is.

"You're much taller than Cristiano, so I need taller heels," she says breathlessly, running her fingers through my hair. My hands on her clearly affecting her as much as me.

"Damn right I am." It comes out as a low rumble. I'm not sure why that matters, but it does. Just proves that I'm bigger and badder than the *tiny dancer*, I guess. Laughing at my own joke, my smile falls away when she steps out of my hold, giving my hair a little tug.

"As much as I would really love to know what that smug smile is all about and think about how I have a place for that crazy talented mouth, I need to get this choreography knocked out."

"Ahhh, you're no fun, Frankie. I bet it'll help get your creative juices flowing." I waggle my eyebrows at her and try not to laugh.

"*Marone*, you're killing me," she says, shaking her head and her ass as she walks to the center of the room, crooking her finger at me to join her.

"You know how hard it makes me when you start talking to me in Italian, Princess…it all sounds dirty." Toe to toe with her now, I look down at her and pray she keeps talking.

On her tiptoes, arms slung around my neck, she whispers in my ear, "You know damn well if I started talking dirty we would never get this done. You'd have me up against the wall before I got a whole sentence out of my mouth, *non è forse vero?*" She places a kiss against my jaw before putting her lips to my ear again. *"Tu mi avresti già alzato la gonna e me lo avresti infilato dentro la figa."*

I groan low in my throat, my cock is now hard as stone and nudging her in the belly as she nips my lobe and laughs seductively. Frankie slaps my ass and leaves me standing there empty handed, wondering what kind of dirty she just laid on me, while she goes and puts the music on. Like nothing even happened.

"You're mean—you know that, right?" I call after her, adjusting myself.

Her smile is all innocence, my eyes travel over her, but her body is pure sin. Put out, I sigh deeply and accept my fate. "Let's get this done so I can take you home and do filthy shit to you," I tell her, winking.

"How well you follow my directions now will be how well I follow your directions later," Frankie says saucily. She's trying to kill me, I know she is.

"I'll be the best damn student you've ever had, Miss De Rosa. Especially if it means I get to dirty up the teacher later."

That gets a breathless laugh out of her.

"Okay, Hitman, time to behave. Do you think that you can follow my lead? I just need to go through the motions with someone to be sure I have it." Her brows are raised in question and I nod in agreement. "Perfect." My arms open to allow her to step in and I try to remember what she taught me all those years ago and place my hand at the center of her back, taking her much smaller and softer hand with my other. "Good. I'll count it out and you just follow, okay?"

Softly she starts counting, and I let her lead me around the studio before I get the feel for it and take the lead, making her smile up at me. I move her in time with the music the way she had. The sensual way her body rubs against me makes me want to pin her to the wall, but I restrain myself, barely, and enjoy the way she feels in my arms. Just like our *Mizpah* charms, our bodies fit each other—her softness to my steel, curves to cuts—we were built for one another.

The music fills the room. "This that ginger dude?" I ask, not missing a step as the tempo changes.

She looks up at me and laughs. "Yes, it's Ed Sheeran. He's good, right?"

I grunt in agreement which causes her to try pinching me, to no avail. "That's what I call zero percent body fat, baby." Her eyes roll skyward making me smile. She's so easy to tease. "This is just like when we were younger, huh, Frankie?" Some of my best memories are of her and I dancing, just like we are now. It helped us both. A lot of my fluidity, balance, and quick feet are because of the hours I spent working on routines for her competitions.

"Mmmm hmmm. I remember, Deac. You used to bitch and moan that all the guys were going to think that you were a pussy too." I can hear the smile in her voice. "I had to constantly remind you that my dad and yours said it was important for a fighter to be graceful, to float around the cage. That they wouldn't think you were such a pussy when you were winning because of the moves I taught you," she recounts in her saucy tone.

It's true, all of it. I'd been worried at first, but then none of it mattered because I got to spend hours with my hands all over Frankie.

Mouth open to tell her just how much of I pussy I'm not, we're interrupted by a knock on the door. We break apart as a young couple comes in. Aware that my time alone with her is up, I lean down and whisper, "Just remember what you said earlier. I'm gonna enjoy dirtying you up tonight, *teach.*" At her gasp, I throw her a sexy smirk and stroll out, waving at the soon to be newlyweds.

"You're in great hands, you two—trust me." A stern look for the groom and a wink at the now blushing bride and I saunter out whistling, thinking about the filthy things I'm going to do to my girl to make her blush like that.

Chapter
TWENTY-TWO

JANUARY IN CHICAGO can suck my balls. I've lived here all my life and I'm still not used to the cold that finds a way to seep into your bones and freeze you from the inside out. Pulling my beanie on, I lock the front door and head for the Rover. Why the fuck I didn't park in the garage when I got home from the gym this morning is beyond me. Jumping into the already warmed interior of the truck, I press the button in the steering wheel and give the command to call the Princess.

"Hey, baby, are you on your way back to the gym already?" Frankie asks, her raspy voice shooting right to my cock.

"No, I was gonna see if you wanted to grab some lunch— I'm starving. I'm not going back to the gym until later tonight," I tell her as I navigate my way down the slushy street.

This close to a fight, I train two, sometimes even three, times a day.

"Oh, that blows, I already made plans with Indie. I figured that you were going to be here training." I hear the disappointment in her voice.

We spend nearly every free moment together, though I haven't been able to convince her to just come and stay with me instead of rooming with Indie. Hell, in the two months that we've been together, I can't even get her to admit we're in a relationship.

"Do you guys mind if I crash your lunch?"

"No, of course not! Do you mind Peruvian?" she asks more excited now that she doesn't have to choose between the two of us. "That BYOB place over on Milwaukee?"

"Yep, that's the one. Is that okay? I can always call her to see if we can go someplace else if you would rather."

"No, that's perfect. Do you want me to pick you up?"

"I have a new student that I'm meeting with in a few minutes to go over her competition schedule, so I'll just meet you there. Indie is probably already on her way."

"All right. Do you want me to stop and get drinks on my way? I know you and Indie like that 'porch rocker' shit. I'll swing by Binny's and grab some on my way since I'm not picking you up. Sound good?"

I'm already turning toward the liquor store, not waiting for her to answer. I won't drink this close to an important fight when I'm training like I am, but the girls can get sloppy if they want to.

"Perfect. Thanks, I have to go, but I'll see you soon."

"You got it, baby." I disconnect the call and turn up the radio when I hear the intro to "The Kill."

Ten minutes later, I'm jogging to the front door of the restaurant, six-pack under my arm, texting Reggie to make sure that he and Trent are with Frankie. Andrew is still out there under the radar somewhere, and fuck me if he thinks he's going to get a chance to lay hands on my girl again.

Spotting Indie in the corner of the enclosed front patio, I head over to her nodding at the hostess on the way.

"What's up, Jones?" I ask as I plop into the cane-back chair opposite her in the vibrant little bistro, plunking the beer in front of her. "I've come bearing gifts for letting me intrude on your chicks-only lunch." Smirking, I whip my hoodie off and pull my dislodged beanie on, pushing it back on my head so it's slouching. I'm sure I have a serious case of hat head right now…ain't nobody got time for that shit.

"Hey, punk. I knew you'd be here. You've crawled so far up our girl's ass lately I fear you might grow a mangina," she deadpans.

How she's able to say the things she says with a straight face is beyond me.

"Where the fuck do you come up with this shit, Jones?" I ask her laughing.

"Where the fuck do you come up with your shirts?" she scoffs, pointing at my Burnout Tee.

Smiling widely, I look down at my "If you Beard it, they will come" shirt.

"You don't like my shirt, Indie? I bet Frankie will. She knows all about the power of the beard." Winking at her disgusted face, I lean so that I'm balanced on the back legs of my chair, waiting to see what crazy shit this bitch says next.

"You're so gross, you know that, right?" she asks over the cat-eyed glasses perched on her pierced nose.

Shrugging in acceptance, I pop a top on a bottle of beer and hand it to her. I need to butter her up a little for the talk I want to have before Frankie shows up.

"So what the fuck is going on with Flashdance? Why is he still hanging around?" I ask as nonchalantly as I can.

Indie looks at me like I really am as dumb as she thinks I am.

"Why do you think he's still here, Deacon? It's not because he's a fan of The Hitman, I can promise you that." Snorting indelicately at my stupidity, she takes a swig from her bottle.

Chewing my lip in frustration, I look Jones in the eyes and weigh how I want to ask this next question without sounding like a total pussy. Then I remember who I'm talking to and know it's useless. She'll hit me with that "mangina" shit regardless.

"It's been a couple months that we've been together now and she still doesn't want anyone to know, like it's some dirty fucking secret or that she's not really my girl. I'm over that shit to tell you the truth. Do you think she still wants to be with Rico Suave or what?" I bite out roughly.

Putting her bottle down, Indie squints her wide green eyes at me like she's trying to figure out if I'm serious. She must see that I am, though I'm really not prepared for her answer.

"Stop being such a cunt about it, Deacon. For fuck's sake, man up!" Shaking her head at me, she huffs out a breath in exasperation.

Indie is the only chick I know that can drop cunts like candy in public for anyone to hear and think nothing of it. I'm pretty sure that the old guy at the table next to us drinking his espresso and minding his own business flinched like someone reached out and smacked him in the face. Looking over at him, I smile and shrug. Ballsy bitch. She and my girl both sound like sailors but look like dolls. It's kinda sexy.

Looking across the table at Indie, I'm waiting for her to expound on her wicked eloquent non-answer. Before she can though, I see Frankie in gray knee-high boots over black leggings bundled up in her pea coat and scarf hurrying down the sidewalk, Trent and Reggie flanking her on either side. I watch as she sashays her sexy ass through the door, whipping off her glasses that fogged up as soon as she came in from the cold.

I get up and head toward the hostess stand to get my girl.

Smiling brightly, she walks right into me and raises her face for my kiss.

"I missed you," she says against my lips.

"I missed you too. Your nose is freezing!" I laugh as I circle my nose around hers, trying to warm it.

Looking up at the boys standing there, I ask, "You guys gonna come sit with us or what?"

"No, we just ate, so we're going to head up to the coffee bar and just chill if that's okay with you, my man." Reggie indicates with his thumb the little area set up on the other end of the restaurant.

"No problem. You see where we're sitting?"

"Yeah, I got it. We'll be able to see you from there."

Lifting my chin in agreement, I take Frankie's hand and start pulling her to our table when she stops abruptly and turns back to look back at the front door. "What's the matter, baby?" my brows drawn down in confusion.

"Nothing, I…nothing. I just thought I saw someone," she tells me, still looking out the wall of windows.

I pull her behind me and look for myself, motioning Reggie over as I do. "Who do you think you saw, Frankie? Andrew?"

"I'm not sure, Deac. It was more like I felt whoever watching and then thought I saw him out of the corner of my eye." She tugs on my hand. "I'm sure it's nothing. Come on, I'm hungry." I can hear the tension in her voice, and so can Reggie who's been standing and listening to us.

Without a word, he slaps my back and heads out the door to check things out, allowing me to relax and focus on getting her to as well. "Come on, your girl is about to stroke out over there," I joke. She laughs and lets me lead her over to where Indie is waiting.

"Hey, hooker! Where the feck have you been?" Indie asks smiling.

Oh, she could say "cunt" loud enough for the whole damn city to hear but not "fuck"? That one is pushing it, I guess.

"Sorry, I have a new student. We were going over what kind of choreography she has planned for her first showing," Frankie explains as I help her out of her coat and toss it onto the empty chair next to Indie.

Pulling out her chair, I lean down and kiss her bare shoulder, inhaling her scent before straightening. A lot of Frankie's shirts hang off her shoulder, sometimes both— they're sexy as fuck. Just that little bit of skin showing and I'm rock solid every time. She smiles at me over her shoulder as I sit down in my own chair. She takes my hand, placing it on her leg. She looks at ease now that we're away from the entrance and prying eyes.

"You two are a little nauseating, you know that, right?" Lip curled at us in mock repulsion, Indie picks up her menu.

"Hey, Jones?"

"Hmmm, yes, asshat?" she asks, not looking up from her menu.

"Eat a dick," I whisper, chuckling as she slams her menu down and looks at me appalled.

"I'd rather eat a puss—"

Laughing hard enough to let loose a snort, Frankie covers Indie's mouth with her hand.

"That's enough, you two. I'm starving, and you and your filthy mouths are going to get us kicked out," she manages to get out in between giggles.

Sticking her tongue out at me, Indie looks over at Frankie all innocent and shit…well, as innocent as a rockabilly chick with colorful ink covering both arms to her elbows and her chest can look, and says, "Yes, Mommy," before going back to her menu.

"Do you want a beer, baby?" I ask, reaching for one in the center of the table.

"No, not yet. I'm still trying to defrost. I think I'll have a house coffee first. I wonder which they'll have today," tapping her fingernail against her lip and then tugging. I groan inwardly…she's killing me. She looks down at the specials posted on an insert and asks, "What are you going to get, Indie? That sandwich you always get with the steak and the egg?"

"Yeah. I really should try something else, but I love it," Indie says, slapping her menu shut. "What are you guys getting?"

I'm just about to answer her when I feel what I'm pretty sure are double-D's pressed into my back. I lean forward as I glance back to find who I assume is our waitress with her fun bags resting on my shoulders. Why are bitches so crazy? It's obvious that I'm here with my girl, my hand on her thigh, her tucked in so tight next to me we could literally share a seat. Scooting my chair forward, trying to break contact, I look over at Indie to see if I'm imagining this shit.

"Yo, sister girl. Rein those things in before you leave nipple prints in my dude's back," Indie issues in warning.

Clearly I'm not imagining things. Leave it to Jones to draw even more unwanted attention to an already uncomfortable situation.

I clear my throat, ignoring the glares being exchanged by the girls.

"Baby," I make sure to use an endearment and to not even glance in the direction of the silicone server, "Are you ready to order or do you still need a minute?"

She doesn't even look my way. Oh shit. Then she starts speaking in rapid fire…Spanish? No. Portuguese? Maybe. She speaks so many damn languages I can't keep up with her multilingual ass. Before I can even decipher which language she's speaking, the waitress is scurrying off and a man who I recognize as one of the owners is coming our way. Now I know for sure it was Portuguese…he's Brazilian.

Smiling warmly, he stops beside our table and leans down to greet Frankie with a kiss to either cheek and speaks to her in Portuguese.

I just look at her as she blushes at his flashing dimples. What the hell is this dude saying to make my girl go all pink? Looking up at him with narrowed eyes, he nods and offers his hand for me to shake.

"Mr. Love, it is good to see you again, my friend. I'm honored to have such a champion in my restaurant and with such beautiful women," he says smoothly, winking at the ladies. Oh, he's good. Releasing my hand, he turns his attention back to Frankie.

"So a coffee then?" She nods and thanks him.

He prattles on in Portuguese, then bowing slightly, he takes Frankie's hand, brushing a kiss to her knuckles.

I still have no idea what in the fuck he's been saying, but I'm done with the girls looking at him like he's Channing fucking Tatum. Squeezing Frankie's leg, lightly drawing her attention, "Princess?" I inquire, eyebrows raised reminding her that the rest of us are lost.

Jumping a bit as if startled, she looks over at me and then quickly down at her menu. She doesn't have her glasses on so I know she can't see shit. Plucking them off the top of her head, I hand them to her. She accepts, glancing up at me with a wide smile.

"Do you know what you want, Deac? Marcelo is going to take our order and he wants to pay for our meal."

Turning to the man who has Indie speechless and my girl flustered—it's gotta be those fucking dimples—"Thank you, Marcelo, but that's not necessary. I'm starving though, so I appreciate you taking care of us personally." I nod in thanks and tell the girls to go ahead with their order.

Once we've all ordered, Marcelo heads back to the kitchen, snapping his fingers at his touchy-feely new hire on the way and they disappear through the swinging doors.

"Deacon, are you seriously going to eat all of that?" The thought of all I just ordered has Indie making sick faces.

I sling my arm across the back of Frankie's chair and laugh.

"Yep. I need fuel, woman. I'm training about ten hours a day right now to prepare for this fight, sometimes more. You burn a lot of calories going at it like that."

"That makes sense, I guess. You're totally treating though, you beast. No way am I paying after all you ordered."

Chuckling, Frankie throws a bottle cap at her, "You weren't going to pay anyway, heifer."

"Whatever, bitch, I might have!" Indie says defensively.

Stretching my legs under the table, I watch the girls and

can't help smiling at their conversation and the way they are with each other. I'm reminded once again how thankful I am that Frankie had Indie when I enlisted. These two are thick as thieves and crazy as shit—they drive me insane and love every minute of it. Especially since whatever had spooked Frankie when she first arrived seems to be forgotten.

Chapter
TWENTY-THREE

ONCE WE FINISH lunch, I send Reggie and Trent ahead of us in Frankie's Range Rover, identical to mine, telling them to just leave it at the gym, that we'll meet them there. Pulling the Princess in to my side, trying to keep us both warm, we say our goodbyes to Indie and hurry through the bitter cold toward my Rover. I used the remote to start it while we were still in the restaurant, so the inside is nice and warm when I open the passenger door and help Frankie in. Going around the front of the truck, I slide in next to her and immediately take her hand. I've always touched Frankie as often as possible, but now that she is actually mine, I always have hands on her. I don't know how our fathers or Cristiano haven't picked up on the fact that we're together. We're inseparable, more so than usual, and I'm constantly feeling her up. Reaching for the radio, she turns it down, leaving her hand on the dial.

"I have to get back to the studio, I'm sorry...I have a class to teach before I go home and get ready for the charity dinner tonight."

I squeeze her hand and glance over.

"That's fine, Princess. I have to be in the gym again any-way."

Cocking her head slightly, she asks, "This is your short training session, right?"

"Yeah, and then we'll probably go over some tape and strategy before we call it and get ourselves ready."

Pressing her chest into my shoulder, she brushes her nose against my jaw and up to my ear.

"I cannot wait to see you in your tux tonight. I don't know how I'll keep my hands to myself." Nipping my earlobe, she places a kiss on my stubbled cheek before settling back into the soft leather seat, raising the volume just as Led Zepplin starts wailing out "Whole Lotta Love." I sing along with Robert Plant and smirk at my girl suggestively.

She throws her head back and laughs then rolls her head against the headrest to look at me.

"You know this has been your ringtone since forever?"

Pursing my lips and nodding at her, I wink.

"Oh yeeeeaaahhh."

She slaps me in the chest and cranks the radio even louder drowning me out.

AFTER THREE GRUELING hours at the hands of my masochist brothers, Sonny finally decides I've had enough for one day. Mav hands me a towel as I step from the ring and says, "Let's head down to the basement and watch some tape. I want to see if there's a weakness we can focus on against Holloway. He's a lot quicker on his feet than you are, but not as smooth."

Shaking his head, Sonny looks over at Mav.

"Holloway's weakness is his boxing all day long. If Deac can get him cornered early on and start swinging, he's got it."

We make our way to the door. Listening to them, I nod in agreement and glance up at the feel of bass vibrating over the floor, rattling the glass as we pass Frankie's studio. I come to a dead stop, causing my brothers to do the same, nearly colliding with me. Mouths agape, we are struck dumb at what we see.

"Holy fuck," I say in awe.

A minute or two have passed as we stare in stunned silence when it's broken by Sonny.

"What are we watching? Should we be watching this?" Sonny asks, not taking his eyes off the five barely covered asses bouncing around to "Wiggle."

"Wh—" Mav clears his throat and tries again. "Why is there a stripper convention going on in Frankie's studio? Not that I'm complaining because, fuck me, look at that, but is this even legal? I have never seen the Princess move like that. Ever. Does she use those moves—no, I don't want to know. Do I?" he asks in reverence.

The only indication that I have even heard him is the elbow to his ribs for thinking dirty shit about Frankie. I have yet to look away from my girl's perfect ass bouncing and ticking in time to the beat, muscles flexing, hips rolling, and then BOOM! She drops to the ground, one leg cocked, hand slapping the floor as she gyrates and thrusts like a motherfucking champion. I'm rock solid and getting harder as I let my gaze roam over her tight, little body.

She has on what look like fucking leg warmers, only sexy, over purple heels. How she dances in them is a goddamn mystery to me. My eyes travel up, touching over toned calves and thighs that I'm desperate to get between, her garter tattoo on full display, stopping at the almost thong thing she's wearing that is most certainly not covering her ass. I'm not sure what they're called because they aren't quite panties yet definitely not shorts, exposing the bottom of both plump cheeks and the dimples in the small of her back just above. I want to look around to make sure nobody else is seeing her this way, but that would mean I might miss something. I'll knock heads later if I need to. Her shirt doesn't cover much either and looks like it has been half chewed off, which doesn't sound like such a bad idea right now. Damp with sweat, her top hangs off one shoulder exposing the tattoo on her back and ends just below her tits nearly allowing a glimpse of the new ink there.

I've not even glanced at the other girls following her lead. I'm completely mesmerized by the moves that my girl is busting out. I think this is called "twerking," but I can't be sure. I'm just gonna call it "about to get you fucked," because that's exactly what's gonna happen if she keeps up with—Jesus. Fuck. She bends over touching her toes, stopping my thoughts dead. Her ass never slowing its bouncing and twitching as she shimmies to an upright position, running her hands over the backs of her legs and over her smooth ass and SMACK! I could chisel stone with my cock I am so hard right now. Blinking, I know that there is no way I'm going anywhere but in there to fuck the Princess.

I push Mav into Sonny, breaking their trance in the process.

"You two go downstairs and do your thing. I'll catch up to you later, much later," I tell them as I head for the studio door just as the class is wrapping up and the dancers, twerkers, strippers, whatever the fuck they are start heading toward the locker room.

"Deacon, you are not going in there," Sonny glances around to make sure no one can hear him and then hisses, "to have sex with Frankie!"

I pat him on the shoulder and laugh.

"Tell yourself whatever you want, bro, but I'm going in there to bend my gir—"

"Ahhhhh, that's enough. I do not want to hear that shit, dude," Mav says, holding up his hand to stop the words about to leave my mouth.

"Up until two minutes ago, I never even thought of her as anything more than the Princess. Holy shit, did you see—you know what? Forget it. We'll see you later, Deac." Pulling Sonny away with him, they turn back to where we were headed before we got distracted.

All I can do is shake my head and smile. I cannot stop thinking about what a fucking awesome distraction it was.

Chapter
TWENTY-FOUR

Francesca

THE MUSIC IS up so loud I don't hear the door open, but I sense him there watching me slip a loose flowing skirt that hits mid-thigh over my hot pants, wiggling out of them once my skirt is in place. The fluttering in my stomach and the smile I can't fight are all the proof I need that I'm not alone—Deacon always has that effect on me. Grabbing the remote control, I turn the volume down, quieting the system.

"You don't have to stop on my account. You know how I love to watch you dance. If you want, you can even show me your new pole routine to go with whatever the hell it was you were just doing," Deacon says, smiling at me suggestively as he walks over to where I'm standing.

"Yeah right, Deac, we have plans tonight. If I go putting my dirty girl moves on you, we'll never get out of here," I joke as I slip my arms around his neck and rub all of my soft spots against him.

His arms instantly wrap around my waist pulling me in tight. "That so, Frankie?"

Shivering at the flinty edge to his voice, I change my mind.

"Maybe we can be late," I say, sighing as his hands travel over the little bumps of my spine.

Palming my ass, he leans down and runs his nose down my cheek. "I love it when you're all sweaty like this. You smell like sex. It makes me so fucking hard, Princess." Inhaling my scent and humming low in his throat, he rumbles, "I'm going to make you do that routine for me when I get you home. My own little private show."

He slips his hands underneath my short skirt, skimming both big hands over the globes of my ass until he's cupping them and his long fingers meet at my center.

I turn my face and reach up to nip his jaw. Tangling my hands in his hair, I pull his head down further so that I can reach his mouth. I swipe my tongue over his bottom lip, eliciting a low growl from him. He opens for me, allowing entrance before he takes complete control, running his hands down to the back of my thighs and lifting me. I immediately wrap my legs around his waist as he starts striding across the studio toward my office, our kisses growing frantic. I can feel his hard cock brushing over the seam of my panties and nudging my oversensitive clit with every step he takes.

"Son of a bitch, I'll be lucky to get these tiny fucking panties ripped off you before I have you bent over your desk," he says into my mouth, his words turning my pussy molten.

"After watching you dance, this is gonna be fast and dirty. I need to fuck you hard, baby. We can do soft later."

I shudder in anticipation and feel him smile against my lips.

"Mmmm, tell me how dirty, Deac," I say in between dipping my tongue against his.

"Fuck," he growls finally making it into my office, slamming and locking the door behind us, pulling the blinds down.

"You want me to tell you how dirty it's gonna be, Princess?" he asks as he sets me down on my feet in front of my desk, kicking the chair out of his way.

I nod yes and watch him through hooded eyes as he reaches forward, grabbing the collar of my shirt in both hands. He rips it swiftly, making me gasp in surprise and thrust my chest toward him, hoping that my bra will meet the same fate as my shirt, because I need his mouth on me.

"You like when I get rough with you, Frankie?" Running his open hand across my chest and then into my bandeau, he cups my breast, testing its weight before rolling my pebbled nipple in between his thumb and index finger. We both watch his hand through the thin material. He smiles wickedly at me and pulls the bra up over my tits but leaves it on.

"Look at you, baby. Your skin is getting all pink for me, Frankie."

Bending, he drags his nose around my nipple and down to the underside of my left breast where he bites and then soothes the sharp sting with a swipe of his tongue. My head falls back on my shoulders, my body ready for him, pussy throbbing in anticipation. Standing up straight again, he gently slaps each of my tits, pulling my gaze to meet his.

"Turn around, Frankie, and put your hands on the desk," Deacon orders gruffly.

My bones feel on the verge of melting. Turning slowly, I do as he says, glancing at him over my shoulder.

"Ahhhhh, fuck. You're so fucking beautiful, Frankie," he says, stepping forward and pressing his hardness against my ass.

My teeth sink into my bottom lip before I release it to smile seductively at him in blatant invitation.

"You keep looking at me like that and you're gonna get fucked," he snarls.

"That's what I'm hoping for, Deacon," I tell him, pushing into his hard on, giving a little wiggle, wanting to make him as crazy as he's making me.

He lets out a low groan before he pulls my hips back, flipping my skirt up over my ass. Placing his hand on my back, he presses, forcing me down on my forearms. Slowly, he slips his fingers into the sides of my panties, drags them down my legs, following their trail with his tongue, dipping into the crevice and licking at the wetness there. Letting them fall and pool around my ankles, he straightens and tangles one hand in my hair, tugging and arching my back while he pushes his mesh shorts down with the other hand.

His mouth to my ear, his stubble scraping against the delicate skin, the scent of my arousal lingering on his lips, he tells me, "You're so wet for me, baby, every time, so fucking wet. I want my cock covered in it, Frankie. I want it dripping with how wet I make your pussy."

As he's talking, he's rubbing the head of his dick against me, swirling it into my wetness and dragging it up in between my ass cheeks and then gliding it back down to tease me. Over and over, until I'm ready to beg him.

"You want my cock?"

"Please, Deacon, I want it," I tell him, my hips rocking against his, completely out of my control.

Tightening his hold on my hair, he whispers, "I'm going to spread you wide open so that I can look at my pussy, Frankie, and it is mine, glistening with how much you want it," ghosting over my clit with his satiny head, making me tremble with need. "Once I see how pretty it is, I'll slam into you, watch as you swallow me up. All of me, baby." Dipping into me slightly to demonstrate, my hips follow his retreat as he says gruffly, "Then I'll pull out so that I can see all of that sweetness covering my cock." He smacks my ass, hard. It throbs and shoots a rush of heat straight through my blood.

My back arched even more, I raise my ass in invitation, praying that he fucking takes it because I am about to come right here, right now, and I'd much rather do it with him buried inside of me. Knowing me and knowing my body so well, he's already aware of what I need.

Laughing softly, he says, "You done with the talking, baby?"

I writhe beneath him in agreement. Which causes his hand to come down on my ass again.

"Hold still, Frankie, or this will be over before we even start," he hisses through clenched teeth. His control obviously slipping.

Pressing back, not caring that I'm begging him with my body instead of my words, he mutters a low string of curses. He untangles his fingers from my hair and spreads my ass cheeks he leans back to look at my pulsing center, just like he said he was going to do. I should be embarrassed, I know I should, but I honestly don't care and I don't have another second to think about it because he slams home, sending me sprawling across the desk and lifting me nearly off of my feet.

"I told you it was gonna be fast and dirty," Deacon says through clenched teeth as he pulls out and slides back in hard and deep.

Pulling completely out, he runs his thumb down to my opening, gathering my wetness and dragging it up to settle *there* before sliding his cock home again, causing me to clench around him. His one hand gripping my ass while he circles my other entrance with his thumb, slowly dipping it in and out to match his thrusts.

As I tense at the invasion, he tells me gently, "Just breathe, baby, I promise I won't do anything that you don't want me to do. I'll always make you feel good."

Relaxing against the hard desk beneath me, I let out the breath I was holding and spread my feet wider, giving him all the access he needs to make my body sing the way that only he can.

"There's my girl, I know what you need, Princess," he says as he resumes the simultaneous thrusting of his thumb and his cock.

Deacon squeezes my ass in his palm and slams into me

hard, hitting that spot deep inside of me, the one I thought was a myth, at the same time as he applies more pressure at my puckered entrance and I'm lost. I try to muffle my cries, but it's nearly impossible, the moan being torn from me in one long breath.

"That's it, Frankie. Fuck, your pussy is so fucking tight, baby. Yessss, milk my cock, Princess, make me come. I want to feel it all over my dick." He grunts as he slides nearly all the way out again and angles in even deeper, triggering yet another orgasm. This one pulls him right over the edge with me.

A few minutes after, I'm still blissed out and would love to just crawl onto his lap for the next few hours but we have to go and get ready for tonight. A contented sigh slips past my lips as I adjust my skirt and my borrowed *Frankie's Place* shirt. I reach up on my tippy toes to place a kiss along Deacon's jaw as he holds open the door of my office letting us into the studio. Just as I pass by him he slaps my ass—hard. Laughing and rubbing my stinging cheeks, I try to look at him sternly, but it's impossible to do while I'm smiling.

"Just when I thought you were being a gentleman," I admonish, shaking my head at him.

"Baby, you should know better than that!" Deacon tells me as he winks and takes my hand.

We are so wrapped up in each other, we don't notice that we're not alone.

"Well, isn't this just fucking adorable? Do you hold hands with all of your friends, Deacon, or just the ones that you're fucking?" an obviously bitter Veronica asks loudly from the other side of my studio.

You have got to be kidding me with this shit. I know that he's fantastic in bed, and out of it, but what the fuck is wrong with these chicks all still trying to get a piece of him? Taking a deep breath, I glance over at him to see how he's going to handle this one. His body is tense, jaw muscle ticking in that way that I shouldn't find sexy right now but do.

"Veronica, what I do with my cock is none of your fucking business," he says, acid and boredom lacing his words.

"You weren't saying that when I was sucking your dick, Deacon!" she hisses.

I can see how angry Veronica is, her body trembling with it, fists clenched in fury.

Holding back my gasp at her words proves impossible. I immediately turn to leave when Deac stops me by putting his hand to the door of my office not allowing me to open it. I don't want to hear what she's saying, her words like a million knives to my suddenly bruised heart.

I can feel his breath on my face, hear him whisper my name on a soft breath like he's talking to himself, as if it weren't meant for me to hear at all.

"Goodbye, Veronica." He tosses the words over my shoulder.

"Just like that, this whole time, we meant nothing to you?!" She stomps her foot, literally stomps it, the heel of her shoe thumping loudly on the hard, wood floor, echoing throughout the gym.

"Apparently not." He shrugs nonchalantly as if he couldn't give a fuck less. Like they're discussing something as mundane as the weather, not what she considers to be their relationship.

It's such a Deacon move. He's telling her that he doesn't care, that he never did, in as few words as possible, and I almost feel sorry for her. Almost.

I can feel his eyes on me, never even glancing her way, just staring down at me, which I'm sure is making her even more irate…not that I care. I refuse to look at him, instead keeping my eyes straight ahead, focused on the glass window of my office door. I do not want him to see how hearing Veronica go on and on about them is hurting me. If I give him the opportunity to make eye contact, I'll be done for and either slap him or kiss him. I'm afraid of both, so I keep my eyes trained forward, my back to him to be safe.

"All for her—your little BFF, the one you spend all of your goddamn time with, put on a fucking pedestal like she's so perfect? You make me sick, Deacon!" she says in a voice that is rising higher and higher, making me cringe at her obvious loss of control.

"Absofuckinglutely." I can hear the smirk in his tone, the cheeky fucker.

I still haven't looked his way, I can't yet. I'm doing my best not to flee past them both, instead zoning in on the pictures that I can see hanging on the far wall of my office. Trying to tune them out and failing miserably.

"You really are an asshole, Deacon, you know that?" she spits.

"I never claimed to be anything else, just like I never claimed that we were together, Veronica. You came to that assumption all on your own, even when I told you repeatedly that wasn't even close to what was really going on. I'm not sure what gave you that impression, but... "He shrugs and shakes his head at her.

"Fuck you!" she shrieks, stomping her foot yet again, making me wonder if she threw temper tantrums as a child. Inappropriate, I know, but it's the first thing that comes to mind.

"Nah, I'm good, thanks," Deacon says to the slamming door and a cloud of overly perfumed air.

I don't see her leave, but I sure feel it in the way the whole dance studio vibrates from the force of her abrupt and rather loud departure.

He waits about three beats before he speaks. The tension surrounding us is palpable and charged, but so very different from the energy that roiled around us when Veronica was here. The atmosphere then had been volatile; this is something I can't quite explain...almost like the universe is holding its breath in anticipation.

"You gonna look at me, Princess?" he asks in a soft, sooth-ing voice, shifting so that he is at my side, leaning his shoulder against the door.

"Have you been sleeping with her?" I curse myself for the breathy quality of my voice, the obvious hurt and disappoint-ment. I don't even know what made me ask. I'm not sure I want to know the answer anyway. Wasn't it me who wouldn't let him put a label on us because I was afraid? Did I give him free rein by doing that?

"I haven't had sex with her since before *that* night," he says, which is what he's taken to calling when I was attacked. I can hear the truth resonating in his words, but how much does that really matter if what Veronica said is true?

"But you let her give you a blow job?" the dismay clearly evident in my words. He had to know that I would ask, that I wouldn't let it go, and I sure as hell wouldn't just take her word for it.

"I did, but Frankie…" He stops talking and takes a deep breath, exhaling forcefully.

"Will you please look at me?" he practically begs. When I don't comply, he drops his head so that his forehead is resting on my temple. I move away, breaking contact. I'm not ready to forgive him yet. I'm not even sure that I will.

"You and I weren't together and it wasn't even like that. It was just one of those things. I was pissed, she was there, and it happened. She wanted to take it further, I didn't, and I made her leave. That's it."

I scoff. He's so ballsy…I don't know why I expected him to sugarcoat it for my benefit. "Just one of those things, huh? We're technically not together now, so is it okay if I go down on Cristiano or let him go down on m—"

Before I can even finish, he's on me, spinning me, my arms pinned above my head, wrists held in one of his hands, the other tracing my lips with a rough fingertip.

"Shhhh, hear me on this, Princess. We *are* together, and the only cock these lips are going to be wrapped around is mine." He taps the center of my bottom lip for emphasis, then leans in to whisper in my ear. "And the only one that's going to be tasting that hot, sweet, little pussy is me."

I'm pretty sure I came in my panties with that last bit. I know I whimpered, and that was before he really started talking dirty. "Now, say some shit like that to me again and I'll wash your mouth out with something other than soap, you feel me?" he grouses.

My mind is reeling, thinking hateful shit about the two of them together, but my body? My body remembers what he feels like inside of me. How he knows it better than I do. Knows what I crave and how to give it to me even when I have no idea. No, my body is betraying me right now and I hate it. I want to hold on to the hurt and anger her visit caused, but instead I can feel the wetness between my legs again. His heat surrounds me, his breath fans across my face, words falling from his mouth so filthy, so fucking hot, so Deacon. Bending so that he can peer into my eyes instead of talking to the top of my head allows him to wedge his hard thigh in between mine. I have to fight myself, beg my body not to betray me even more by rocking against it.

I pull out of his grasp, and he lets my arms fall, making room for me to push back slightly so that I can take a breath and clear my head a little. I grasp at my fleeting anger that is slowly being overcome by lust, even though I can still feel the lingering effects of just having him buried inside of me.

Looking down, I focus on his chest, on the tattoo that spans across it.

"When am I the only one, Deacon? When does it stop?" I ask him softly, my anger and lust being replaced with sadness, leaving me feeling defeated.

Making eye contact, I can see his hurt, and even regret,

but it doesn't even come close to mine. This, this right here is what I had been afraid of. This all-consuming need to be with him but never really being enough because no woman ever has been. Where does that leave us when all is said and done? How could we ever go back to what we were after we've had a taste of what we could be?

Shaking away the sadness that has seeped in and taken over, I let the anger rise to the surface, because that is the only way I'll come out of this alive. Broken and incomplete in a way I wasn't aware was possible, but alive.

"You let Veronica suck you off because you were pissed. Do you hear yourself right now, Deac?" I ask. "How long ago was it? So help me God, if you fucking say last week, I will kick your ass, Deacon," I tell him deadly serious, my fight returning full force at the thought.

He looks away from me, the ticking muscle in his jaw making me nervous. I don't even want to know anymore, I just want out.

"I would never cheat on you, Frankie. Whether you want to admit it or not, we are together. It's just you and me, Princess," he says softly, reaching to brush hair off of my forehead and tuck it behind my ear.

I try my best not to react to his words, to his gentle touch and his habit with my hair.

Staring at his muscled chest I ask flatly, "When, Deacon?"

"The night you were supposed to come to my place from the bar. She showed up and told me that she saw you leave with Cristiano. Said that you guys were practically fucking in the back of a cab." He says the last through gritted teeth, his body hard. I laugh incredulously at him. "You mean to tell me that Veronica fed you a line of shit that you believed and it pissed you off so badly that your dick found its way into her mouth? You know what, Deacon? Fuck you."

I manage to get out from between him and the door but

don't make it far before he grabs my arm and jerks me back to him.

"I'm not fucking proud of it, Frankie. I get pissed and I do stupid shit, but I don't want to be that guy with you. I just—I fucked up. I want to deserve you. I'm trying, Princess," he says earnestly.

I have nothing to say to that, so I stay quiet, concentrating on getting my breathing under control.

He clears his throat, startling me a bit.

"I didn't ask before because I didn't want to know the answer or give you a reason to question me about what went on that night when you didn't show up. I had no right to ask you, but now, now that we're together I have the right to ask."

He steps in front of me, making it so that he can see my answer as well as hear it, his hold on my arm never relenting.

"Did you go home with him that night?"

"Pfft. I hate to tell you, Deacon but your rights went to shit the moment that *she* walked through the door. Not because you let her blow you, but because of *why* you let her do it." I spit the words out, glaring at him.

"Did. You. Take. Him. Home?" he demands in a danger-laced voice.

I just stare unblinkingly at him in answer.

"Did you let him inside what is mine, Frankie?" His tone deathly serious, the volume rising yet the tone lowering menacingly at the same time.

I yank my arm out of his grip. "I'm not yours, Deacon. You won't let me be because of things like this. You, letting your temper lead you around by your dick." I wasn't going to tell him that what he thought was Cristiano and I practically fucking was actually a friend bringing me down from a panic attack. Cristiano was the only one there for me, and I won't apologize for that. But then Deacon pushed me too far and my temper now matched his own.

"Why can't you just tell me the truth?" he accuses.

"The truth? You want to know the truth? I was having a panic attack and he helped me through it," I shout. "I needed you. Again. And again you weren't there for me. Do you see a pattern here, Deacon?" I ask, my eyes narrowed and glaring. "I need you, you need a blow job. I suffer twice."

He flinches as if I'd hit him. The hurt that washes over him is like a blanket, covering him completely. "You blaming me, Princess?" His voice is strained when he asks. "You blaming me for his sins? For a panic attack I didn't know you were having? Why didn't you tell me?" Shaking his head, he pins me with his beautiful, sorrowful eyes, which right now are murky with pain and guilt.

I don't really blame him. I'm angry. I just want him to hurt like I'm hurting and to understand that this fight isn't just about Veronica. It's bigger than her.

His voice, which a moment ago had been pitched low, is now raised in anger and accusation. "You want to put that all on me? Go ahead if it will make you feel better. I already blame myself for not being able to save you from him that night. Remember this though, both times I wasn't there when you needed me is because you wouldn't let me be," he bites out frustrated. I've thrown him.

"None of that shit matters now though, does it? Just answer the question, Frankie." I'm not sure why he's putting so much importance on this. To ease his own guilt maybe? I won't allow it and refuse to answer him, crossing my arms over my chest. It does nothing but infuriate him even more.

"Did you fuck him?" he yells loud enough to echo around the dance studio and bounce back at us from every corner.

"No!" I scream just as loudly, stretching on my tiptoes to get in his face. I poke him in the chest. "No, you asshole. I was still thinking about how much I wanted you. You better believe I'll fuck him now though," I hiss as I spin on my heels and stalk away.

I don't even flinch when I hear him roar "Fuuuuuuuuck," followed by the tinkling of glass as he puts his fist through what I'm guessing is my mirrored wall.

Chapter
TWENTY-FIVE

DEACON

CHEST HEAVING IN anger, I don't even register that I'm bleeding all over the fucking place until I nearly slip in the blood pouring from my hand. Running my good hand through my hair, tugging at the long strands, I take a moment to get my shit together. I need to go after Frankie and talk this shit out. I knew that she'd be pissed if she ever found out about that night, but I honestly didn't think that she'd leave me, and I definitely didn't think that she'd go to Cristiano or blame me for everything. Frustrated, I glance around the studio looking for a towel or something to wrap my hand in. Spotting one, I snag it and head to the door, yanking it open. I run right into Sonny.

"Hey, brother. Good thing you were in there, I just spotted Veronica getting into her car and she looked pis—"

It's then that he notices my hand in the towel red with my blood.

"Son of a motherfucker!" he spits out under his breath. "Where's the Princess, Deacon?"

"I don't have time to do this shit right now, Sonny. I have to find Frankie." I go to push past him but he steps to the side blocking me.

"She knows, doesn't she? Veronica came here like I told you she would and ran her fucking mouth." Shaking his head at me, he huffs a breath in exasperation.

"Not now, Jameson! I need to talk to her. You can lecture me later. Right now though, fuck off." Brushing past him, I make it about two steps before he spins me around by the shoulder. I cock my arm ready to throw when someone hooks my arm stopping me.

"What the fuck is going on? Deac, calm the fuck down, bro!" Mav grabs my wrist and holds my injured hand up, looking at me with raised eyebrows.

Muscle in my jaw ticking, I yank out of his hold.

"What happened to your hand and why the fuck are you swinging on Sonny? Somebody better start talking," he demands, looking between the two of us glaring at each other.

"This dumb fucker got caught up just like we told him he would," Sonny tells him.

Mav looks confused and then it dawns on him, "Frankie."

"Yeah, yeah. Deac fucked up again. Just like he always does, right? You two can stand here and talk about what a fuck-up I am, I need to go find my girl." As I turn to leave, I nearly mow down my father.

I start cursing under my breath. "I can't catch a fucking break today!"

My pop doesn't even say anything, just holds out his hand. He's so used to my temper getting the best of me it doesn't even faze him anymore. It was the reason I started fighting in the first place. It was an outlet for all of the anger roiling through my blood. Though I haven't fought angry since I was a punk kid.

Placing my injured hand into his waiting palm, "Pop, I don't have—""

"You gonna tell me why you're bleeding all over my gym two days before a fight and throwing punches at your brother, Deacon?" he asks as he unwraps the towel and inspects my injuries.

"I gotta go find Frankie, Pop. I messed up."

"Frankie?" he asks, looking up at me over the top of his glasses.

I wince, nodding. We hadn't talked about telling our fathers yet, but it looks like mine is about to find out.

"You two, go get ready for the charity event," he tells my brothers, not breaking eye contact with me.

Leaving us alone—well, as alone as you can be in the middle of a crowded gym—I know I'm going to have to tell my dad everything.

"Pop, can we talk about this later? I promise I'll tell you everything then," I plead.

"Son, you're not going anywhere until we clean up this hand and make sure that you don't need stitches. While I'm doing that you can tell me what has you all fired up and what the hell it has to do with the Princess."

Following him passed the lockers to the First Aid room, I hop up onto the table while he gathers the supplies he'll need.

"Start talking, Deacon."

I sigh deeply and explain to him all that's happened since her birthday, omitting the night with Veronica and that Frankie and I are now together.

Head bent over my hand, which is now clean and bandaged, he takes a deep breath and lets it out slowly.

"Ever since you were little, the two of you had a connection. I honestly thought that by now you would be married, on your way to having a family of your own."

Shaking his head he continues, "She was the only one that could calm you down when you let your hot head get the best of you. It didn't matter that a lot of the time it was her that you were losing your temper over." Chuckling at the memories he looks at me with a sad smile on his face.

"Deacon, you're a lot like your mother—all fire and passion

with a quick temper. They're some of the qualities that make you a great fighter, but you have got to start thinking before you act. You're twenty-seven, a grown ass man. It's time to start acting like it. Fix this shit with Frankie, Deac. I won't have you and your impulsive actions fuck with the relationship we all have. We're a family. Fix it and then get your ass to that dinner. No excuses." Nodding once, he makes sure that I understand and then leaves me with a pat on the back.

Hopping down, I head for the parking lot at a jog. I have to make this shit right.

SLAMMING THE ROVER into park, I bound up the stairs to Indie's front door, knocking twice before I throw it open and rush in. I come to a screeching halt when I see him sitting on the couch in the front room.

"What the fuck are you doing here, Flashdance?" I snarl clenching my fists, ignoring the instant discomfort in my left one.

After looking me up and down in my disheveled state like some pile of shit he stepped in, he meets my eyes.

"So Indie was telling the truth. You are with Frankie," shaking his head, not trying to mask the disgust the thought brings him.

I'm too pissed to play games with his ass right now.

"Did she call you here?" I ask through clenched teeth.

He snorts his disdain at me.

"Clearly you've already screwed it up. That's got to be some new record, Deacon, since I just talked to her the other day and she never even mentioned anything going on between the two of you." He flashes me his teeth in a grimace like he's saying "tough break." "I guess it's a good thing that I'm staying in town. She'll probably need a friend to be there for her."

I'm about to lose my fucking mind and take his ass to task when he snaps his fingers and points to me. "Hey, we have something in common now! Well, besides Francesca." He giggles like a little fucking girl.

Not taking the bait, I stay silent, feeling the heat from my temper race through my veins, heating me from the inside out until I feel like a volcano ready to fucking blow. When I do, somebody better hope I don't kill this asshole.

Sensing that I'm not going to engage him, he shrugs and goes on.

"Sadly, my girlfriend and I have, how do you say? Split up? Yes, that's the term," he says, playing down his knowledge of American slang. "So we're both single now, you and I."

His smug smile falls from his face as I advance on him, chest heaving. I'm stopped in my tracks though when Frankie walks into the room with Indie. Looking from me to him and back to Rico Suave, she walks over and puts a hand on his arm and speaks to him in fucking Spanish, not so low that I can't hear what she's saying but too fast for me to understand any of it, taking my mad to a whole other level. I just stand there seething as she speaks, trying to follow what she's saying to him.

She gives him a sad smile, squeezes his arm, and goes to move past him down the hall to her room.

Livid, I stand there and watch her walk away. Pointing a finger at him, I give his ass one warning.

"Stay the fuck away from her."

Leaving Cristiano and Indie standing together, I stride to Frankie's door and open it without knocking. Spinning around, her shoulders fall in defeat when she sees that it's me, knowing that there's no way in hell that I'm leaving without talking this out.

"Deacon, I really don't want to do this right now. I'm tired. I'm tired of it all, and I just don't have the energy to hash shit out tonight." She takes in a deep breath and says softly, "I'm sorry for what I said earlier. I don't blame you, for any of it. I just—I don't blame you." Turning her back to me, she walks over to the dresser and starts pulling out what she'll need for the banquet that we need to be at in a couple hours.

"It doesn't matter if you do or not, I do. I'm not going to give you time to decide this isn't right, because you know it is. We. Are. Right. Frankie," I say emphatically as I stare at her reflection in the mirror.

"Deac, let's not do this, okay? I don't want to be hurt or upset by you and the things that you do. I want to go back to the way we were. I just—I want to be friends again."

I can hear the quiver in her voice and see her lip trembling. I never wanted to do this to Frankie. I never cared about who I hurt in the past because I never bothered to stick around long enough to see the aftermath.

Coming up behind my girl, I bring my arms around and lightly grasp her delicate wrists in my hands, caging her in so that she has to listen to me. Speaking to Frankie's reflection, I press my front into her back.

"I can still taste you on my tongue, Princess." My voice is low and gravelly with emotion that I'm not used to hearing.

"My cock is still sticky from being buried inside of you. I can smell myself on you, baby, and it does something to me—it makes me fucking crazy." Leaning in, making sure not to break eye contact, I bury my nose in her hair, inhaling our mingled scents, dragging it down her neck, and placing a soft kiss on her shoulder. "Tell me how we forget about that, Frankie. Explain to me how I go back to loving you from a distance and pretending. Because right now, I don't see how it's even a possibility."

Closing her eyes, breaking our gazes she huffs.

"I never said that we would be able to forget, Deac. I said I just want to go back to the way we were and be friends." Pushing against me, I let her break free. "I can't be like this. I don't want to feel this way or wait for the next girl to show up knocking me down a peg and breaking my heart a little in the process because she wants a piece of what I have. I am a strong woman, Deac. I have overcome a lot in the past few months, but I don't think I can be strong enough to survive you."

Seeing tears hanging from her lashes threatening to fall, I pace away from the sight in frustration. I want to put my fist through every fucking thing in this room right now. Slowly taking a deep breath to calm myself, I lean against the wall, crossing my arms over my chest to try to keep my heart from falling the fuck out at her feet.

"What do you want from me? You want pretty words? Huh?" I ask her in a voice beat down by love. "You know that's not me, Frankie. I can't be someone I'm not, but I can be the man that loves you because that's the man that I am. Whether you believe it or not." Looking at her profile and her trembling chin, I wish that she would just look at me. I need her to see the truth in my words since my actions have fucked me. On an exhale I continue trying to convince her. "No matter what chick shows up, none of them will matter. Not one of them has ever even come close to getting *what you have,*" I say vehemently. "You have me, Frankie. All of me, and that's never gonna change."

Shaking her head, she looks me in the eyes. Crying openly now, she whispers on a broken sob, "I don't want all of you. All of you hurts too much."

Straightening at the blow of her words, I take one step toward her and then stop. My head reeling from the hurt, confusion, and a million other emotions fucking with me right now. Is she for real? Once again I pour my heart out, bleed all over the place and bare my soul, and she tells me that she doesn't want me? That she survived that animal, Andrew, but she can't survive me? What more is there to say? What the fuck else can I possibly do to prove to her that I'm in this? I fucked up, yes, but I have never even thought of touching another woman since we got together. It's always been her.

As I watch the tears slide soundlessly down her beautiful face, I shake my head, huffing out a breath in disbelief. Looking at my girl I let my temper rise to the surface.

"Do you know how many women I've fucked? How many I've let blow me?" I ask her angrily. "Because I sure as hell don't! They were just places for me to stick my dick." Ignoring her hiccupped gasp I go on. "I do know how many I've made love to though. I know that it's her face I see when I close my eyes. The one face I've always seen no matter who I was fucking." I take one last calming breath, my fists clenched to stop from dragging her into me and kissing her into believing me. "Romantic? No, not really. But the truth rarely is, Princess."

With that, I'm done fighting with her, for her to believe in me, us. For now. I stride out of the room. Out of Indie's house and away from the only woman that has ever meant shit to me.

Chapter
TWENTY-SIX

PULLING UP TO my house I'm not surprised to see both of my brothers' vehicles along with my dad's truck in my driveway. They love the Princess too and I know they're worried…I don't need this shit two days before a big fight. After the charity dinner, we are supposed to fly out to Los Angeles where the fight is being held.

I run my hands roughly through my hair and pull, letting out a deep breath to try and clear my head before I go in there and face them. How in the fuck am I going to tell them that I fucked up so royally I lost my girl? The pain in my chest just thinking those words is almost unbearable. I hurt to my soul right now and have absolutely no clue what to do to make it stop. To top it all off, I can't back out of this banquet tonight and there's no way she won't be there…it's for her mom.

How in the fuck am I going to sit at a table with her and pretend like she didn't just rip my heart out and hand it to me? I slam my palm against my steering wheel in frustration and throw the door open, slamming it hard enough to shatter the window. Turning away from the damage, I stalk to the front door, grab a potted plant at the bottom step and throw it to the ground, smashing the clay pot against the pavement, then viciously kicking at the debris. Hands on my knees, I try to get control of my temper but it's pointless. I want to wreck shit and do irreparable damage to everything in my path, to destroy everything around me so that it matches the chaos inside me. Whipping my keys into the front yard in disgust, I start up the steps. As soon as my booted foot hits the first stamped concrete step of my porch, my dad is waiting for me, hands in his pockets.

Breathing deeply, I look at him but avoid making eye contact. "Pop, I'm not going tonight. I—" I pause, huffing loudly, and continue, "I'm just not going. Make a bigger donation in my name or something."

Finally meeting his eyes, I expect disappointment, but find compassion and understanding, which make me feel even more like shit.

Opening the door wider, he nods.

"Let's take this inside where it's not so goddamn cold, Deacon."

I shuffle past him and head right for the stairs, ignoring my brothers and Trent. Once in my private suite of rooms, I go right to the liquor cabinet in my office and pour myself a Scotch, but just as I'm about to throw it back, my pop booms in his don't-fuck-with-me tone, "Deacon, you better put that glass down right this fucking minute. I will not have you throwing everything away, all of your training, because you screwed up and got your heart broken. You have already compromised this fight by injuring your hand."

Eyes downcast, I look into the amber liquid, knowing that he's right. In complete despair and abandon, I sling the still full snifter at the fireplace and watch it shatter, sending shards of glass and expensive alcohol flying in every direction. I'm on a roll tonight with the breaking of glass.

"You feel better now, Deac?"

Staring out the window, I try to reel in the anger and hurt that is consuming me right now, and shake my head no. My throat feels raw, like I've swallowed all of the fucking glass that

I've managed to smash in my anger.

"You know there's no way that you can miss this banquet tonight. It's important to us, to the Princess, and to Guy. You give the organization ten percent of your earnings, son. It's not an option."

He's right, and I knew it even when I told him that I'm bailing on it that I simply can't. Guy and my dad set up this foundation years ago to honor Isabella, Frankie's mother. She was an advocate for people suffering from Post-Traumatic Stress Disorder when she was alive, and my pop and Guy took it a step further in her death by starting a charity in her name. This dinner is held every year to raise funds for the organization and just having me on the guest list helps to sell plates.

Looking at him over my shoulder, I finally find my voice.

"I know, Pop. I'm just all fucked up in the head right now, ya know?"

Turning my gaze back to the window, I can see his reflection in the pane.

"Deacon, I know that right now you are in a bad place, but I need you to focus. You don't have the luxury of calling in sick or just skating by with your head in the clouds somewhere."

Coming further into the room, he sits on the arm of one of two chairs flanking the fireplace, careful not to step in any of the broken glass.

"You have to clear your mind, Deacon, of all of it. All the hurt and pain, the anger. You have to let it go until this fight is over. You can't go at Holloway half-cocked and full of fury. Either you'll kill him or get hurt because you're not thinking straight." Exhaling loudly he continues, "Neither is an option, son. I need for you to understand that."

Turning, I grip the back of the worn leather desk chair. "How do I do that? I just want to get fucking lit and pass out so that I don't feel this way anymore. Tell me how to forget it all when I can still smell her on my skin, Pop, because right now I don't want to remember any of it."

Looking me in the eye, he says solemnly, "If she's worth it, Deacon, you can't forget. A woman like Frankie won't let go, you just have to learn how to cope with the loss or fight to keep her." Shrugging apologetically, he says, "Unfortunately you aren't just any man and your responsibilities are bigger than your problems. We have to figure out how to get you past this for the next few days until you have the time to dedicate the energy needed to fight or move on."

Dragging my eyes away from him, I look at the picture just past his shoulder, at how happy Frankie and I look in it. The canvas print that hangs above the fireplace had been a gift from her. It's of us on base when I came home from my third and last deployment. I remember it like it was yesterday.

I'd been looking around the gymnasium for my people when someone jumped on my back nearly knocking me down. She was hanging on me like a little spider monkey, her legs wrapped around my waist, arms around my shoulders, me smiling back at her, and Frankie smiling down at me. I was holding on to her legs and she had an American flag in her hand, the only point of color in the black and white picture. It'd been this day that I decided not to reenlist. I couldn't leave her anymore, I hated not seeing her every day, and I missed my friend. The other part of me.

How did everything get so fucked? I bring my eyes up to meet my dad's.

"Aren't you gonna ask me what I did, Pop?"

Pursing his lips, he shakes his head and shrugs his shoulders. "Nope. You fucked up, that much I know. I'm certain that you didn't hurt Frankie intentionally, and I see that whatever you did is hurting you too, so I think that's punishment enough." Standing he puts his hands on his narrow hips. "Whatever you did doesn't much matter now, Deacon, because you can't turn back time and undo the wrong. All that matters now is what you're going to do about it, son." He heads for the door, stopping at the threshold. "Go get your monkey suit on. Carter hung it in your bathroom. Be downstairs in fifteen minutes or we'll be late. You can drive with me since it's too cold to ride in your truck without a window."

I turn to my bedroom to get ready, sighing in defeat and wishing the whole time that I could just stay home and drink myself numb.

COASTING TO A stop in front of the Field Museum where the charity event is held every year, Trent waits in line for the valet behind rows of limos and flashy cars. Impatient to just get this night over, I lean in between the front seats where he and my dad are sitting. "I'm just going to get out here and go inside."

As I'm reaching for the door handle, my pop stops me. "You can wait a few minutes and we can go together, Deacon. Don't be so eager to get inside, okay?" he says with a knowing look.

I want to get in there to see Frankie and he knows it. What he's telling me, as subtly as he can, is that there's no way in hell he's letting me loose by myself tonight. For the first time in my life, my pop is going to be my wingman. I'm not sure how I feel about that.

We finally make it inside and are making our way to our designated table, not stopping for small talk along the way, which I'm grateful for. Nodding at Mav and Sonny who are already seated, I glance around looking for Guy and the Princess.

"They're not here yet, Deacon," Mav says quietly as I sit in my seat making sure that I sit next to an empty chair, hoping that's where Frankie ends up. I feel crazed right now fighting the need to see her and hoping that she doesn't show up at all. I know Pop is right and I have to control my desire to put everything I have into fixing things with Frankie, but I can't do that yet. It's too much, too soon. But I also don't want her to think that I'm finished fighting for her, for us.

All thought stops when I hear Guy's booming laugh. Scanning the room, I see them speaking with Nina, the woman that heads the foundation. Standing beside him is my girl. She looks gorgeous in her floor length gown, deep red with beading that glints in the lights and candles around the room. Indie is with her in a vintage dress that hits her mid-calf and puts her colorful skin on display.

"Deacon? You okay?" my pop asks in a low voice from his seat on my right.

I take my eyes off of her long enough to reassure him that I'm not going to lose my shit just yet.

"I'm all right, Pop."

Reaching for the glass of ice water in front of me wishing it was something much stronger, I bring my eyes up from the table to watch them as they make their way toward us. Indie's looking at me like she wants to junk punch me. To be honest, I'm not entirely sure that she won't.

As they reach the table, my brothers, father, and I stand, shaking hands and greeting Guy. The whole time I have my eyes on Frankie, who still hasn't looked in my direction as she kisses my dad on the cheek, smiling sadly at him.

"You look beautiful," I tell her in a husky voice.

As breathtaking as she looks, I can see that she's been crying and that she isn't happy about being here, the little frown lines bracketing her lush, cherry lips a dead giveaway. Nodding her thanks, she takes her seat, which, much to my dismay, is not next to mine. I turn my attention to Indie now that I've been dismissed. I don't hide my pain from her—I'm too tired to even try tonight.

"You look beautiful too, Jones. Thanks for coming with her."

"I would never miss this, just like you wouldn't," she says, squeezing my tuxedo clad arm, letting me know that she sees how hard being here is for me. Thank fuck, because I can't fight her too right now.

I dip my chin in acknowledgment, sit in my chair next to Guy, and try to seem interested in the conversation, even though I'm drawn to the woman across the table, her every movement and breath affecting me. When the band starts playing a surprisingly good version of Adele's "One and Only," I'm about to say fuck it and beg her to dance with me. If I can just put my hands on her, I can convince her to forgive me. Coax her into talking to me at the very least. As I push my chair back to stand, Guy says jovially, "Ah, here he is. I thought that you would not make it, friend," in way of greeting.

Turning my head slightly when I hear the unmistakable Spanish accent reply, I lock eyes with Cristiano as he rounds the table to shake hands with Guy, nodding in greeting to my dad and brothers on his way over to the empty place next to Frankie.

Her eyes fly to mine, our gazes colliding. She shakes her head in denial when I glare at her accusingly. The hurt written all over me. He leans down before sitting and places a kiss on her cheek, making eye contact with me as he does, much the way I used to do to Drew to taunt him and remind him who Frankie really belongs to.

The tension at the table is palpable and obvious to everyone but Guy who goes on to thank Cristiano for coming and apologizing for not inviting him sooner.

"Thank you for inviting me, Guy. I know how important this night and this foundation are to you and the *Princessa*. I—"

"Don't call her that. Ever," I bite out harshly before I can even think to stop myself, the spoon in my hand being bent to shit like it's nothing more than plastic.

Placing a hand on my arm in a seemingly innocent gesture, my Pop presses his fingers firmly and says in a warning tone low enough for only me to hear, "Deacon, that's enough. Lock it up," before sitting back and smiling, trying to ease the startled expressions on the faces of everyone at the table.

I can feel my brothers watching me, ready to spring into action if need be. They know I am barely hanging on to my temper right now, and with Frankie sitting there statue still, delicate hands clenched into fists beside her water glass, I'm glad that I can always count on them to have my back.

Cristiano smiles at me in that smarmy fucking way that he has as he places his arm on the back of Frankie's chair, letting his fingers brush against her bare shoulder, causing her to tense. She may be upset with me, but my girl knows me and how volatile I can get. Especially when it comes to her.

"As I was saying, I know what this means to Francesca, and what is important to the *Princessa* is important to me," he says, all the while never breaking eye contact with me or stilling his hand on her skin.

Looking down at the mangled silverware in my hand, I try to regain some control, but I've got nothing, and in a tone so lethal it makes even me a little nervous, I quietly seethe, "I'll tell you one more time, do not call her that."

Slowly bringing my eyes level with his, I see that he's not feeling as brave as he was a minute ago and that just fuels me further. Ignoring my dad's hand on my thigh applying pressure and Guy's curious gaze, I sit a bit straighter and in the same deadly calm voice, "If you don't get your hands off of her, I'm going to personally make sure that you never dance again. I will break every bone in your motherfucking body if you lay one more finger on her, and that's a promise, *amigo*," I say, mimicking his words from earlier.

Cocking my brow, I turn my attention to his now still hand and work on regulating my breathing as I watch his hand and then his arm fall away. Satisfied that I've made my point, I look toward a visibly upset and embarrassed Frankie, but she won't meet my gaze—not that it matters because she will not find any apologies in my eyes. I glance at Indie who is the only one at the table enjoying my little display, if the smile on her face is any indication. Hold tight, Jones, I'm just getting started.

Turning my attention to Guy who is clearly confused and understandably a little angry at my outburst, "I'm in love with your daughter and whether we're together or not, I'll be damned if I'm going to let that asshole or anyone else for that matter touch her. I apologize for not telling you sooner, so that this scene here could have been avoided, but that's all I'll apologize for."

Gasping audibly, Frankie stands, throwing her napkin down on the table, and nailing me with a withering, watery glare, storms away from the table. Indie, hot on her heels, looks back at us over her shoulder and mouths, "I've got her." I'm not sure if she is reassuring me that she will take care of Frankie or warning me away.

Brushing off my dad's vice-like grip on my thigh, I too get up.

"Now, if you'll all excuse me, I'm going home to pack before I start flipping fucking tables or breaking jaws." I make sure to stare down Rico Suave as I deliver my parting speech.

Turning to my brothers, I point a finger in Flashdance's direction.

"Take care of my girl and watch him," and then stalk away without another word, not looking back at the mess I've just left in my wake.

Chapter
TWENTY-SEVEN

FIGHT NIGHT:
Deacon "The Hitman" Love vs. Michael "The Tank" Holloway

THE SWEAT IS pouring off of me. The ticking sound of the speed bag competing with The White Stripes blasting from every speaker in the hot-as-fuck gym that Carter rented out for us. We've been here two days, in this sauna, since our L.A. branch is under reconstruction. Slamming my fist into the leather one more time, I turn and head for the ring, motioning for one of the guys that Sonny got to spar with me to suit up. I slip in between the ropes and grab my gloves from the corner. I'm in the process of pulling them on when my dad and Sonny walk in from the offices.

"Deacon, what the fuck are you doing, bro?" Sonny yells at me from across the gym.

Ignoring him, I tilt my head from side to side, popping my neck, bouncing on my toes, trying to ease some of the tension that has held me prisoner since I walked out of Indie's place two days ago.

After her birthday party when we didn't speak, I was a fucking wreck—drunk all the time if I wasn't fighting and fucking whatever came my way. Now though, I can feel the swell of rage pulling me under. I was hurt the last time, disappointed, and I allowed myself to drown in a bottle. Now, I'm all that and more. I know what it means to really be with her, to have Frankie, mind, body, and soul. I don't have the luxury of self-soothing with a bottle of vodka and some stranger this time. My pop won't let me go to that place no matter how badly I want to.

If I'm not training, I'm thinking about Frankie and how she quit us without even trying. Yeah, I fucked up, but that was before I made a commitment to Frankie. I let myself down by not following through with the promise that I had made to myself to be a better man for her. I never set out to hurt the Princess, and once I claimed her, there is nothing and no one that could ever tempt me into being disloyal to Frankie in any way. In her heart, I know that she knows that. She's running scared right now, and I'm pissed at us both for letting it happen. So fuck her, and fuck me, for this drowning feeling that I can't shake, which only pisses me off more.

Sonny shouting angrily breaks into my thoughts.

"Yo, Deacon! Get the fuck out of the ring. We have the fight in less than four hours. We need to get back to the hotel and rest up."

Still ignoring my brother, I give the poor fucker I'm about to tear apart the signal to go ahead and come at me. Unfortunately for him, he does. I let him charge me and swing wildly, ducking his punches easily. I come up at him from his left side and counter with a combo that has him staggering back, but not far enough out of my reach as I hit him with an uppercut under the chin that knocks him out cold. Standing over him, I'm not prepared when Sonny steps in between us and pushes me back forcefully. Stumbling a bit, I don't think about what I'm doing when I swing on him, connecting with his jaw with a right hook before I sweep his legs, causing him to hit the canvas hard enough to knock the wind out of him. Eyes narrowed, I'm seeing red and seething with anger. I'm just about to hit him again when I'm tackled from behind and pinned down with a forearm to the back of my neck. Mav's face comes into focus at the same time as my pop's gym shoe-clad feet come to a halt in front of me.

"Let him up, Maverick. He's done now."

"Pop, he just knocked out his sparring partner and then took Sonny down. He's out of fucking control!" my brother says in exasperation, his minty breath warming my already over-heated skin.

Cheek pressed against the mat, I let them discuss me like I'm not here, as if I can't break his weak ass hold whenever the fuck I want to. Clearly, my dad is thinking the same thing.

"Mav, if Deacon wanted to continue on this stupid fucking rampage of his, he would. You're not containing him, son—he is containing himself. Now let him up before he decides to take you out next. Your little brother is obviously in the business of throwing temper tantrums today," Pop says in a very unamused voice.

Getting in a cheap shot by using the forearm across my neck as leverage, Mav finally gets off of me, allowing me to get to my feet to face the firing squad. I don't look at any of them, the adrenaline coursing through me, making me feel even more out of control than I did when I hit my brother. Was I sorry that I hit Sonny? Yeah. Did I care? Not even a little right now. Feeling all of their eyes on me, I sigh deeply, as if they're boring me. I focus on my hands, yanking my fingerless gloves off.

"We done here, Pop?"

Tossing them behind me, I watch them over my shoulder as they land in the corner before I turn back to my dad and meet his steely gaze.

"Yeah, we're done, Deacon. Head on back to the hotel with Trent. We'll come that way as soon as I look at your brother's jaw." The last was said to make me feel bad. It doesn't work.

I know why he's letting me go without giving me shit over hitting Sonny. He's trying to let me get myself straight, rein in the mad taking over. That isn't going to work either. On bare feet, I turn and hop out of the ring, stalking over to my duffel, stopping only long enough to put my shoes on. I pull my Black-hawks hat low enough that hopefully nobody recognizes me as I slide into the back of the car Trent already has waiting at the curb. He tosses me my phone.

"Carter called, said to tell you to give him hell tonight."

It's the same thing he always tells me before a fight. I grunt in acknowledgment, palming the phone and typing out a text without even thinking about it. *"Are you going to be there tonight?"* Before I can hit send, I shake my head at myself, disgusted, and shove it in my pocket. I'm not ready for her answer. I don't want to give her the opportunity to say no. To anything. I'm giving her space because I have no choice right now. These next couple of fights will make or break my career and I am already at a disadvantage with my fucked up hand. My pop was right—I have worked too hard, *they* have worked too hard, to get me where I am to throw it all away because of a broken heart. I just have to keep it together for a little while longer. Stick and move. Stick and motherfucking move.

BACK AT THE hotel, I spend the time waiting for them to come knock on the door doing sit-ups, pushups, shadowboxing, and showering over and over, in that order. I can't shake the feelings that have taken me over completely since I left the gym. I run hot and cold from moment to moment and have to talk myself out of hopping on the next plane out of here, straight to my girl. The only thing keeping me from doing just that is the very small possibility that she's here in Cali for the fight. Before all of this—her, me, us, the breakup—she would've been here. Nothing would have been able to keep her from being in my corner. That thought alone is enough to set off my already volatile temper. Reaching for the towel on the bar, I step out of my fourth shower of the night. Rubbing the soft cotton over my too tight skin, I look at my reflection in the mirror, my eyes locking on Frankie's name on my chest.

Soft fingers flutter over the elegant letters, "When did you do this Deacon?" Blue eyes framed by thick lashes meet mine before searching my face, then come back and hold me there, nowhere to run. "Why?" she asks softly.

Shrugging nonchalantly, "It's not the first ink I've gotten for you, Princess, and I'm sure it won't be the last either." Chuckling, I pull her into my side trying to put an end to this conversation.

"Yeah, but this is different and you know it," she says, looking down at the feminine curves of black inside the angry red heart. "Please tell me, baby. I won't be upset or judge. I know that you were probably angry with me." Leaning forward, she places a kiss over the tattoo, her lips lingering, and then they're gone and she has me pinned with those blues again, the ones that see everything, see me.

I groan and look up at the ceiling.

"Frankie, it's not a pretty story. I don't want to bring any of the stupid shit I did to this place," I say, raising my arm to encompass the bed that we've just fucked each other stupid in.

Meeting her gaze again, I see that she is not going to budge on this, the stubborn ass.

Huffing, "Fine. So I was listening to some music, drinking—heavily and about to do something that we won't talk about," I say looking away from her, the muscle in my jaw bulging from the strain of me clenching my teeth so hard at having to tell her the next part.

"The song 'Un-thinkable' came on and I stopped what I was doing to listen to the words, pulled ou—"I shake my head at my slip—she doesn't need the specifics. "Anyways, Drake said some shit about living for destiny and having more of a thing and ink over his heart for his girl, and in that drunken moment, it just seemed like I wanted to—no, I needed to

do it. I don't know if I thought somehow it would make me feel closer to you or what, but I was doing it no matter what." While I'm talking I've been drawing figure eights over and over along her back and still when I feel her lips on her name again. When those same lips find their way up the side of my neck to my mouth, I breathe in relief.

In between soft kisses, she whispers, "I love it, Deacon, thank you." Kiss. "Play me the song." Kiss. "I don't want anyone else to share that with you." Kiss. "Only me." Kiss. "Ever." Kiss. "Then I want you to play me a different song." Kiss. "Our song."

Determined to torture myself, I stride back to the bedroom in my suite, grab my phone off the dock and glance through the texts and calls that I've missed from Carter, Trent, and whoever else doesn't matter because they aren't Frankie and pull up my Spotify, setting it to play "Un-thinkable," then add our song to the queue. I lie down on the bed to listen. Allowing the sadness to overtake the anger for a time, letting it bring a binding around my heart to add to the uncomfortable pull of tension weighing me down, I listen until the last chords of "You Got What I Need" play out. The words hanging in the air like a reminder. I feel them wash over me and then I tune them out and shut down. Effectively slamming the door on all the love that memory brought to the forefront and immediately surrounding myself with all the ugly shit I've been feeling instead. The anger I can handle, work it to my favor. Love and sadness and the bullshit that comes with them make me weak, and I have no fucking time for that shit.

Chapter
TWENTY-EIGHT

I SIT STOICALLY on the table, staring at the wall over Sonny's shoulder as he methodically wraps my hands in the bright pink tape that Frankie bought me that I never got around to replacing. I think about the last fight and who was taping me then. Her movements were not as jerky and agitated as my brother's, then again I hadn't punched her in the face hours before either. Seeing Mav and my dad out of my peripheral talking to the babysitter sent by the EWF, I let my thoughts swirl and for the first time in my life I don't even want to fucking be here. In this moment I want to give up because I don't fucking care. The notion is so foreign to me it makes me irate that I've been brought to this.

Closing my eyes, I think about the fight and try to get my head in the game as I feel Sonny start his prefight rubdown. The silence in the room is deafening, the tension adding to the heaviness inside me. Opening my eyes, I'm startled to find my pop staring at me. I look away, swinging my gaze instead to the bruise covering Sonny's swollen jaw, and still can't find the strength to give a fuck. Focusing on my pop again, I allow myself a moment of weakness.

"She here?" I ask gruffly.

Shaking his head no, he starts to say something, but I cut him off by hopping down from the table.

"Let's do this shit then, yeah?" Yanking open the door, I stomp to the tunnel and wait for my intro music, not bothering to see if my team is behind me. The one person who has always been in my corner, the only person I want there isn't. So fuck it, fuck it all. This may be an important fight, but I have yet to get my heart in it.

As soon as my song starts, I start for the Octagon, my home, the place I need to be right now to release the fury and despair that I feel. I stand impatiently at the bottom of the steps, just going through the motions as they check me out and the cut man tends to me. Scraping my hair back into a tight bun, I step into the cage and wait for some relief. I get none. Looking around the arena, I see the blur of faces as I raise my arms in greeting, though not in my usual fanfare. I'm making my way back to my corner to wait for Holloway when I see the ring girls for the evening. When Veronica blows me a kiss and laughs as she takes her seat next to the other bikini clad chick, I want out more than ever.

By the time The Tank enters through the gate, I'm way past ready for it all to be over. I don't pay attention to anything that the ref says or the taunts from Holloway; all I hear is white noise and the rush of my own blood coursing through my veins. As soon as the bell dings, I spring into action, following his dancing and bouncing form as he circles me trying to find an opening to lay me out. I never even give him the chance as I land a high kick to his temple, then as he staggers back, I get a grip on the back of his head and bring my knee up as I pull his face down, connecting with his nose, bringing an instant gush of blood. Not pausing in my assault, I unleash a flurry of left and right hooks, not letting the pain in my left hand slow me down. I follow him as he slides to the mat still taking my hits, until the referee slides in between me and a nearly unconscious Holloway, stopping the fight, nearly taking one of my punches himself. Chest rising and falling rapidly from the exertion, I don't wait for them to announce me as the winner—I already know I am. Without more than an arm raised briefly in acknowledgement, I storm out of the cage, letting the gate slam against the outside of the cage when I throw it open. Not slowing, I charge back down the tunnel I had come from only minutes before, knowing that I'm going to catch hell from all sides and still not able to find my give a fuck.

I HEAR TRENT on the phone talking to Reggie about the fight, telling him that we're on our way back to the hotel now. Reggie, being the head of my security, takes his job very seriously. Since I'd made him stay behind with Frankie, he sent Trent and some new guy, Bo, with me on this trip. I don't give a fuck who he sends where, as long as he keeps Frankie safe. Andrew still hasn't surfaced and I need eyes on her in case he's planning something. I usually never have this much security, but with things the way they are, it makes everyone feel better that Frankie and I are covered. This checking in bullshit is pissing me off though—I don't need a fucking keeper.

"Ask him if she's okay," I demand kicking underneath Trent's seat.

He locks gazes with me in the rearview mirror and nods in acquiescence. Satisfied, I go to watching the lights flash as we speed by. I'm not sure how Reggie knows Bo or what his deal is, but I know he's one hell of a driver. Maneuvering through the shit traffic of L.A. like its nothing. I pull my phone from my duffel. Scrolling through all of the missed calls, I notice that I already have one from Derek, the President of EWF, and about fifteen from both Carter and Mav. Since the two of them work together on all of my PR stuff, I'm assuming that they are busting ass on damage control and probably have received a call or two from Derek as well. I keep flipping, not finding what I'm hoping for, and go to my texts, stopping when I see one from Indie.

> *Jones: Hey, you. Just wanted to wish you luck tonight and let you know that WE'RE watching. Knock him dead, asshat. On second thought scratch that, it's probably frowned upon. Just win the damn thing, okay?!*

Smiling faintly for the first time in days, I shoot off a reply.

> *Me: Thanks, Jones. I'm sure I'll be in a world of shit, but I won, so fuck it.*

Hitting send, I lean my head back and close my eyes. I want to grill her on why the Princess didn't come. What she's doing. If Rico fucking Suave is there. If she's okay. Someone tell me again why I can't just go get my girl. Lock her up somewhere and make her love me. I pinch the bridge of my nose with my calloused thumb and forefinger, exhausted despite the adrenaline still shooting through me. I'm already tired of fighting myself, convincing myself that I have to wait and it's only been two motherfucking days. Not expecting a response, I'm startled when my cell dings with an incoming message.

> *Jones: We saw. WTF was that all about, dick? She's really upset and if you tell her that I said so I'll kick your ass! You're probably gonna get fined, huh? She's on the phone with her dad now, speaking Italian, don't know what they're saying.*

> *Me: Why is she upset? She okay, Indie? Fuck the fine.*

> *Jones: She's upset bc you're so angry. She's worried.*

> *Me: Yeah, well, if she's so worried there's an easy fucking*

solution.

Jones: Not that easy, caveman.

Me: Whatever. Gotta go.

Phone switched off, I throw it back into my bag and go back to watching the city fly by.

"Hey, Deacon?" Trent's voice breaks through the silence.

"Yeah?" I bark out.

"Reggie said that Frankie is fine, hasn't left her place all night and…nobody came over. It's just the two girls."

Reggie's way of letting me know Cristiano hasn't been there. I nod but don't say anything to him.

"He also said that he's staying the night."

Whipping my head in his direction, "Why the fuck is he sleeping there, did he say?" He hasn't slept there in months. Then again she's either been in my bed or I've been in hers during that time, and I can protect my girl without his help. Wiping the sweat from his brow with the back of his hand, he brings his gaze back up to mine in the mirror.

"He said he doesn't think she should be alone." Shrugging he holds his hands up in "don't shoot the messenger" fashion and goes back to texting.

Whatever the fuck that means.

I curse under my breath and reach for my phone again. As I wait for it to fire up I think about all I want to say and wonder how much of it I'll actually get out. Should I call or just text her? The phone comes alive in my hands and I look down at the picture of me and Frankie wrapped around each other laughing, me kissing her on the cheek. I stroke a finger over our smiling faces and then swipe it away, opening up to the apps. I hover over the call button and then switch to the text.

Me: Reggie will stay there, he'll keep you safe. Don't fight him, please. For me.

Tapping the send button, I sit and wait for a response, my leg bouncing up and down in agitation. When three minutes go by and I still don't get one, I shoot off another text.

Me: You don't need to text me back. Write this shit down though, one fight down, two more to go. Don't think I'm not coming for your ass, Princess.

I let out a deep breath and wish like hell I had a drink. I'm just about to tell Bo, the stunt driver to stop at the next liquor store he sees when I hear the ping of my phone, letting me know I have a text message. Palming my phone, I look down at the glowing screen to see,

The Princess: Bumper Cars, Deac <3

Bumper Cars? What the fuck does that even mean? I huff out an exasperated breath about to man up and just fucking call her when it dawns on me. It's a song. Spotify app open, I search the title and put my earbuds in to listen. It's so Frankie it makes me feel closer to her, and then I stop to actually listen to the words. They say so much, tell me the things that she's afraid to say, the things she's fighting. Her pain comes through in every word. My girl. She loves hard, but she knows me better than anyone else and that's where her fear lies.

By the time we reach the hotel I've listened to the whole album and text her once again, letting her know that I hear her. I'm here and I'm not going anywhere.

ME: Little Do You Know

Chapter
TWENTY-NINE

Francesca

I HANG UP the phone and toss it onto the cushion next to me, sighing in relief. My dad is livid. He's pissed with Deacon for the stunt he just pulled, and he's upset with me for contributing to his volatile mood. When Gaetano De Rosa isn't happy about something, you bet your ass everyone is going to hear about it.

Indie leans her head back, resting it against my leg. "You gonna be okay if I head out for a while, doll?" she asks from her spot on the floor. Indie knows that watching Deac act out the way he did is killing me. He's a professional, and up until now, has always acted as such. I'm disappointed in him, but at the same time, I get it. I brought him to this. I brought him to this, brought *us* to this fucked up place where I switch between guilt, sadness, and anger. Same as him, I'm sure. All because I couldn't fight him or my feelings for him anymore. I didn't mention to Indie the text message that he sent while I was talking to my dad. I probably should have responded back with a little more than the song, but I'm just not ready to let him in even a little right now. He owns too much of me; I'm weak when it comes to him.

Sighing, I look down at my friend. "Of course I'll be okay. Reggie is here with me." I hate that they feel the need to babysit me, but I appreciate the hell out of it—more than they know!

I tuck my feet underneath me and curl up in the corner of the couch looking over at Reggie, who has been on the phone since the fight started. Touching base with the guys I'm assuming. "You're not going anywhere are you, Reg?" I ask him, hoping that he's staying here again.

"I'm not going anywhere—you're not that lucky," he tells me in his gruff yet gentle tone that he only uses with me.

I smile at him and turn back to Indie. "See, I'm good. Go have a good time." My world might be crumbling down around me, but I don't want her to be a casualty of the devastation.

Indie pops up from the carpet and gives me a kiss on the cheek before she heads for the door. "I'll catch you two crazy kids later," she calls out. Poking her head back in, "If things go the way that I'm hoping, it'll be a late night, so don't wait up. And if you hear screaming, don't come to the rescue unless you want to join in," she says with a wink and closes the door behind her.

Reggie looks over at me and I just shrug, and we both start laughing. "You know that bitch is crazy, right?" he asks good-naturedly

"Yeah, I know she is. I love her anyway though."

I grab the remote and start flipping channels before the highlights from the fight start playing. I don't want to hear them analyze what has gotten into Deacon. I'm just about to give up when I'm paralyzed by the picture filling every bit of the sixty-inch TV hanging on the wall. The blood in my veins turns icy as I stare into the brown eyes of the man I had thought myself in love with. As my body involuntarily starts, I sit trembling and listen to them talk about things I can't wrap my mind around. *"District Attorney Andrew McAvoy wanted for questioning in connection,"* my eyes lose focus of the man on the screen, *"to an ongoing investigation involving his fiancée, Francesca De Rosa…hasn't been seen…high profile federal case."* Heart racing, ears buzzing, I can feel a cold trickle of sweat making its way down my spine. I only catch bits and pieces as I struggle to hold myself together. *"Ponzi scheme…McAvoy uncovered over three hundred million dollars…possible human trafficking…drug cartel…his whereabouts…paramount to the conviction of…"*

The TV flicks off and Reggie comes into view, putting his hands gently on my shoulders to stop my motion. Without realizing it, I had begun rocking back and forth, my arms wrapped tightly around my body, but not tight enough to stop the quivering that started from the inside and worked its way out.

"Hey now, Frankie, I'm here, girl. You're okay," Reggie says softly, squeezing my shoulders, comforting me and bringing me back from yet another attack. Another attack where all I want is to pull at my hair, yank at the memories just out of my reach, grab answers, and run with them. And Deacon. I want Deacon. Swallowing back a sob, I fight to still my swaying.

"There she is. Where did you go, Frankie?" he asks, rubbing his hands briskly up and down my arms as if to ward off a chill.

"I don—I…did you see that?" I question.

Nodding solemnly, "Yeah. Yeah, I saw. Did you know anything about the case that he was working on?" Reggie asks. I shake my head no, rubbing my hands over my face and into my hair, tugging tightly at my scalp, trying to get my thoughts from being so jumbled. "No. We never spoke about his cases. He said that it was a breach of client-attorney privilege."

"Yeah, well, he always was an uptight prick," he says, trying to lighten the mood, though it's the truth. I'd settled for Andrew as an adult just as I had for Cristiano when I was younger.

Reggie stands and paces over to the recliner he'd been sitting in when his phone starts to ring. Silencing it, he turns back to me. "How often are you having these attacks, Frankie?"

Raising my eyes to his, I start to deny it, but see the look of determination on his face and think better of it. "Since the beginning," barely a whisper. "I haven't had a bad one in a while though," I tell him.

"Does Deacon know?" Reggie asks quietly, arms folded over his chest.

"I never told him that I was having them regularly. He knows of only one. I didn't have many when we were together and if I did he was asleep and I'd had a nightmare or whatever." My voice trails off.

"Don't you think he deserves to know? Don't you think you owe it to yourself? You're obviously having problems dealing with what you went through and I know for a fact he's always been your anchor, just as you've always been his."

All I can do is stare blankly at him, because I know he's right, but if I admit it, I'll cry. I'll curl up in a ball and cry until I can't cry anymore.

"He can't know right now, Reggie. He can't. There's too much at stake for him and he's already acting reckless." Determined to get my way with him in this, I cross my arms defiantly. My stance matching his own.

"He's half out of his mind because you're not at his side, Frankie." It's the first time Reggie has ever raised his voice at me. "You know how he is, and I hate to break it to ya, but it's only gonna get worse." What he says is true. I know it is but it doesn't change anything. I still love him, but I'm still scared and he still messed around with Veronica. All because he thought I was with Cristiano, when all I wanted, all I needed, was him— that night and now.

It's always going to be him. Even when it's not.

Chapter
THIRTY

DEACON

ONCE BACK HOME in Chicago, shit goes downhill fast. I got my ass handed to me by my pop the whole flight, and then Guy the moment we landed at Midway the night of the fight. Derek Elliott came by personally to pay me a visit at the gym, reaming my ass and letting me know none too nicely that this time the fine for me storming out of the cage in a show of poor sportsmanship is fifty grand, next time it would be double, and if I'm dumb enough to do it again, there would be a disciplinary hearing. Just what I fucking need. Added to that shit, Veronica's ass keeps popping up wherever I am, and twice now the Princess has seen her hovering. Short of knocking a chick out, I'm not even sure what to do about it. My dad will not kick her out when she shows up at the gym, because she hasn't done anything to merit it, so I just ignore her. I have not said one single fucking word to her since the other day when she popped up at my house and couldn't get through the gate and I had a few choice words for her.

Things are still a little strained between Sonny and I, but that's probably because he's still sporting some discoloration from the fading bruise on his jaw and I still don't give a fuck.

Seeing him come toward me now as I hang up the chains I was using for my workout, I'm a little surprised. I lift my chin in greeting.

"What's up, brother?" I ask as warmly as I possibly can when I feel anything but. It's not even him that I'm angry with, but for whatever reason he's getting the brunt of it. Maybe it's because he was right about shit going down the way it did with Veronica telling Frankie.

"You might want to hide out somewhere—Veronica just showed up and she brought a friend," he says with the same chilly note, looking at me expectantly, waiting for the words to click.

"Fuck. Sylvia?" I ask on a frustrated groan.

"Yep, and Frankie is here teaching classes all day." Stuffing his hands into the pockets of his track pants, he spreads his feet, planting them firmly in front of me, eyes narrowed. "Why the hell does it seem like every time I turn around I see her?"

"Because you fucking do, Sonny!" I shout angrily. "Everywhere I fucking go, there she is. Frankie has already seen her here a couple times. I—"

I'm interrupted by the sound of raised voices coming from the front of the gym. Turning to look that way, I see the Princess in her favorite Frankie's Place shirt, the ripped out collar making it hang off of her shoulders, and a pair of black leggings stopping at her calves showing off the sculpted muscles of her incredible legs with the aid of her hot as fuck black heels. The ones with the bright pink soles that match the lettering on her shirt. Taking in the scene, I see that not only is Frankie there, but Cristiano is with her, and they're having words with none other than Veronica and her skanky fucking friend. I'm not sure what has me more pissed off: the girls here causing a fucking ruckus or the fact that Frankie and Flashdance are standing so close to each other.

I ignore Sonny cursing under his breath next to me and

stride toward the group. I step in between Frankie and the two girls, all of whom are pointing fingers and hurling insults. I don't spare *him* more than a glance. Just enough to see he's aggravated, though I think it has more to do with me swooping in than the little catfight about to go down.

"What in the fuck is going on here?" I bark at Veronica and Sylvia.

As calmly as I can, I look back over my shoulder and ask softly, "You okay, Frankie?" my eyes scanning her face and body to make sure, although I know they didn't touch her.

Nodding, she glares around me at our unwanted visitors. So close that she's nearly pressed into me, the heat radiating off of her and coasting over the bare skin of my back sending little electric shocks licking at me, through me, making the ink that covers it feel alive. I don't have time to revel in having her this close before I feel a hand running up my chest. I whip my head back around, swatting it away as I do.

"Oh, come on, D, I brought your favorite sex toy," Veronica purrs as she curls her fingers around Sylvia's, tugging her closer into her side and batting her fake eyelashes at me.

Snorting indelicately behind me, Frankie tenses. Then Rico Suave goes and opens his big fucking mouth and I feel the tenuous hold I've had on my temper over the last couple of days being tested to its limit.

"Ahhhh, I see. You are here to toy with Francesca, to make her jealous, *sí*? Did you not know that they broke up? He is free to do to you what he wants," he says in his accented English with a shit-eating grin that is about to get him hurt.

From somewhere to my left, I hear Sonny warn gruffly.

"Be very, very careful, Cristiano. My brother is operating on a shorter fuse than usual. He laid me out; he won't hesitate to lay your ass out too."

"I only speak the truth, *amigo*, she is no longer his concern and therefore they are both free to do whatever and whoever they want." Shrugging his shoulders, he looks back at the vultures waiting for the chance to swoop in.

I can feel the tension rolling off of Frankie still safely behind me.

He has his mouth open to speak again when I cut him off.

"Are you insinuating that you're fucking my girl?" I growl, turning fully now, forgetting all about the two pains in my ass watching in rapt fascination at the fight unfolding. Facing him, my back is still to Frankie, which is good, because God help this motherfucker if she gets hurt when I snap because of his mouth. Not if, *when*.

"Is that what you're saying? That the Princess jumped from my bed to yours?" I snarl vehemently, shifting on my feet, ready to put him down. "You better be real fucking careful how you answer that question. Either way, it isn't going to end well for you. I can guaran-fucking-tee it." I take a step closer to him, but stop when I feel Frankie's trembling hand land briefly in the center of my back. The soft touch sears my skin and makes me crave more before she snatches it away.

"Deacon, please," she implores. "Cristiano, that's enough," Frankie says firmly, trying to skirt around me but unable to get past the arm I hold out to stop her.

"It is okay, *mi amor*, he won't hurt me here in front of everybody. Plus, he better get used to you being with other men. He lost his chance——"

Wrong answer, motherfucker is the last thought I have before I snatch him up quick by his throat and slam his ass to the ground. Kneeling next to him as he tries to catch his breath, I bring my face within an inch of his. I can feel Sonny pulling back on my arm, not to drag me away but to ground me.

"Hear this, motherfucker, you ever think of telling me about what I lost or what I need to get used to and I'll end your shit, you feel me? Do you honestly think I care where the fuck I am or who may be around?" I laugh sardonically at his stupidity. "I'll tell you what's never gonna change no matter how badly you want it to. I'm always gonna be here, wherever she is, in her life. She'll always be mine, even when she doesn't want to be." Smirking at his laid out form, I let my brother pull me back to a standing position.

Slowly Cristiano struggles to rise up on his elbows and then hisses, "You are no better than that animal that attacked her, you know that? You are violent and a danger to her. The only difference is you'll kill her when he could not."

Frankie lets loose a broken sob bringing my attention back to her. Covering her mouth with her hand, the bracelet dangling from her wrist, I focus on the charms against her soft skin as I concentrate on not killing Cristiano.

Raising my eyes to meet her watery gaze, I say in a voice layered in threats, "That's where you're wrong. I'm worse than he is." My voice shakes from the rage I feel at his accusation. "I love her enough to kill for her. I'm trained to hurt people, my hands and body weapons. I wouldn't think twice about killing someone with them to protect Frankie. Wouldn't matter to me if I went to prison for it either." I meet his glare, mine full of hate before turning my attention back to the Princess. "That makes me more dangerous than him on every level. Not to her though, never to her," I say for her benefit, regardless that she knows I would die before laying hands on her. My lips kicked up in a sad smile, my voice gravelly with too much emotion, "Even when she won't fight for us, I'll go to war for her."

With my words hovering in the air around us, I reach out, touch her face with just the tips of my fingers, running them from the softness of her cheek over her trembling lips before stalking out, leaving them staring after me.

Stopping at the front desk, I grab a shirt out of the display case and pull it over my head. Pointing in the direction I just came from, I tell Julia, our receptionist, that Veronica and Sylvia are banned from the gym indefinitely. To mail them refunds if they've already paid and to deactivate their cards. I can't do shit about seeing them on the EWF circuit, but I damn well can stop them from coming in here and fucking with Frankie and making my life any more miserable. I gesture to Trent and Bo, who have been watching the whole thing but know better than to step in, that I'm ready and the three of us head out into the brutally cold night. I don't give a fuck how clean I'm supposed to stay during my training—I'm getting lit tonight and nobody's going to stop me. I've earned that shit by not doing the damage to Flashdance that I really wanted to.

MAV THROWS A bottle cap at me as he sits on the island watching me cook.

"You know you have to get your ass back to the gym, right? We can't keep working out here. You need sparring partners; I'm done letting you throw punches at me in your basement, dude."

Snorting, I glance at him over my shoulder.

"You make it sound like we're in a dungeon. I have the same setup down there that we do at the gym, Mav." Shaking my head, I turn back to the stove and the rib eye steaks I have on the grill pan.

"Deac, it's been weeks. You can't avoid her forever and you have a pretty important fucking fight coming up."

He's right. I know he is, but I just haven't been able to go there yet. I don't want to see her with him, and at least at home I can be as mad as I want and I'm not in any danger of going to jail for killing entitled assholes. I have my reasons; they're just gonna have to do shit my way. I need back in the gym though. If not to train, then to know that she's close by. My mind is so all over the place. One minute I don't want to be anywhere near the gym because she's there and he might be too, the next minute I'm jonesin' to be there, just to be near her. Love hurts. It hurts like a fucking kick to the balls.

I face my brother and lean back against the counter, crossing my arms over my chest. Looking around, I'm reminded of the first night Frankie and I had sex, all of the words that were said and the wicked things we did right here in the kitchen. I bring my focus back to Mav.

"You're right, bro." Nodding in agreement.

"Right about what?" Sonny asks as he comes in carrying the six-pack that he went out to get.

Grabbing one out for himself and another for Mav, he stows the rest in the fridge, pulling out a bottle of water for me. My brothers and pop are being extra vigilant after finding me passed out drunk and not answering my phone for nearly two days after my little altercation with Cristiano.

"Make a gym time for tomorrow and line up some punks for me to beat up and toss around."

Brows raised, he watches me for a second before responding.

"All right then. Done." Taking a swig from his bottle, he looks at me over the rim a little pensively.

"Spit it out, Jameson. I know you want to fucking say something." Uncrossing my arms, I pull a platter out of the cabinet and wait for him to tell me what he's thinking.

He sucks his teeth and clicks his tongue, and finally he says, "Do you want me to work around Frankie's schedule? She's there a lot more often now, but I can work it out, Deac. I mean, you can't dodge her forever, but I need you focused, and with them teaching couples classes…" He trails off.

Breathing deeply, I set the steaks down on the counter.

"Are they together now?" I ask in a low voice.

Mav is quick to jump in.

"No, no. It's nothing like that at all, Deacon. They're just teaching a class to couples, mostly people wanting to learn a dance for their wedding." Mav hops down from where he's been sitting, grabbing the condiments I set out and brings them over to the table.

Once we're seated, my appetite all but gone, I eye the beer in Sonny's hand. Before I can snatch one for myself, Sonny cuts in, "You can't be drinking right now, Deac. We've let you slide with training here instead of at the gym, and that's only because you have such a fantastic setup. This fight is too important to let you fuck around with your conditioning, my man. Sorry."

Flipping him off, I pile steak and veggies onto my plate and dig in. He's right. This is it—I have to beat Billy "The Kid" Dair and I'll get my chance at the strap. I have to channel all of this pent up anger I have, the hate and rage banging at my insides to get out, and take this fucker to task. Once I have that locked down, there's nothing that can stop me from getting my girl. I just have to keep my fucking head a little while longer, do this shit in order. Stick and move, stick and motherfucking move.

There's nothing more important to me than Frankie, but what kind of man would I be, how formidable a fighter, if I gave it all up to chase after her like some kind of pussy? Do I want her? More than my next breath, but I also know I have to be worthy of her and being a quitter will not make me worthy of the Princess. I'm not saying that she couldn't, wouldn't love me if I lost. I could never love a bitch who operated on that level, but I know my girl and she'd lose respect for me if I threw it all away, and that's unacceptable. It's go time. She may be my biggest weakness, but in no way does that make me weak— quite the opposite. There is no room for pussies in the cage. It's do or die, and I'm ready. I have a lot of work to do, a lot of fighting, and I know that the toughest fight won't be for the belt but for Frankie.

Chapter
THIRTY-ONE

Francesca

ONE OF THE things I love about dancing with Cristiano is that I don't have to think. He leads and I follow, which is good because my mind is constantly on Deacon. I miss him so much it hurts. It isn't just my lover, my boyfriend, that I miss, it's my best friend. The person that I go to for everything has been snatched away from me and I feel bereft without him. I need him. My heart physically aches from the Deacon-sized hole dead center.

I'm scared more often than I want to admit, and I don't know who to turn to. I'm surrounded by these big, tough guys, all of whom care for me, but I only need one. I know that all I have to do is reach out. To tell him about the phone calls, the letters, and the pictures, and he would take care of it all, of me, but there is no way that I can right now. He has the fight coming up and he's still hurt and angry. I know that's why he hasn't been here to train. He was barely able to restrain himself the last time I saw him here, and truth be told, Cristiano is lucky that he didn't do worse. He deserved it and I don't blame Deacon for reacting the way he did. I know what it must do to him to see Cristiano and me together, the same as it tore at my heart every time I saw Veronica hanging around. Worse because him and I are constantly touching one another, in each other's arms. It's pretty hard to dance without touching your partner. I'm just ready for all of this to be over. I want to not hurt any more, to not cry myself to sleep and pretend for everyone that I'm fine. I gambled on Deacon and I lost. Broken out of my thoughts by Cristiano dipping me nearly to the floor, I gasp, startled.

"Where are you, *mi amor?*" he asks smoothly, as he kisses the corner of my mouth. His lips would have landed their target had I not turned my head. He's becoming more and more bold with his advances. I would be lying if I said that I'm not flattered, maybe even tempted, because I am, but then I fight past all of that pain and confusion and let my heart remind me that it's no longer mine to risk. Deacon is right -- I'm his girl whether I want to be or not.

Swinging me gracefully back into his hold, he smiles sadly at me and places another kiss on my temple. "I'm having dinner with some of our friends, join me?"

"Thank you, but no. I have a class that I want to prepare for and I'm more tired than usual this week. We've been really busy. Thank you again for all of your help, Cristiano." Stepping out of his arms, I shoo him away. "Go, get out of here. I can handle the rest."

He bows with a flourish, then turns and saunters out whistling. I can't help but smile at his dramatics.

I look up from my sound system when I hear someone tapping on the glass that separates the studio from the gym. Smiling, I motion for Mav to come in. Norah Jones is singing "I've Got to See You Again" for about the tenth time when I hit mute, silencing the stereo. I'm concerned as soon as I see the edgy look on Mav's usually carefree face

"Hey, Princess. You left the blinds open," he says in a flat tone, blinking slowly like that is supposed to mean something to me.

Ummmm...okay.

"I don't usually close them, Mav," I tell him with a little laugh like he's being silly, which he kind of is.

"You should if you want privacy; everyone in the gym saw you and Cristiano in here. *He* saw the two of you, Frankie."

Mav crosses his arms over his chest, widening his stance, and continues to stare at me as if I should know exactly what he is getting at, and I truthfully do not have a clue.

"Privacy? We were working on a routine for one of my students and her partner, Mav. I don't need privacy for that. And who is '*he*'?"

I am completely baffled by this Maverick. Out of the three Loves, he is the most laidback, and for him to be confronting me about anything is out of character.

"Deacon, Frankie. Deacon could see you. Was that kiss at the end choreographed as well or what?" he asks with a disapproving look.

I don't even bother to answer him. This is absurd.

"Look, I don't know what's going on between the two of you, but we just got him back in here training. Deac has been more reckless than I've seen him in a very long time and completely unmanageable, and I'm not blaming you, but it's kind of your fault, 'ya know?" With raised eyebrows he goes on, "It's impossible for him to train like this, and you kissing Cristiano for everyone to see after dry humping each other all over the dance floor for the last hour is enough to put him over the edge." There's a muscle pulsing in his jaw as I stare at him in utter disbelief.

"Dry humping? Really, Mav? It's called the tango, you asshole, and trust me, Deacon doesn't care as much about what I do with Cristiano as you may think," I snap, although I know that to be a bald-faced lie. He cares very much. I'm just trying to diffuse the situation. Before I can get another word out though, he interrupts me.

"That's bullshit, Frankie. You didn't see him when you were hurt—he was a wreck. Hell, we all were, but Deac—I'm just thankful that it was me that found you and not him, because as painful as it was for me, it would've killed my brother." Maverick shakes his head, remembering a time we all just want to forget. "The man never left your side the whole time you were out. We had to make him go and take showers, and even that was a battle. He was shattered by what happened to you. He's just as wrecked now—it's just a different kind of hurt he's battling. So trust me, I know he gives a shit about what's going on with Cristiano."

Now it's my turn to cross my arms over my chest. I try not to let what he said affect me. I can't imagine what it did to Deacon; the very thought has tears pricking the backs of my eyes. Looking away from him, I tell him, "I'm not with Cristiano so there's nothing to hide from him. I love Deacon, Mav. Whether he and I are together or not, I love him."

I turn my eyes to the glass wall of the studio, sighing. "It was one of the reasons that I was leaving Andrew that night. I was so confused about my feelings, I knew that there was no way that I could go through with the wedding plans when I felt so torn. I thought that Deacon and I might actually have a shot."

"So what the fuck happened, Frankie. I don't get it!" he huffs, completely exasperated.

"You know damn well what happened. Veronica showed up." I laugh grimly. "She showed up and ran her mouth about how he was waiting on her and I believed her, because that's the Deacon I've always known. The manwhore with girls lined up waiting to get a piece of 'The Hitman,' but this time I was one of them and it hurt."

"Oh, come on, you knew he wasn't waiting for her. Veronica is a liar and he has been done with her for a long time. She started getting clingy and he stopped taking her calls. You—"

"It doesn't matter that he wasn't waiting for her! You and I both know what happened when she got there," I interject, pain lacing my words.

Of course he knows. The Love brothers are close and they don't keep anything from each other. It's one of the many things I love about them.

"So what, this thing with Cristiano is to punish him or something?" he snarls.

"He messed around with her because he was pissed at me, Mav. She told him that she saw me leave with Cristiano, and instead of calling me to ask about it, he let Veronica blow him." My hands curl into themselves, my fingernails cutting into my palm. "Had he called me, he would have known that I was in bed, alone, thinking about what the fuck those two were doing and trying to keep another panic attack from kicking my ass. However, he didn't. He did what Deac does, and I'm okay with that now." Yet another bald-faced lie. "I have since come to the realization that I cannot bear to lose Deacon in my life completely, and if we continue with our relationship, I will, I have! He's too much for me, Mav, and I'll never be enough for him."

Lips trembling, I swallow back the lump in my throat and smile sadly at him.

"I need him, Maverick. He is my person, but we can't be more than friends. I cannot be one of *Deac's girls,* and with Deacon, that's all I would end up being. Maybe not at first, because it's me, but eventually that's what would happen."

Blowing out a breath, I straighten my spine, managing to fight back any tears that were threatening still and hold his probing gaze.

Eyes saddened by what I just shared, he nods his head in acceptance, but his words contradict the action.

"I get it, Frankie. I get that you're scared and why, but you could never be just one of *Deac's girls*. You may not see it, but you are Deacon's only girl, always have been." With that, he spins and strides out the way he came.

Well, fuck. He doesn't get it. He says he does, but he can't, and I don't dare let myself believe what he said. It would be way too easy to just forgive Deacon for the thing with Veronica, but I cannot set myself up for that. Especially now. If anything happened to him, I would never forgive myself. If he gets hurt during one of his fights or drops out now because of me, again…I wouldn't be able to deal with that. He's worked too hard to get to where he is. *I've* worked too hard to help him reach this point and he's too close to fuck it up. This hurts now, but losing him completely would be unbearable. I have to keep my heart safe from any further hurt, and I have to keep him out of harm's way at the same time. I'm protecting us both. Even if he doesn't see it that way. I know that although he isn't in my face that he is fighting for us. Keeping his head down and biding his time and I know that no matter what I say he won't stop fighting until he's ready. He will eventually get over the pain of losing me. My recovery though is questionable at best.

Chapter
THIRTY-TWO

DEACON

FUCK THEM IF they think I'm going back to the gym when those two are there. Watching that fucker put his hands all over my girl is one thing, seeing him kiss her another thing entirely. They thought my ass was volatile before. Just wait! I have only ever felt this kind of all-consuming, simmering right below the surface, ready to spew out of every pore and annihilate everything and everyone around me rage one other time, and that was when Frankie was attacked. They can find another gym or we can keep on training at my place—I don't care. All I know is that I am not going back there. I want so badly to say fuck it all and break Cristiano for even thinking that he can have my girl, but I have to play my shit straight. I won't even allow myself to think about it being too late. I can't. That just isn't an option.

Coming to a stop on the slushy mess of a jogging trail, I plant my hands on the top of my head and breathe deeply, the crisp air making my lungs burn. I have a month before the next fight, and once I win that I have four months to get ready for the championship. I'm on my way to Mav's to meet with my brothers and Reggie. I know that they want to bang out a game plan after that shit fest that went down the other day. I'd ended up knocking out two sparring partners and dislocating another's shoulder. Pop's pissed and both Mav and Sonny are nervous. Fuck, even I'm a little nervous about how hot I'm running. I take off at a faster pace the last half mile to my brother's brownstone, hoping to shake all of the negative shit swirling around in my head by abusing my body. Once on his stoop, I take the stairs two at a time, knocking quickly before I turn the knob.

"Yo! Where you assholes at?"

I hear Reggie boom from the landing that they're in the media room. On my way past the kitchen, I snatch two coconut waters out of the fridge and go to see what the guys are getting into. Striding into the sitting area with its comfy, worn, black leather theater seats and recliners, I drop into the one nearest to me. As I sit, I raise my chin in greeting at the three men watching my every movement. Slowly, watching them watch me, I take my beanie from my head, finger comb the strands back into a rubber band, and crack open one of my bottles.

"So what's up? We staging my intervention or what?" I ask before I chug down the water.

Laughing, Mav shakes his head.

"You're way past that shit, brother." Shoving a handful of popcorn into his mouth, he smirks over at me.

"No, Deac, we're hammering out your training schedule and Reggie is here to go over a few things about who needs to be where and when," Sonny says from his perch on the arm of a recliner.

My gaze swinging in Reggie's direction, I ask sharply, "Who's with the Princess now if you're here?"

He just looks down his crooked nose at me, like I've just insulted him. "Calm down, my man. Trent and Bo are both with her. I'm not going to leave her alone, especially right now."

I sit up straighter, narrowing my eyes at him. "What do you mean especially now? Is there something going on? Has she heard from Drew?"

I'm just about to get to my feet when Sonny pushes me back down, holding me in place. I hadn't even realized that he'd made his way over to where I'm sitting.

"He means with all of the extra media and attention the fight is stirring up. She's fine, Deac. None of us is going to let anything happen to her." Sonny gives my shoulder a squeeze. I relax back into my chair not nearly as appeased as they think they have me. Reggie doesn't say shit just to say it, and that's the second time now that he's made a comment that makes me think there's something more going on. My brother walks over to the island-sized footrest separating my section from Mav and Reggie's. He sits, hunching forward, his elbows on his knees.

"Speaking of Frankie, I have your training schedule all worked out and your gym times don't overlap with any of the classes she doesn't teach alone."

Smart man. He's avoiding any mention of Flashdance because he doesn't want to test my temper today. He's learning. Probably doesn't want to get hit again.

"We'll be doing the majority of your hours on the ground level. Pops has them setting up the temporary cage again right now. We'll be all set for tomorrow's session." Pausing he looks at me sternly, wearing his coach mask now. "It's the best I can do, Deacon. You're just going to have to man up."

Glaring at him, I grit, "I know what the fuck I have to do. You just need to make sure he stays away from me. I'm all done holding back, you feel me?"

Eyes focused intently on mine, trying to read me, he nods his head in agreement.

"Fair enough, Deac. I'll try my damnedest, but you gotta work with me, brother. We have to work that mad out of you somehow, some way."

Snorting, I just smirk at his attempt to compromise.

"Yeah, well, I fuck and I fight so…" I shrug looking away and then bring my eyes back to his dark and assessing gaze.

"One isn't happening at the moment because my girl is off dancing with some fucking prick, so fighting it is. Just keep lining up the sparring partners, Sonny, and don't get pissed when I lay their asses out." I break the seal on the second water and take a swig, smirking at his resolute expression.

Letting out a string of curses, Mav stands.

"You, little brother, are the biggest fucking pain in the ass. Your acting out bullshit is a little more serious than simply being all ass hurt. You could injure someone, Deac—badly."

I say nothing, looking him right in the eyes. I don't have to. He knows that right now, I don't give a fuck.

"All right then, I'll have Carter print up extra release forms for the guys stupid enough to spar with you to sign."

Snatching up his phone, he heads out of the room to presumably call Carter.

"Now that that's all worked out, let's figure out what Reggie has planned so that we can eat and get some rest. You're in the gym at six tomorrow morning," Sonny says with a little more glee in his voice than I like.

We turn our attention to Reggie, switching gears to focus in on the business he needs us for.

"Well, since we're going out of the country for the Dair fight, I think that if the Princess stays back, that I should hire on one more guy to go with you guys. I trust Bo and Trent, but I think we need another body." Smoothing a hand over his stubby Mr. T-style mohawk, he looks at me and Sonny, waiting us out.

I don't care if no one goes with me as long as the Princess is covered. Opening my mouth to tell him that very thing, Sonny answers for me.

"Do whatever you need to do to make sure you can stay here with Frankie and not worry about what the hell is going on in Brazil. Hell, hire two more guys so that you have a replacement if you need it," he says, shrugging his shoulders nonchalantly.

We all trust the man with our lives, Frankie's included.

I watch him for a second and try to figure out if there was anything to his comment earlier or if he really was just talking about all the hype over the fight. I'm not sure I believe that; I think there's something going on and that they are keeping me out of the loop because they need me concentrating on Dair and not on something that we pay Reggie to handle. They have to know though that there is no way in hell that I'm going let them handle keeping the Princess safe while I sit by with my dick in my hand waiting for instructions. Not finding what I'm looking for—the man has a poker face that would make any hustler proud—I look over at Sonny.

"Is that it then? There's nothing else we have to go over?" I question, turning toward Reggie. "You don't have any concerns that I need to know about? Because you know if there is something going on that you aren't telling me and I find out, or something fucking happens to Frankie, that shit is gonna get ugly as fuck, right?"

Reggie shoots eyes over at Sonny, quickly bringing them back to me.

"Everything is fine, Deacon. I will not let anything happen to her, and I swear to you that if I run into a problem that I can't handle, I'll come to you. I got her, bro." Nodding solemnly, he doesn't break eye contact with me.

The conversation ends when Mav calls from the kitchen to come and eat before there's nothing left.

"STOP DANCING AROUND him, Jamie! Get your fucking guard up and be ready. If you're afraid of him, then get the fuck out of there," Sonny screams from outside the cage at the second sparring partner of the day. Watching him put his guard up and come toward me hesitantly, I just laugh to myself. This fucking guy. Dipping to the right, I get him with an uppercut in his ribs that folds him over on himself, allowing me to get him with a left right under the chin, and its lights out for Jamie. I start toward Mav and Sonny as they send the medic in to tend to Jamie's weak ass.

"Get me some fucking guys that can take a hit, Mav. These fuckers are a joke." I take a swig from the water bottle that Sonny hands me.

"Deacon, it's not easy finding these guys, let alone better ones. Nobody is volunteering to be knocked the fuck out, asshole. You have everyone talking about how crazy you've been lately. Maybe if you toned that shit down some, you could make my job a little bit easier."

The three of us turn when we hear the door slam closed. *She* has me more out of breath than any of the guys I've sparred with today just by standing there against the door. Being on the ground floor has really worked well. I haven't seen Frankie since we started training down here, which is both good and bad. I need to see her, but I can't take seeing that fucker with her and that seems to be the norm lately. As she makes her way to the cage, I can see that she's nervous, apprehensive.

"Hey, Loves." Smiling hesitantly, she stops just inside the door of the cage. Mav and Sonny wave their hellos, still agitated with me and a little wary over her impromptu visit.

She fidgets, tucking her long, blond hair behind her ears. She looks at my brothers, and then her blues finally settle on me, though they don't quite meet my gaze before darting away. "I'm sorry to interrupt you guys…this will only take a second." She's talking to Sonny and all I can do is take her in.

Letting my eyes travel down her jean-clad legs to her gray, suede, calf-high boots and back up over the swell of her ass, and further to the cream-colored, fuzzy sweater that is completely backless except for the gold chain at the very top that hangs in between her shoulder blades. Jesus fuck. She's so beautiful it hurts. My gaze lands on her profile. I watch her lips move and remember what they felt like on my skin, wrapped around my cock, moving against my neck as she begged me for more, deeper, harder, moaning my name. I'm brought out of my dirty thoughts when she turns her attention to me and my now rock hard dick pressed painfully against my cup.

"I don't want to bother you, but I tried to give Reggie the night off and he said that you were the only one that he was taking days off from. Can you just let him know that it's okay, please?" Staring somewhere in the area of my chin, tugging on her bottom lip, she waits for my answer.

I glance at Mav, my eyes narrowed. He just shrugs, though he and Sonny both look as apprehensive as the Princess did just a few moments ago.

"Why would I give him the night off, Frankie?" I ask in a bored tone when I'm anything but.

"We were invited to a ballroom dance competition as judges. It's not exactly somewhere you take bodyguards, and even if it were, I can't get a ticket for Reggie this late." Still not making eye contact with me, she alternates between chewing on the inside of her lip to plucking at it. It's driving me insane.

"We? Who's we?" Squinting I wait for her answer, praying that it's not who I think it is.

She sighs, sounding defeated.

"Cristiano and I." I can barely hear her she says it so quietly.

Muscle pulsating in my jaw, I purse my lips in thought, trying not to lose my shit. The pain that those three words cause, unbearable.

"So have him wait outside. There's no way that Flashdance can keep you safe if something happens," I bite out snidely.

Shifting from foot to foot, she peers at Sonny over her

shoulder. I can see that he subtly shakes his head no. She turns back to me bringing her eyes to mine. For the first time since she's been down here, our gazes lock and hold. She takes in a deep breath.

"We're going to St. Louis. Overnight. The hotel is fully booked because of the competition, so I can't get Reggie a room. I tried."

I stare at her, blinking slowly. I let what she just said wash over me and sink in. My girl. My girl is going away with Rico fucking Suave and is standing in front of me telling me about it so that I can call off her security detail. So, what? They can fuck in private? Fists clenched at my sides, I grind my teeth, that ticking muscle in my jaw morphing into a painful pulsating bulge. I'm not sure which emotion to dial into first: the anguish that is ripping through me or the rage about to boil over. Dropping my head, I stare at the mat under my bare feet for a second, trying to reel it all in, not paying any attention to Mav when he says my name in warning.

Slowly raising my eyes to hers, I say in a pleading voice, "Please tell me, Princess, that you are not down here asking me to pull Reggie so that you can go on some romantic fucking getaway with your little boyfriend." Rubbing my chest in the spot where my heart used to fucking be, I beg her with my eyes as well as my words. Right here, this moment, I feel more out of control than I ever have. The riotous feelings are a living thing inside my body and I want to bleed them out of me. I want them gone. All of them. The love, the hurt, the anger. I just want to be numb. It's a total mindfuck, making me feel reckless out of pure desperation.

Eyes searching her face, I find my hands balling into fists again as I stare at her, willing her to tell me that it's not true.

"Frankie? Tell me that isn't what's going on right now." My voice is thick with the pain her visit has brought.

Sonny steps in between us, and putting a hand to my chest,

he pushes me back a step and I let him. I let him because I'm in a daze since she still hasn't said anything. He knows that I would never hurt her. I would die first. But he also understands what this has done to me, to my temper. I know that he's just trying to diffuse a bad situation before it gets worse. Reaching around my brother, I snatch her arm gently and draw her closer, a little too quickly, in my need for her to answer, making her stumble into Sonny. It forces her to brace herself with a steadying hand against his back. She looks at me, tears in her eyes. Pain and regret reflected in their beautiful depths.

"Princess?" Heart racing wildly, I search her face, landing on her blues, imploring with everything in me. I just need one word. Just two letters. Finally she puts a stop to the panic that is about to set in and consume me.

"No," shaking her head vehemently. "No, Deac. I would never—it's not—he's not—No," she says clearly, resolutely, so that there is no way that I can misunderstand.

Releasing her arm, I nod once in acceptance, relief.

"He goes. Mav can call Carter and he can figure out a place for him to stay. Your boy's ability to dance does nothing for my faith in him to keep you safe. You're mine to protect, like it or not, so deal with it. Reggie goes." Turning my back on all of them, I stride to the other corner, slipping my gloves back onto my shaky hands, effectively shutting them out and letting them know I'm done with this whole goddamn scene. Thank fuck Mav had these guys sign waivers—their day is about to go to shit.

Chapter
THIRTY-THREE

PULLING UP AT the EWF offices downtown, I park the Rover in the underground garage and take the elevator up to the top floor. They are doing the final interview for the piece that will run the weekend of the fight. They have already had cameras at the gym recording my training and brief interviews that they have been airing all week.

On my way up, I shoot off a quick text to Frankie, I can't stop myself. I hate how we left things the other day and I hate even more that she went away with him. I had a game plan that I had to stick to but she needed to know that I was fighting for her. Always fighting for her.

> Me: *Two more fights to go. I hope you're ready for the make up sex. I'm going to fuck you like I hate you so I can show you that I love you.*

Quickly pushing send I realize that I probably should've gone with something romantic or some shit but I'm still pissed and still me. To soften the text a bit I send another.

> Me: *You Got What I Need*

The doors open, depositing me into the plush lobby. I walk to the reception desk where there's a beautiful, mocha-skinned woman I've never seen before operating the phones. She must be new or a temp because her dress is baring more cleavage than most bikinis and that's not how Derek Elliott runs his federation. She smiles hungrily, thoroughly eye fucking the shit out of me. Biting the tip of her pen, she purrs, "Well, hello, you must be Mr. Love. I've been expecting you." Leaning forward, she rests her tits on her forearms, pushing them up and causing a nip slip that I know she's aware of.

It does nothing for me. Not even a twitch of my cock. Before Frankie, I would have had this chick bent over the desk, balls already slapping against her ass. I smile coldly, maintaining eye contact.

"You can put those things away, sweetheart. I'm Mr. Love, but I'm not your guy."

She looks up at me from under her lashes, licking her bottom lip.

"A little birdy told me that you're too much for one woman to handle. I can call a friend who would be more than willing to help me out. We can be very," she pauses for effect, "*helpful,* Mr. Love."

What was with all of these chicks offering threesomes lately to try to sway me? Did girls really talk about this shit with each other? I keep my tone firm and even, my face impassive.

"Obviously you have your information wrong. I'm handled just fine by one woman. You're not her. Now, can you let them know that I'm here for my interview?" Not waiting for her to answer, I turn to the sitting area, take a seat, and wait.

Finally sitting down with the interviewer, I'm relieved to see that it's Brendan, a standup guy who I know won't try to dig and will keep the questions about the fight and not what is happening in my personal life. I shake hands with him, settling back in my seat. He gets the cameraman positioned where he wants him and gets my mic on and tested.

After all of the usual questions about my strengths and

weaknesses, what I believe my opponents' strengths and weaknesses are, training methods, things I'm doing differently and the like, I think we're finished. Then he goes in a direction that I wasn't prepared for.

"People are talking, Deacon."

I bark out a short amused laugh. "Oh really?" Quirking my eyebrow, I wait for him to explain that cryptic comment.

"They are. They are saying that you're angry, that you aren't yourself, and that it will most likely affect your fighting. Is any of that true?" All of a sudden, Brendan is a dick and I'm not as relieved to see him as I had been.

"I don't know if you've noticed, but I'm a fighter, we get angry. If people are talking, that means they're scared. If they're casting doubts about my capability to fight at the best of my ability, then they must be praying that it's true. Am I angry?" Shrugging, I say in a detached tone, "I guess we'll see once I get into the cage in Brazil. You say angry, but I say hungry. There is a lot on the line, and if starting rumors makes people feel more confident in the outcome of this fight, then so be it." I rap my knuckles against the table top. "I'm here for one thing and one thing only, and it for damn sure isn't to make nice. I'm here for the strap."

It's a lie—I am angry. I would never admit that though, because I know, and clearly so does Brendan, that an angry fighter makes for a sloppy fighter. That's something that I have to work on, and fast. Because there is no way I'm losing this fucking fight. I'm not sacrificing this time to get my girl back just to lose. That is in no way part of the plan. Stick and move. Stick and motherfucking move.

Never breaking eye contact, I take the mic off my shirt as I stand, tossing it on the table in between us before turning and walking out. His interview is over.

Chapter
THIRTY-FOUR

LATE AS HELL, I come out of my room carrying my bag. In search of my ringing cell phone, I jog down the steps. I'm able to find it and swipe my thumb over Carter's name before it stops ringing.

"What's up, my man?" I ask as I reach for my wallet and keys, checking to make sure that the back door is locked.

"Ummm, hey. You okay?" he asks tentatively.

"What the fuck kind of question is that, Carter?" I stop what I'm doing and wait for him to explain.

"Well, it's just that…well, there's a picture in the paper." Pausing, he takes a deep breath.

Why the fuck is he being so dramatic?

"Yeah, and? You know I don't get the paper, dude. Just tell me what the fuck you're trying to say. The car is going to be here."

Looking at my watch I curse. "Fuck, it should be here and I'm trying to get shit together still, so can we do this later, bro?" Stalking to the front of the house, I key in the gate code and am about to turn off the music when he says, "There's a…ummm, a picture and an article in the Trib. It's of Frankie and Cristiano from when they judged that competition in St. Louis," he says in a rush.

My hand hovering over the off switch on the radio, I stop and listen to the song plays, telling me to say something and I feel like putting my fist right through the speaker.

"Send it to me," I tell him gruffly.

"Deacon, I don't think—"

"Yeah, well, you should've thought about that shit before you called to drop this on me minutes before I'm set to leave for the fucking airport for one of the most important fights of my life, but you didn't. Send. The. Fucking. Article," I thunder.

When I hear a horn blasting from the drive, I stab at the end button while slapping my hand over the power switch on the stereo. I grab my bag, locking everything up. I'm proud of myself for my even breathing and for not breaking anything until I hear the ding of an incoming message and look down to see my girl and Flashdance all dressed up, sitting with his arm draped behind her chair and her smiling at him with a caption that reads:

"Have local dancer and her ex-partner and longtime lover reunited? By the looks of things I would say it is a definite possibility. The two seemed comfortable with one another when they sat on a panel as guest judges and were even seen canoodling at a night club later that evening. Is romance in the air for these two again? We sure hope so."

I grip my phone so tightly I'm sure it's going to crack. I'm pulled from my thoughts when Mav opens the door to the SUV he hired to drive us to the airport.

"Yo, fuckerface! You coming?" He laughs thinking his shit is funny.

He quiets abruptly when he sees my face.

"You saw it? Sonofabitch motherfucker," he spews.

"Were you gonna tell me?" I ask, deathly calm.

"Deacon, bro. We are days away from a fight. An important fucking fight. We were going to wait until after you beat

Dair to tell you." He looks at me apologetically, begging me to understand.

I get it, and I'm not mad at them for not telling me. I wish I hadn't fucking seen it at all. Whatever. I have no time to think about this now. Seems like I'm having to remind myself of this much more often lately, but shit needs to be done in order. Stick and move, stick and motherfucking move. I have to remember that, or I'll kill someone.

Chapter THIRTY-FIVE

FIGHT NIGHT:
Deacon "The Hitman" Love vs. Billy "The Kid" Dair

WE'VE BEEN IN Brasilia, Brazil for five days preparing for tonight. The weigh-in last night didn't exactly go as planned. "The Kid" and I had some words and almost came to blows. I'm sure I'll be hit with yet another fine. This shit with Frankie is costing me a fortune. My pop and Guy are both here too, so I have four of them pissed off, giving me hell, and ripping me a new asshole. At least the sparring partners here in Brazil are a little more of a challenge, though it hasn't stopped me from putting a hurting on all of them, frustrating the hell out of Mav and making him work even harder to find me more.

"Deacon, can you come here and look at this real quick?" Pop calls from the small TV that they have set up in the corner.

I stalk over to them, rubbing a towel over my hair and chest. "What's up, Pop?"

He and Guy are watching tape on the oldest fucking TV I have ever seen.

"Look at this, what do you see?" Guy says pointing at the grainy screen.

I lean forward, squinting to get a better look. After a few moments, I see what they're talking about.

"Dair has a weak jaw. He wobbles like a fucking top with anything heavier than a tap." I straighten and I see them both nodding their heads in agreement.

Pop points at the men fighting.

"Did you see that? Jab, jab, down to his knee. Now watch this."

He fast-forwards to another bout.

"Look there, uppercut to the chin, dropped to his knee. Same thing in the next fight."

"How didn't we see this earlier? Me, Sonny, and Mav have been watching him fight all season," I ask, confused.

Guy pauses the video.

"These were his last three fights. I think that he may have taken a hit and softened it. We aren't sure, but that is now your target," he says excitedly, which only makes his accent more pronounced.

I nod.

"Okay. I'll wobble him then," I tell them shrugging non-chalantly.

My dad glares at me, shaking his head in exasperation.

"Deacon, it isn't going to be that easy. I need you to be focused. Calm and collected is the only way to beat this guy. You can't go in there like a powder keg ready to blow like you have been during training and against Holloway. Do you understand what I'm saying to you, son?" he implores.

Looking between the two of them, I see the worry on their faces, in the tightening around their mouths and eyes. I want to put them at ease but I won't lie to them.

"I can't. I am all out of calm and collected, Pop. I've been trying for months to get a hold of it and haven't been able to, so I'm adapting. That's the best I've got right now and it's going to have to be enough to win. I won't lose this contest," I assert and I mean it.

Win here, take the strap in Vegas, and then get my girl.

Stick and move. Stick and motherfucking move. If I keep saying it enough, maybe it'll sink in and I'll start believing it.

HERE IN BRAZIL, I'm given a whole locker room to get prepared for the fight, instead of just a room like most arenas. My team is still at the hotel, but I was going crazy there so I headed here instead of staring at the fucking wall in my room. I am slipping my board shorts on, Frankie's Place in bright pink over my ass and my sponsors down each leg in the same color, when I hear the door behind me open up. Turning, I'm about to tell whoever it is that they're going to have to find somewhere else to shower when I see that it's the Princess. My breath catches in my suddenly too dry throat. I want to kick my own ass when I feel the excitement at seeing her here. For my first thoughts being that she's here. In Brazil. For me. And that she's beautiful.

Slowly I turn my back on her to give myself a second to get my shit together. I try to ignore the fact that she's wearing her "Hitman" shirt, the one that falls off her shoulders over a pair of shorts, and of course her requisite fuck-me heels.

"What are you doing here?" I bite out in aggravation.

I look at her and all I see is that picture in the Trib and the words written beneath it.

She clears her throat delicately. I can feel her coming closer and my body tenses.

"Deacon, I wouldn't miss this. I know that we aren't in a good place right now, but that doesn't change how important you are to me."

A derisive snort escapes me as I turn, pinning her with eyes I know are wild with emotions. Emotions that I don't want to feel right now.

"What do you want from me? I don't have time for this shit

right now."

"Deacon, please, I—"

"You what? Please what? You made your choice, I get it. So again, what do you want from me?"

"I just want to talk to you, to see if you're okay. This fight is a big deal, Deac, and I'm scared for you. I just want to be here for you." She's sincere—I can hear it in her voice. I just don't care right now.

I feel all the anger and hurt simmering just below the surface and I know that it's too late. There is no way I can hold it in any longer because right now the feelings are just too fucking much. All of it, her being here, is just too fucking much.

Scoffing at her, "You want to be here for me, Francesca?" I spit out, using her full name because I cannot bear to call her anything else right now.

I stand straight, hands balled into fists, my chest heaving. Forcing myself to ignore how she flinches as the name registers with her, as if I've reached out and smacked her in the face. I try to drag in air, but all I get is a coconut-scented lungful. My body trembling, I want to grab her and crush her to me, but I can't and that only feeds the pain and anger inside of me right now.

"So what? I'm supposed to thank my lucky stars that now you want to be here for me? Where's Cristiano tonight?" I ask, his name like fucking acid on my tongue.

"Deacon, I've always wanted to be here. Always. We just want—"

"I. Want. You," I roar, slamming my fist back into the locker I'm standing in front of, the soft metal caving without resistance. "I only wanted you, Frankie. Don't fucking tell me what 'we' want."

She'll never understand how hard it is for me to ignore the tears silently streaming down her face. I shake my head to try to rid myself of the sight. I can't let them affect me. Her pain is apparent, but I hurt too and I just can't afford to right now.

Blowing out a deep breath that does absolutely nothing to lessen this feeling that I'm suffocating, I look away from her.

"I can't do this right now with you. I have to get ready for Dair." Turning to face her again, I plead,

"You're gonna get him killed, Frankie. I'm so fucking heated right now, so out of fucking control I can't see straight, and that's…do you know how dangerous that is, how dangerous you are—for him?"

On a sob she nods her head and moves past me toward the exit, stopping in the doorway. She turns hesitantly, immobilizing me with her watery blues and quivering voice, "I know you don't believe me, Deacon, or you don't want to hear it, but I do love you. I love you enough to let you go, because in the end, we would have only hurt each other more than we already have. If that's even possible."

Blinking slowly, I focus on her trembling lips for a heartbeat before meeting her eyes. "I never wanted there to be an end," I tell her matter-of-factly. Not waiting for a response, I stride away, locking myself away in the First Aid room to wait for my brothers and pop. As the door is closing I hear her whisper softly, "Little do you know." That song. Those words. They give me hope, but I tamp it down. I can only focus on fighting one person trying to hurt me at a time and she's already had her turn, now it's Dair's.

AT THE ENTRANCEWAY into the arena, I stand in the shadows waiting for my intro music. Pop is replacing Mav as one of my two corner guys tonight. I'm not sure if it's because he thinks he'll be more helpful since we've changed tactics or because he is afraid of what the fuck stunt I'm going to pull tonight. Bouncing lightly on my toes, I wonder a little myself.

I'm doing my best to keep it locked up, but knowing she's here is fucking with my head, adding fuel to the fire. My dad nailed it earlier—I'm like a powder keg ready to blow. That's exactly how I feel and my detonation isn't something anyone will see coming or even be able to stop. Myself included.

When "Radioactive" starts streaming throughout the arena, I snap to attention. I will my muscles to loosen as I let the drum beat, which is what I love so much about this song, flow over me and hope for it to slow my racing pulse and ease the tension throughout my body. Inside and out, pulling me taut. Forced to give up on the relief I'm unable to find, I follow the team out to the Octagon and pray that "The Kid" survives this fight. Survives me.

If I didn't already know about his weak jaw, I would have figured it out ten seconds after the bell sounds. He's so busy guarding his wobbly chin that he leaves the rest of his body wide open, allowing me to unleash some of the pent up anger overrunning me right now. I can hear my pop and Sonny yelling at me to slow down, that I'm going to tire myself out, but I feel nothing but determination and ice coursing through my overheated blood, and neither of them has me pulling back. I'm able to catch him with a quick jab to the kidneys and then another. He lets his guard fall enough for me to land a left hook to his face and a left uppercut that shatters his jaw and wobble he does.

The crowd erupts in thunderous applause and screams, so loud I can feel their voices. As everyone celebrates around me, slapping me on the back in congratulations, I'm led to the center of the Octagon by Sonny, who obviously isn't going to let me bolt again. Waiting for the official announcement, I let my eyes scan the arena, telling myself that I am not looking for her, lying to myself. Finally finding her, I'm able to catch glimpses of her through the chaos going on around me in the cage as she stands with Guy, Trent, and Reggie just on the other side of gate. My gaze zeroes in on her. I can see the tears falling from her eyes. Her lips tremble as she smiles at me, but it does nothing to soften the godforsaken look in my girl's eyes. The same look I'm certain she sees reflected in mine.

My arm thrust in the air by the referee in victory, the crowd is brought to an even more deafening level. None of it matters, not like it should. I'm lost in Frankie's blues. Two fights down, one more to go. Get the belt. Get my girl. That's my end game. Stick and move. Stick and motherfucking move.

Chapter
THIRTY-SIX

Francesca

I'VE BEEN BACK from Brazil for almost a week now and have received either a picture or phone call every one of those days, not to mention the three that were waiting for me when I returned. I have no idea how they're getting past Reggie and the new guy he has with me when he isn't around himself. I do know that I can't do this anymore. I'm exhausted and stressed to the point of making myself sick. I called Detective Adams, and she and Flores will be here sometime tonight to pick all of the pictures up and work on tracing the numbers that the calls came from. I kept every one and didn't touch them, other than to open the envelopes. There are no signatures but I know who they're from. The threats, the accusations, and cryptic messages…I've heard them all before, on that night. On the plus side, I haven't convinced myself lately that he's watching me or that I smell that same sweet scent that I have nightmares about. That was probably because after my panic attack, Reggie has amped up my security. I think he's trying to make me feel more secure, which it does…to an extent. In fact, the only reason that security isn't camped out on the couch right now is because Adams and Flores are on their way here.

Pacing around Indie's front room, Damien Rice is streaming from my laptop. I stop to listen to the words, thinking how the eerie tempo and melancholy lyrics are haunting and so appropriate to the battle that is raging within my heart. I debate for the millionth time whether or not I should call him. I want to, but that last confrontation with Deacon killed something inside of me. As much as he hurt me, I hurt him that much more. Never have I seen Deac look defeated by anything, until me. I did that to him. I put that look in his eyes and the fire in his heart that burned through him and scorched everything in his path. We flamed bright and then crashed, losing everything in the process. I know that we love each other, but I'm not sure that either of us can survive this kind of chaotic, passionate, infinite love. But I'm not sure we can deny ourselves of it or its soul crushing beauty either.

My braid hanging over my shoulder, I finger the tip as I bite the inside of my lip in contemplation. I'm staring down at my phone about to make the call when a text comes in. I'm disappointed when I see that it's not from Deacon. Although I never respond to the texts he sends, not after that one time, they still connect me to him and I need that little piece of him.

Cristiano: I miss you. Can I see you?

Inhaling deeply, I reply.

Me: Not tonight, I have something to take care of. Soon.

His reply is almost immediate,

Cristiano: I'll look forward to it, mi amor. xx

Not bothering with a response, I go back to pacing, my bare feet slapping against the oak floor. I know that Deacon saw the picture of Cristiano and I in the Trib and I know how it looked. Yes, we were—are—comfortable together, and yes, we were "canoodling" in the club, but I'm blaming that on the copious amounts of alcohol he had been drinking and the utter despair I had been feeling over the scene with Deacon earlier in the day. It always comes back to Deacon. I'm afraid that no matter what I choose to do or whom I choose to be with, that it always will. Nobody will ever live up to him. An impossible task to even attempt.

The song ends and the even more fitting sound of Madilyn Bailey's version of "When I Was Your Man" fills the room. I'm manic with my music lately, not allowing for silence to eat up any space that I occupy. Afraid of my own thoughts and shadow at the moment. Sighing loudly, I unlock the phone and pull up Deacon's picture. I take in his sexy smirk, and my own mouth tips up into a sad smile. Blowing out a breath of air, I let a curse slip past those same lips as I hit the call button. My finger tapping out a nervous beat on my thigh, I listen waiting for the call to connect.

I'm startled when there's a knock at the door, followed by the chimes of the doorbell. Slowly lowering the phone to my chest mid ring, I reach for the knob, cursing my lack of shoes not allowing me to see out the peephole. It doesn't matter anyway—I'm not expecting anyone but Detective Adams and her partner. Opening the door wide, I immediately start to tremble uncontrollably. Blood running cold, I shake my head from side to side as if that can ward off the vision in front of me.

"Hello, Francesca, aren't you excited to see me, darling?" Smiling, he steps closer to where I stand stunned and frozen to the spot.

I can faintly hear Deacon, calling my name as I gasp out on a terrified breath, "Andrew?"

TO BE CONTINUED...

Acknowledgments

I WAS TOLD that writing these would be harder than writing the actual book. They were right. I worry that I'll forget someone who was so important to getting me to this point. I've made a list. I've checked it twice and still, I'm certain people are missing. If by chance you are that person, I didn't mean it! Every single one of you deserve a thank you, a hug, a damn medal for taking this ride with me. None of it would have happened without each of you there by my side. Thank you. From the bottom of my heart, thank you.

I'm acknowledging people in alphabetical order. I'm not actually that anal, but for some reason that's how I wrote my list out (don't judge me). First though, I would like to start with my readers. You'll have to forgive me because I am total shite at hearts and flowers so, bear with me.

To My Readers:

To even be addressing "my readers" is surreal! I never thought in a million years that this day would come. That I would put my words out there and people would actually enjoy them. I can't thank you enough for taking a chance on me, a woman who wanted to just do something for her. Something that let her know that she wasn't just "mommy" or "Sug." You took a chance on me and my filthy mouthed fighter and thank you will never be enough.

Amy:

You, my scary stabby spice are invaluable. You're my friend, my sister, Deacon's trainer. You hit me with tough love when I needed it most and talked me through every bump in the road, especially in the aftermath when the easy part of writing was finished. You were never too busy, my questions and complete lack of knowledge, never an issue. I have learned a great deal from you throughout this process and I can't thank you enough for always making time for me no matter what you had going on. For every name change, plot change, c-punch and "NO" I thank you. You believed in me, supported me and guided me through and I will always love you for not letting Fat boy Slim win in the end. I love you #OZ

Beta Berries:

Who & RA, you ladies and your encouraging words, constant laughs, love and support kept me going! You let me torture you with half scenes, rewrites, more half scenes and weeks long breaks in between new stuff and I love you for every second of it. #dirtygirls

Cara:

My donut eating sprinting partner. I know that I say it all the time but it's true. If it weren't for you, this book would never have been finished. Every night, whether you had things to do or not, you made sure you set aside sprinting time for me so that I was able to reach MY goal. You read and researched, talked and listened anytime I needed you to and you never once complained even though you had your own thing happening. You never stopped encouraging for a second and your belief in me and my ability to finish and finish well is what kept me going. We bonded over douchebaggery and AT but that was only the beginning of the #ELC and a #synopsislesssister-hood. I love you my soul sister. My wildly inappropriate #notdeadOpie. Long live #teamstickyDandredsolocups and thank you for always being the friend I need exactly when I need her.

Cherry:

Years ago I fell in love with your books and on a whim reached out to you through email. I will never forget the immense surprise, awe and total fangirl moment when I saw that you had responded. Not only did you respond but you answered my questions in great length and offered to buy me a cup of tea when we met in person to answer any more that I might have. You made a forever friend that day. But you're more than a friend and mentor. You're family and I love you more than you'll ever know my African American lovey!

Coco:

My Indie. My monk. My so incredibly dope friend. You hate Deacon. HATE him. Yet you pushed through with your monkness and made sure that I wasn't going to fall flat on my face. Your generosity never ceases to amaze me. You go above and beyond all day every day in every way. I stopped trying to stop you a long time ago because I know that you do what you want, but know that not a second goes by that I don't appreciate every one of those gestures big and small. You're my soul sister and I'd be lost without you and my words would still be in the yellow pad app of my phone. I love you friend. Even though you hate my guy and every book I've ever tried to make you read. No matter what, we'll always have music and our insane love for everything British.

Deacon Originals:

Tam, Thistle and Goldie, what can I even say to you girls to thank you for always being there when I need you? Your faith in me never wavered, my biggest cheerleaders and champions. No matter what shite was happening in your lives across the pond you always made time for me and my boy. I left you hanging on more than one occasion and you may have cursed and threatened me but you never gave up on me. You taught me to believe in myself and my ability to write well and while I'm still working on that you never fail to remind me every day with your kind words and dirty f-bombs that I love more than anything! You never stop thanking me for allowing you to be a part of this journey but it's I who should be thanking you for coming along for the ride. Love you my proper lady, my Scot and my Reggae queen.

Elites:

You ladies have been my rock for more than two years now. We were thrown together and made to sleep in the same beds as strangers and amazingly enough we came out of it with a bond so true no amount of snoring or terrible bar service could ever break. You are and always will be, my Ohana

Jodi the Bibliophile:

I forced an ARC on you. Seriously FORCED it on you just because I wanted to give you something for all of the times you tagged me in posts and made me laugh my ass off at your wild inappropriateness. To say that I was floored that you actually read Love Hurts would be an understatement. You didn't know me, We weren't friends and yet you not only read my book you shouted your love for it from the mountains and I am so completely humbled and grateful and fucking out of my mind in love with you for that! You're super stuck with my ass now as you are the trailer to my park. I love your face you C-U-Next-Tuesday!

Jules:

My book pimp! I asked you to read Love Hurts because I needed a fresh pair of eyes and because I valued your opinion.

Never did I expect you to pimp it all over town! Lol I love you to bits Jules and can't thank you enough for our friendship.

Kari:

My graphic artist QUEEN! Thank you so much for always having time for me and my constant need for teasers and banners last minute! You're the best doll!

Kristy:

I'm not sure if I told you, but it was you who inspired me to finally get serious about my writing again and to find the courage to share it with people. You, an everyday woman just like me. Mom, wife, cook, chauffeur, losing yourself in the monotony that goes along with putting others needs before your own. Thank you for writing Driven just to prove that you could because it forced me to write Love Hurts for the very same reason. Thank you too for always having time for me and my silly questions. Even at your busiest you never turned me away. I love you to bits Switzerland.

Lauren:

My photographer, cover artist and very dear friend! I can't thank you enough for putting up with me and our quest for a mystical unicorn who turned out to be not so mystical. You are beyond wonderful and I'm so grateful to get the chance to work with someone as talented as you are and even more so to call you a friend! Love you lady!

Lisa:

The very best editor I could ever have hoped for! Thank you so much for never trying to change my voice and for your limitless patience for me and my jacked up tenses. You helped me to make my story what it is and I am so incredibly thankful and proud of what we've accomplished. Thank you from the bottom of my heart, I can't wait to work on book two! I'm dying to see where you'll read from next!

Melissa and Sharon:

Thank you two crazy ladies so much for taking me on when you didn't have too! I am so grateful and know that my release wouldn't have been nearly as fantastic if it weren't for you! Thank you!

Ninfa and Jilly Bean:

Thank you so much for putting your hands all over Deac. Your love for me, your friendship is something that I can never thank you enough for. Never have I met two more giving women. You give freely no matter what it is and I'm in awe of your pure hearts. You'll never know how much I appreciate you ladies and all of your love and support. You're my little beta tag team and I can't wait to do it again.

PCVPPC:

I have no clue where to even start with you ladies. Every moment of every day, one of you is around for whatever one of us might need. Sisters, anchors, sex experts, friends and so much more. There's not a thing we can't talk about and not a single time that I've felt let down by any of you. Your dedication and support have brought me to tears more than once and I'm not just talking about on this particular journey. You are all more amazing, more appreciated and more loved than you'll ever know. Family by choice.

SSWC:

We started as three and now we're five and I couldn't be more proud of all that you ladies have accomplished. Kittyho,

Creeper, Sauce, Woody and Cali, you girls have been a constant for the last few months. A safe place where we can all be us and new and a little clueless. This journey was better because we took it together. Love my ladies.

Stephy poo:

My go to girl for EVERYTHING! I never have an issue that you don't try to solve! You have become one of my dearest friends and I love you for tolerating my filthy sailor mouth, my constant "can we know him's," total lack of internet knowledge and just every other ridiculous thing that I hit you with! You're a gem and I am so very thankful that you put up with me and all my crazy! Thank you for being you! I couldn't love you more!

To the bloggers:

Big and small you all are what makes this Indie book world go round! There are so many of you to thank for taking a chance on a debut author that I don't even know where to start! There are a few of you that went above and beyond because you believed in me and my writing though: A Book Whores Obsession, Schmexy Girl, Smart and Savvy with Stephanie, Our Five Cents, Angie's Dreamy Reads and my girls at Romance Bytes. Thank you all so much from the very bottom of my heart! I don't know if people realize just how much work goes into running a blog but I do and I thank you for even taking the time out to promote me whether it was once or one hundred times. You aren't required to do any of it and do it because you love to read and support authors. I think that you're all rock stars no matter if you have ten followers or thousands. Thank you, so much for all that you do. The Indie book world wouldn't be where it is without each and every one of you!

About the Author

MANDI BECK HAS been an avid reader all of her life. A deep love for books always had her jotting down little stories on napkins, notebooks, and her hand. As an adult she was further submerged into the book world through book clubs and the epic-ness of social media. It was then that she graduated to writing her stories on her phone and then finally on a proper computer. A nursing student, mother to two rambunctious and some-what rotten boys, and stepmom to two great girls away at col-lege, she shares her time with her husband in Chicago where she was born and raised. Mandi is a diehard hockey fan and blames the Blackhawks when her deadlines are not met. Love Hurts is her debut novel and she is currently working on the next in the series along with whatever other voices are clam-oring for attention in her mind.

Connect with Mandi

Website
http://www.authormandibeck.com
Facebook
https://www.facebook.com/authormandibeck
Twiiter
https://twitter.com/authormandibeck
Goodreads
https://www.goodreads.com/book/show/23367669-love-hurts
Instagram
http://instagram.com/authormandibeck/
Spotify
https://play.spotify.com/user/manranbeck

CPSIA information can be obtained
at www.ICGtesting.com
Printed in the USA
LVHW03s1755081018
592819LV00014B/1562/P